Tw....

Part Four
Books 11, 12 & 13

Katrina Kahler

Copyright © KC Global Enterprises Pty Ltd

Table of Contents

Book 11

Unexpected!

CHAPTER ONE

Casey

The day after the election assembly was unlike any other school day I had ever experienced. When Ali and I walked the hallways together, there was an outpouring of congratulations to each of us. As Ali adjusted the signature braid that hung over her shoulder, her smile was full of pride and mine was a mirror image.

It was like the scene from a dream. Everyone was happy to see not just Ali but me as well. Kids who I had never officially met before waved in my direction or gave me a thumbs up. If this was what it meant to be a school leader, then I was in awe.

I still couldn't believe that these people, both my classmates and teachers had voted for both Ali and I. With Ali as captain and me as the vice-captain, the positions were perfect for us. I was still learning to be more outgoing and confident, especially with giving speeches. Whereas my twin was a natural and would easily step up to the challenge. With her guidance, I was sure that I could do the same.

Now we were linked by more than our appearance and the fact that we were twins. I could stand proudly by her side while we worked together as leaders of our school.

Reaching to brush a few stray strands of hair from my face, my fingers touched the badge that was pinned to my shirt. The word 'Vice Captain' stood out clearly above my name.' Apart from the word 'Vice' and my name, the badge was the same as my sister's. I felt so proud to be wearing it but it would definitely take some getting used to. It announced our position to anyone walking by and I supposed the only thing flashier would be someone shouting our titles through a megaphone. Everyone's eyes seemed to slide to the badges that Ali and I wore as we strolled the halls into class, and I was overwhelmed with pride.

"Hi, Ali!" a pretty girl called out with a friendly smile.

This was immediately followed with, "Hey, Casey!"

The girl disappeared amongst the crowd of kids before I could catch a good glimpse and I wondered if she was from the grade above us. It was a little strange to hear others calling our names, even though we'd never met. But the assembly had introduced our faces and names to lots of kids, parents, and teachers who we didn't previously know. It was such an unusual sensation that would certainly take a while for us to adjust to.

I then spotted our principal, Mrs. Jensen smiling broadly at us as she passed by. "Good morning, Ali. Good morning, Casey."

"Good morning, Mrs. Jensen," Ali and I said at the same time.

I knew I had Mrs. Jensen to thank for pushing me to apply for a captain position. It was a good thing that she did. Even though I was reluctant to compete against my sister, I'd be so jealous now if Ronnie had my spot because I'd been too shy to put my name in the ring.

"All this attention is so weird," I said to Ali under my breath.

"I know," Ali grinned. "I haven't had this much attention since my first day here."

Little did she know that I had never experienced attention like this. Ever! I'd grown up in this town, and everything had always been much the same for me. I went to school with the same kids each year and attended events with all the same faces.

But meeting Ali had changed that and I never wanted to go back. With her help, my self-confidence had grown. Even though I would still have to face my fears when it came to speaking to an audience, with Ali by my side, I knew I'd be fine.

Then there was my crush, Jake Hanley, the boy who was always in my thoughts. His handsome face popped into my mind and distracted me enough that I walked right past my locker. It wasn't until Ali grabbed hold of the strap on my backpack that I turned back.

"Whoops," I said, grinning as I reached to spin the combination so I could open my locker door. "Too much going on in my head right now!"

"You looked as though you were daydreaming," Ali laughed.

"I was," I nodded, a pink blush creeping over my

cheeks.

Ali smiled and looked down at her badge before opening her own locker. I felt so happy for her. As much as she had fitted in from her very first day, moving to a new town and a new school couldn't have been easy. She was so disappointed to have missed the opportunity of being captain at her old school, but things had fallen into place for her. She deserved the role so much and after going through all the trauma of her adopted mother's death, it was wonderful to see her smiling and happy again. If her adopted mother was still alive, she would be so proud.

Across the hallway, someone scoffed, breaking me from my thoughts. Glancing over my shoulder, I saw Ronnie and Holly huddled against the wall, both staring at Ali and me.

We could easily hear Ronnie's voice above the noise around us. "Anyone would think they were royalty."

"They're making it out to be such a big deal," Holly replied. "It's not like anyone outside of this school cares."

Ronnie glared at me. "I know!"

"Don't listen to them," Ali whispered.

I bit my lip. It was hard when Holly and Ronnie insisted on bothering me whenever they could. I caught an eye roll from Ronnie before I turned around to close my locker.

Ignoring them, Ali looped her arm with mine as we walked towards the classroom. She seemed to have confidence in every situation. I wanted to be the same. Ronnie and Holly insisted on targeting me most of the time, and I knew it was because I was the less confident one and I always let them get to me.

Because Ronnie had congratulated me after the election, I was hoping things would now be okay between us. What a joke that was! As if she'd change overnight just because I was wearing a badge. If anything, she'd probably become even worse. To see me elected when she'd had her own hopes set on a captain position would have irritated her no end. I could understand how she felt because if I were her, I'd be feeling the same way. Regardless though, I'd do my best to keep my jealousy to myself.

I just hoped I was strong enough to ignore her. With Holly whispering in her ear, I was sure the pair were up to something. Those two were the worst.

Mrs. Jensen's voice carried down the hallway and I stopped in my tracks. But it was Ronnie who she was referring to. "Ronnie, have you met up with your mentor yet?"

I grabbed Ali's arm and moved discreetly to the side, keeping my back against the wall. I wanted to hear what Mrs. Jensen had to say. She had a bright orange cord in her grip and I watched as she passed it to Ronnie. Immediately I noticed Ronnie's name printed in bold text on the label.

"Here is your lanyard," Mrs. Jensen said in a serious tone. "Now please be sure to check your duty schedule.

There is a list of expectations attached and I've emailed it to all the hall monitors. With less than two weeks left of the semester, this is your chance to practice so you'll be prepared when you start back next fall. I have every confidence in you, Ronnie. And I expect that you'll rise to the challenge!"

"Thanks, Mrs. Jensen," Ronnie said in her fakest voice.

I knew it well. It was the same voice she used whenever she spoke with teachers or parents. The problem was, she was so convincing, which was why no one ever believed me when I spoke up about her bullying.

She whispered to Holly as she headed past us into the classroom. I overheard her comment. She was clearly unimpressed. "I saw the email. Why did she have to announce that in the hallway in front of everyone? And now I have to wear this ugly thing! It's embarrassing!"

Ali smirked at me as we followed behind Ronnie and Holly.

"I'm not wearing this all day long." Ronnie frowned at her friend as she sat down at her desk. "That is not going to happen."

I sat down in my own seat which was right next to Ronnie's. From the corner of my eye, I saw her pull off the bright orange lanyard and shove it into her backpack.

"It's not that bad," Holly tried to reassure her.

"Then maybe you should wear it!" Ronnie scoffed back.

Holly wrinkled her nose but said nothing else. Groaning in frustration, Ronnie turned to face the board.

Brie, who was already in her seat behind me, tapped me on the shoulder. She had heard every word from Ronnie as well. We gave each other a knowing look. To see Ronnie finally put in her place was the best thing ever. Even though she liked to tell people what to do, we knew that the hall monitor job was not at all what she had wanted. Hopefully, her popularity would suffer when she was forced to report kids who broke the rules in the hallways. If that happened, it would serve her right.

"How are you feeling today, vice-captain?" Brie grinned.

"It feels so strange," I admitted. "But it's good. Really good!"

After all the drama I had gone through over the past few weeks, I never thought I'd finally reach the other side and be happy with the results. The badge pinned to my shirt was proof that it had really happened.

Brie smiled at me. I knew she was proud. She had never been interested in applying for a leadership position herself, but she was so happy for Ali and me.

Although I was excited, I was also a little nervous. The scariest part was the speech we were required to present at the awards ceremony the following week. I knew I still wasn't the best at giving speeches, and I felt anxious at the prospect of speaking in front of a large audience again so soon. But at the same time, I had Ali to help me and almost a week to adjust to the fact that I was now a school leader. The hard stuff was over, and with Ali's support, I should be fine. We made a great team, and I was looking forward to what was ahead.

Taking another quick glance down at my badge to make sure I really wasn't dreaming, I smiled to myself. When I saw Ronnie staring at me, her eyebrows raised in mock disgust, I inhaled a deep breath and ignored her. I was the one wearing the school captain badge, whereas instead, she was forced to wear a bright orange lanyard. Who did she think she was, anyway?

Determined not to let her get to me, I focused my attention on the board, the smile remaining at the corners of my lips while Ronnie huffed out an exasperated sigh beside me.

CHAPTER TWO

Ali

Arriving at school that morning was a dream come true. Though my dream hadn't even come close to the warm feeling that I experienced when I walked the corridors.

I couldn't help smiling at all the happy faces. Even kids and teachers who I hadn't met before were acknowledging me. Many of them must have voted for me and I just hoped I'd be the captain they wanted. I promised myself to do as much as I could to make that happen.

With the memory of my adopted mother in my heart, I knew I could do anything I set my mind to. She'd repeated those words to me often enough, and I would always remember them. It warmed my heart to think of her. She would have been so proud.

Touching the badge at my shoulder, I pressed my fingers against the surface. A wave of butterflies fluttered in my stomach over everything I'd accomplished since arriving at this school only a short time ago. Achieving the captain position had once been a dream but I'd made it a reality, and I was still struggling to believe it had actually happened.

I watched Casey and Brie chatting to each other from their seats near the front of the classroom. Through our connection, Casey's happiness reached me. Everything had worked out for both of us and I was so glad.

As I focused on my twin, I recalled my fear when I thought she would win the captain position over me. Even though I'd suggested the idea to our principal and had meant every word, I would still be hugely disappointed if Casey had been elected captain instead of vice. I'd have supported her, but deep down, I'd be jealous. While I knew I shouldn't feel that way, I couldn't help it. I was just glad that everything had fallen into place and we'd both managed to get the positions we truly wanted.

Beaming to myself, my mind wandered to thoughts of my dad and Jackie, my birth mother, and the fact that they were going out on an official date. All I wanted was to see Dad happy again. He and Jackie were perfect for each other and for him to be with her made so much sense for our family.

Their first date was planned for the weekend and Casey and I couldn't wait to see how it all turned out. I texted with my twin for hours after Dad made his announcement. Recalling that moment made me smile. It was so romantic and so sweet. Now it was up to Dad to impress Jackie so we really would end up as an official family.

Our teacher's voice sounded across the room and I glanced in her direction. "Alright, class. Pay attention, please. I have some exciting news for those of you who haven't made plans for the summer yet."

Everyone settled in their seats as Mrs. Halliday waved an orange sheet of paper in the air. I looked at her with interest. There had been so much going on that I hadn't really thought too much about the upcoming vacation. But as Mrs. Halliday spoke, a tingle of anticipation grew inside me.

"There is a brand new summer camp not too far from here that will have its official opening this summer," she explained as she scanned the faces staring back at her. "Apparently, it's already been advertised online and in the local papers, but there are still some vacant spots available. The organizers are hoping for maximum attendance and have notified a few local schools with the information. If anyone is interested, you'll need to be quick to book. Otherwise, you'll miss out."

She then flipped the lights off and turned on the projector screen. "I found some video footage on their website so you can see what's included. It's pretty impressive. If I was your age, I think this is a camp I'd love to go to." She smiled as she navigated the links on her laptop.

All of a sudden, a popular song sounded through the speakers along with an opening photo of a beautiful campsite. Everyone's eyes were focused intently on the screen. The video transitioned to display scenes of the camp facilities and the various areas of the campsite. Cabins were scattered across the hillside and at the bottom of the hill was a winding river. Rope swings were attached to trees where several canoes were secured as well.

When the video panned to an aqua park complete with four different water slides, the entire class gasped in surprise.

"That looks so cool!" Jake, whose desk was right near mine said to his friend, Sai.

I agreed with him completely and so did everyone else. Murmurs of excitement swept through the room as the video continued to play. I'd been on a few summer camps before but none that had included a real aqua park. In the past, I was overjoyed with just one slide into the pool but this place had four!

We were then shown footage of the cabin interiors and eager comments sounded around me.

"Those cabins look so modern and new!"

"Yeah! So much better than the cabins at our school camp!"

A voice could then be heard detailing the activities of the camp. There were so many on offer but there were several that stood out...rock climbing, a high ropes course complete with something called the Leap of Faith. Both of these looked scary, especially as I had a fear of heights but I would still love to try them. There was also archery, bush-walking, a two-day hike where the overnight stay was in tents, and the most exciting of all...a double looped go-kart track. At the mention of that, the whole class went crazy.

"A go-kart track!" Sai gasped loudly. "This place looks so awesome, Jake! We should totally go!"

Jake gave him an enthusiastic nod. It was obvious both boys were super keen. There were a few grumbles around the room, but they were from kids who already had plans for the summer. Some were organized to go to other camps and were now wishing they were attending this one instead.

As for myself, I hadn't even remotely considered something like this. Over the past couple of summers, I'd stayed at home to be with my mom. Because it was so soon since the funeral, I hadn't planned to go anywhere this summer either. Dad had arranged to work from home so he could still care for me. But other than hanging out with Casey and doing some fun things around town, I hadn't given the summer much thought. After seeing the video footage though, I wondered if this camp was something fun for me and Casey to do.

My twin turned in her seat, her eyes wide. I nodded at her. The more I considered the idea, the more excited I became. It would be like the school camp we went to in the fall, but it would be so much better now that we were sisters instead of two girls who just looked alike and barely knew each other. We wouldn't need to swap lives and could enjoy it without all the drama we'd experienced the last time. Plus, it looked like the best camp I had ever seen or heard of.

It appeared that several other kids were also interested. But according to Mrs. Halliday, there weren't too many spots remaining. When my eyes fell on Casey again, I focused on flooding her mind with my thoughts. Instead of looking excitedly back though, her expression suddenly drooped and with a shrug of her shoulders, she turned back towards the front. What was the problem? She had been excited a moment ago. What happened? I wished we sat close enough for me to ask her. This camp looked like the best place for a summer with my sister, I couldn't understand what could possibly be the issue.

Jake's voice filled my ears again, and my own

shoulders slumped. Perhaps Casey wanted to spend the whole summer with him instead. But he seemed interested in the camp too. There was no way of knowing if he was thinking of going unless I asked him. But I didn't want Casey to be upset if I encouraged him when she had already made other plans.

Brie turned in her seat and gave me a thumbs up. I did the same in return.

That was promising. If Casey's best friend was interested, surely between the two of us, we could convince Casey as well. If we all went, we'd have the best summer ever. I was certain of it.

After my mother died, I wasn't sure I'd ever feel like this again, but with the summer camp coming up just at the right time, it had to be fate.

And now that Dad was dating Jackie, I wouldn't feel bad about leaving him. Besides, he'd be busy working anyway. This was the absolute best solution to keep me busy and Dad would have to agree.

With that thought, my mind was made up. All I had to do now was persuade Casey.

CHAPTER THREE

Casey

The moment Mrs. Halliday started the video about the new sleep-away camp, my eyes were glued to the screen. It looked so beautiful and so much fun, and I knew if I went that I'd have a fantastic summer.

It looked very different compared to our school camp. This one had so many more activities, the cabins were modern and best of all, there was a real aqua park with four amazing water slides plus there was a go-kart track. The idea of all that was almost too much to comprehend. As well, the camp extended for several weeks. I imagined leaving my family for so long. If Ali and Brie came, it would be perfect. Sleeping in a cabin or in a tent under the stars with them would create so many fun memories. And I'd get to know Ali even more than I already did.

I turned in my seat to see if my twin was interested. We'd been so busy, we hadn't really discussed any plans for the summer, but by the sparkle in her eyes, I knew she wanted to go too. I could easily see she was just as excited as me.

But then reality struck and my excitement shattered into a million pieces.
Even if Mom agreed to let me go, she could never afford the cost. Camps were always so expensive. She had already paid for the school field trip one and struggled to afford it. She didn't earn enough to have spare cash left over for vacations or camps, especially the long camps that were held during the summer.

Usually, my summers were spent with Lucas, my

annoying brother, and I had to try to avoid boredom. It wasn't fair that I would once again be his live-in babysitter when I had an amazing opportunity to have the summer of a lifetime right in front of me.

Brie's family often went on vacation for several weeks during the summer. This left me to binge watch television, causing Grandma Ann to give me the evil eye for doing so. There weren't many parks or things to do within walking distance, so unless Grandma Ann was around, we were stuck at home for most of the day.

Brie had mentioned that her family may not go on vacation this summer and I had at least looked forward to having her and Ali around. But even Brie seemed keen on the camp. She leaned forward, tapping me encouragingly on the shoulder while the narrator of the video told us all about the fun things I'd miss. These were things I wouldn't have the chance to experience because I'd be forced to stay at home with Lucas...while everyone else was having the time of their lives.

"This looks so cool!" Brie exclaimed. "Since Dad started his new job, my family doesn't really have anything planned this summer. We should go. All of us." She turned eagerly in Ali's direction.

I couldn't bear to disappoint them. If they wanted to go, I wouldn't stop them. And besides, it seemed as though they had already made up their minds. They didn't have a younger brother to take care of and their families obviously had plenty of spare money to spend.

My stomach sank. Even if it was remotely possible that Mom could afford to send me this year, Lucas would complain. He'd say it wasn't fair for me to go if he was stuck at home with nothing to do. I could already hear his whiny voice in the back of my head. And there was no way Mom could afford to send both of us. Now that I was almost thirteen, she was relying on me to take care of my brother while she was at work. She would definitely want me to remain at home.

Once again, Lucas was ruining my fun. I wondered if that would ever end or if I'd lose out on fun things for the rest of my life because of him.

I wished Mrs. Halliday had never even mentioned the camp. I rested my chin in my hands, willing for the video to stop so I could forget all about it. But it was too late. Now both my sister and my best friend would probably go, leaving me utterly alone.

Ali's voice popped into my head, reminding me to be positive. I was sure it was our connection reaching me across the room. My mind spun with possible solutions. The only way I could go was if someone else watched Lucas. Mom would never be able to afford to send me to camp and pay for a babysitter, so that was out of the question.

I supposed I could rely on Grandma Ann if—and that was a big if—Mom actually allowed me to go. But then I remembered Grandma Ann was planning to visit a friend across the country at some point this summer. I had no idea for how long but she was obviously not going to be around to care for Lucas.

I tried to think of another solution but came up blank. So much for positivity. It appeared as if the world was against me, desperate to make me miserable when all I wanted was to have a normal experience for once.

I sighed and sank into my seat. My boring summer played out before me…long days in front of the television while Lucas bounced all over the place. I'd check my phone for messages from my friends who wouldn't be able to get back to me since they'd be so busy at camp. Or, they'd continually send me amazing pictures, added to the ones they posted on Instagram, making me hate my own summer even more.

My throat ached, and I tried to swallow. I ground my teeth together in an attempt to stop the negativity from snaking through my body. It was so hard.

Glancing over my shoulder, I looked at Jake, thinking that at least he'd be around. But that idea floated out of reach the moment I saw his smile. Mrs. Halliday had passed out the orange fliers so that anyone who was interested could take one home to show their parents. The bright orange sheet sat on my desk untouched but Jake was intently reading the details and taking in every word.

His eyes darted between the orange flier and his friend, Sai. They whispered to each other and high-fived a few times. We hadn't discussed summer plans, but I had hoped he'd be around.

My chest ached. Were he and Sai considering the possibility of going to the camp? I didn't really have to ask that question because I already knew the answer.

It'd be bad enough having Ali and Brie away but if Jake was gone too, then I really would be all alone. I had no other friends to hang out with. Would bickering with Lucas be the only interaction I'd have?

I covered my face with my hands. This was so much worse than I anticipated. Was I doomed to be a couch potato while everyone else made memories this summer?

I didn't open my eyes again until Mrs. Halliday flicked on the lights. As my eyes adjusted, big black spots dotted my vision. I wished I could disappear into one of those dots.

"Can you slide over?" Brie asked, sitting on the edge of my seat beside me. She placed her hand on my back and leaned closer. "I'm texting my mom about the camp. If we're going, we need to get on the list before all the spots are taken."

I blocked her from Mrs. Halliday's view. My skin heated to an uncomfortable level. Now I had to disappoint Brie by telling her I couldn't go.

Mrs. Halliday stood at the front of the room holding packets of paper in her hands. "Alright, everyone. I know that was very exciting. But it's time to get on with our day. We have a lot of revision work to cover before your end of year exams. These are your review sheets."

While Mrs. Halliday passed out the packets, the new summer camp was all anyone could talk about. Our teacher would end all the side conversations soon, but I wished she'd do it quickly.

The twisting in my stomach continued. At the same time, my new badge pressed against my cheek as I reached into my bag for my books. I couldn't believe the morning had started off so well and now I had to face tests I wasn't prepared for…followed by a long, lonely summer.

CHAPTER FOUR

Ali

Throughout the rest of the morning classes, all I could think about was camp. Luckily, most of the classroom time was spent revising what we'd already learned during the semester and I didn't need to pay too much attention. I already had a good grasp on the work so I wasn't worried at all.

Now and then, I'd catch a glimpse from Casey and it seemed like she was struggling with the revisions. The moment I had a chance to talk to her, I decided I would offer some help. I might even suggest that she come to my house after school so we could do some revision together. I didn't want her missing out on camp because of her grades. There was no way I could allow that to happen.

In the past, I had actually completed a history test for her. It had been another of our swaps that had almost ended in disaster. I shuddered at the memory. Although Casey had ended up with an A on that test, I certainly couldn't repeat the experience. And besides, I needed to do my own test so I'd get a decent grade, myself. Maybe I'd just try to do what I could to make the tests easier for her. It would be like helping her with her speech. She really was very smart but tended to be distracted. Although I knew that was probably due to living with Lucas. As cute as my half-brother was, he had a lot of energy. Casey's house wasn't a very good place to study when he bounced around so noisily most of the time.

But Casey seemed less and less happy as the morning ticked on. Eventually; I stopped focusing on her because it brought my mood down too.

Pushing all negative thoughts from my head, I tore a sheet of paper from my notepad and wrote down a list of things I wanted us to do together at camp. I added three exclamation marks to the last item on my list. When I read it through, my insides rippled with excitement.

Camp Bucket List

* Visit the aqua park every single day and try every single slide
* Canoe together down the river
* Use the rope swings to jump into the water
* Become expert at archery
* Conquer the advanced rock climbing wall
* Complete the high-ropes course and do the Leap of Faith
* Ride the Go-Kart track (take turns at being the driver!)
* Learn how to play waterpolo
* Learn a new cheerleading routine that Mrs. Caldwell will love!
* Camp out under the stars
* Cook our food on a real campfire
* Meet heaps of new friends!
*Have the best time of our entire lives!!!

By the time recess rolled around, I was bursting at the seams to show my bucket list to Brie and Casey. As soon as the bell sounded, I hurried to the door where they were both waiting for me. "That camp sounds so amazing! I can't stop thinking about it!"

"Me too!" Brie grinned. "I'm so glad my parents didn't make any plans for this summer. Normally, we're out of town, but I *really* want to go to this camp. I wonder how many spots are left?"

"I hope at least three!" I couldn't bear the thought of one of us missing out.

"Imagine a two-day hike and sleeping out in tents. We could have a campfire and everything. It sounds soooo fun!" Brie's eyes sparkled as she spoke and I pictured our campsite in my head, my own excitement brimming over even more.

At the same time, I watched Casey closely. She hadn't said a word since we left the classroom. Was she worried about her grades or was she worried that Jake might not be able to come with us?

"What do you think, Casey?" I prodded as Brie pushed open the doors that led to the courtyard.

"I don't know," Casey muttered. "Sounds like fun, I guess."

"Of course it sounds like fun," I said, trying to encourage her.

Whatever was on her mind needed to change. There was no way I could enjoy myself without her being there. "There is so much to do. The campground looks so beautiful. And that aqua park will be amazing. We'll have the best time together."

"Come on," Brie prompted. "Why aren't you more excited?"

It was exactly what I wanted to know.

"Did your mom make plans this summer? I know she doesn't normally," Brie frowned.

"No plans," Casey said.

"Then what's the problem?" I asked.

Casey sighed. "I don't really think Mom will let me go."

My stomach dropped. "Why not?"

"She just won't," Casey said, digging the toe of her sneaker into the ground.

"Just ask her," Brie insisted. "Hopefully she'll say yes. I'm sure my mother would call and convince her. You're nearly thirteen. Surely she'll think you're old enough? But we need to sign up right away, or we'll miss out on getting a spot. How about you, Ali? Do you think your dad will let you go?"

Casey turned to me and I looked back at her encouragingly. "I'm sure my dad will be fine with it. He'll be working, so if I go he won't have to worry about me being bored. And our mom will want us together, Casey. This will be so much fun. You can't miss out!"

Casey frowned and then sighed again. "Mom won't be able to afford to pay for both Lucas and me. I can't do

25

anything on my own without him wanting to do it too, but it means paying double. That's why I've never been able to go to a summer camp. And besides, she'll want me to look after him while she's at work."

My spirits lifted. The problem wasn't with Casey not wanting to go, it had to do with money. My dad earned a lot so my family never really had to worry about that. I also thought Dad would agree to help cover the cost for Casey if I asked him. Casey was my sister, after all. I was sure he wouldn't mind. In fact, he'd probably insist on it. And Jackie would appreciate him wanting to help.

Maybe Jackie could afford for Lucas to go to a day camp where he wouldn't have to sleep-over. It would be a win-win for everyone.

I kept my idea to myself, wanting to make it a surprise for Casey. I couldn't wait to get home and check with Dad. When I called my twin later and told her everything was organized, she'd be over the moon.

"I know it'll be so much better than the other camps I've been to," Brie said. "Especially with those modern cabins and that aqua park. Four huge slides. How crazy is that! Plus, so many activities…the go-kart track and the Leap of Faith! There are so many cool things to do. I can't believe there are still spots available!"
She eyed Casey encouragingly before turning back to me. "Have you ever gone to sleep-away camp, Ali?"

"A few times" I replied, my own eyes still on Casey. "Not for a couple of years, though. Before my adopted mom got really sick."

"You had fun, though? Right?" Brie asked, nudging me. She was trying to help me convince Casey that the camp was a good idea. I had it covered though.

"Absolutely!" I beamed at her. "But this one will be even better with all of us together. We'll meet a heap of new kids from other schools and we'll have an amazing summer. I even heard Jake and Sai talking about going, so they'll be

26

there with us as well."

"They're going too?" Casey asked, her brow creasing.

"And we won't have Holly and Ronnie to worry about!" Brie added. "I overheard them talking and they're both going on vacations with their families."

"See! It's working out perfectly!" I smiled. "We really will have an amazing summer!"

I hoped Casey could feel our connection. I wanted her to know that I was handling all of this and she had nothing at all to worry about. I could hardly wait to ask my dad. I already knew his answer and I imagined Casey's surprised expression when I told her the news.

It couldn't happen quickly enough!

CHAPTER FIVE

Casey

For once in my life, I wanted recess to end. Ali and Brie wouldn't stop talking about camp. Ali had even made a bucket list of the activities she thought we could do together. And she kept flashing it at me. I just wanted to grab it from her and toss it into the nearest trash can.

Neither of the girls realized I wasn't going with them. I had no choice. If I had the money and someone else to care for Lucas, then I would have texted my mom and asked her to sign me up immediately. But that wasn't the case for me. Mom didn't have the money and there was no one to mind Lucas.

Not wanting to spoil their mood, I tried to keep out of the conversation as much as possible. Meanwhile, my stomach sank to the ground and a dark cloud settled over me. I couldn't help it, but disappointment flooded my bones. If I couldn't go, I kind of expected Ali would refuse to go too. Brie was often busy over the summer and in the past she'd gone to camps on her own, but I thought Ali would be different. She was my sister after all.

Her situation was so different from mine though and she always seemed to get what she wanted. Her father had truckloads of money. If she wanted clothes, she asked for them and her father swiped his credit card. If she wanted to redecorate her room, I was certain her dad would hire an interior designer with a snap of his fingers.

While I knew I was exaggerating, I couldn't help feeling that way. In my life, every experience was the opposite to that of my twin's. Mom had enough money to fill our freezer with food, pay the bills, and that was it.

If the situation was reversed, I wouldn't go to the camp without Ali. Surely a caring sister would insist on staying behind. Right?

But if she suggested the idea, I would tell her to go. She had the means to do it and I didn't want to ruin her summer. Even so, she could have offered. At least that would have helped me feel a little better knowing that she cared; instead of abandoning me without a second thought.

All Ali could do was talk to Brie — *my* best friend — about how much fun they would have over the summer. She tried to "reassure" me. But she barely knew anything about my situation. She hadn't begged for years to go to a sleep-away summer camp and was always denied. She wasn't forced to stay at home with her little brother while everyone else was enjoying their summers out of town. No one ever denied Ali anything.

It wasn't fair.

I glanced away, desperate to find an excuse to leave. Across the lot, I caught Jake's eye. He waved to me and I waved back, but my heart wasn't in it. I bet if he were sitting with us, he'd go on and on about the camp too. We hadn't made any plans together, so he probably wouldn't think anything of signing up and going. He probably thought that I would automatically go as well.

In the short time we'd been hanging out together, I had never brought up my family's money situation. There hadn't been a need until now. Either way, Jake would probably sign up too. Everyone's parents wanted them to have fun experiences as kids. But none of my friends had a mother who could barely afford everyday necessities, let alone an expensive summer camp.

With every second I thought about the incredibly boring and uneventful summer ahead of me, my mood worsened.

Then, out of nowhere, all the nervousness and anxiety

about our last camp situation abruptly bubbled to the surface. It was impossible for Ali not to like Jake. He was adorable, sweet, and so friendly. If she went without me, I bet after several weeks of her and Jake being cozy by the fire, he'd probably fall for her. It was bound to happen. She looked like me, except she was better at so many things. And she had a ton of money and could go to any fun event (or camp) she wanted.

Ali would return from the summer with Brie as her best friend and Jake as her boyfriend. Because Chris and our mom had started dating, they'd probably end up getting married. We'd move into Ali's beautiful house, and then I'd have to watch my crush be in love with my sister.

The gray clouds that filled my mind thickened, and when the bell finally rang, I was overcome with despair.

On the verge of tears, I didn't want the girls to know how upset I was so I sprinted into the school, leaving Ali and Brie to walk along behind me. I knew they were excited, but I couldn't believe they were willing to go to the camp without me.

I didn't get too far though as there was a crowd of kids blocking the hallway entrance. Ronnie's voice carried over the group just as Ali and Brie appeared at my side.

"What's going on?" Brie asked.

"Keep to the right!" Ronnie's voice sounded over the ruckus. "Clear the hallway, keep moving. The bell has rung, people... now get to class."

We all shuffled as a group toward our classrooms. Ronnie had her hair tied back in a braid and the orange lanyard was hanging in full view from her neck. No kids stopped by their lockers or congregated in small groups under her watch. If they did, she immediately went over to them and forced them to move along.

"Who is that girl?" someone asked.

"Whoa, she's pretty bossy about this," another girl frowned.

I couldn't believe Ronnie was taking the job so seriously. I knew she liked to be the center of attention, but this was unlike anything I'd ever expected from her. Didn't she realize how much the other kids would dislike her if she kept being so pushy? I understood she had a job to do, but she could have been a little nicer.

Although, when had Ronnie been nice to anyone without immediately smirking and saying horrible things behind that person's back?

As we shuffled along toward our classroom, I spotted the reason for Ronnie's behavior. Mrs. Jensen stood by one of the classroom doors, chatting with another teacher. Ronnie's gaze darted between the principal and the kids filing past. She was clearly behaving this way for Mrs. Jensen. This whole thing was an act, anything to impress the teachers.

Mrs. Jensen moved towards Ronnie and said something. I hoped she was telling her to pull back a little, but the way Ronnie smirked at me told me otherwise.

She locked her eyes on mine. "Don't dilly-dally."

I wasn't dilly-dallying. That comment was completely unnecessary. But I couldn't say anything with Mrs. Jensen nearby. I had to try to be a model student around the principal, especially now I was wearing a leadership badge. Besides, if I complained about Ronnie, she'd be sure to make my life even more miserable. I still had a lot of school years left with both Ronnie and Holly. Those girls always held a grudge, so I kept my complaint to myself.

I couldn't resist an eye roll in Ronnie's direction though. I was the vice-captain of our school and hadn't done anything to deserve to be singled out. Who did she think she was? I touched my badge, having the urge to point it out to her; to remind her that I had a higher position than her.

Thankfully, Ali spoke before I could do or say something I'd later regret. "I can't believe Mrs. Jensen was impressed with that."

I shook my head in annoyance and my skin prickled. Between not going to camp, the prospect of Ali becoming closer with Jake and Brie, and Ronnie's attitude, I wanted nothing more than to escape the school grounds. I needed space from all of this, but I knew that wasn't possible, at least not for another few hours.

Remembering the smiles across Ali and Brie's faces as they'd discussed the camp, I tried to change my attitude.

As difficult as it was, I had to try and stay positive in the way that Ali always insisted I should.

CHAPTER SIX

Ali

Through the rest of the day, I was desperate to tell Casey about my plan. I knew she was upset and I hoped she wasn't mad at Brie and me for going on about the camp. But we were excited and wanted Casey to feel the same way.

Her mood continued to worsen but until I had my dad's approval, I had to keep the secret buried inside me until I was sure he'd say yes.

With that thought, something else occurred to me. I hadn't actually considered whether my dad would allow *me* to go. Brie had asked me that question and I was sure I knew the answer. But what if I was wrong? What if he decided it was too soon since Mom's death?

Surely though, if I told him how important it was he would have to agree. Besides, he'd be busy working and if I went to the camp he wouldn't have to worry about me. He could go out with co-workers — something he rarely did — or spend more time with Jackie. It would be so cool if Casey and I came back from camp and our parents were closer than ever.

I was determined that everything would work out in our favor and when the final bell of the day rang, I hurried from the classroom, barely waving goodbye to Casey and Brie. As soon as Dad agreed, I'd call Casey straight away. I pictured the surprise on her face when I told her and I impatiently scanned the cars in the lot, searching for Dad's SUV.

Sprinting between the other parked cars, I was out of breath by the time I finally reached him. "Hey, Dad," I said as I flung the door open and hopped inside.

He grinned at me. "Whoa, there. I thought you liked school? What's the rush?"

I tilted my head in his direction. "No rush."

He made a show of looking out my window. "Looks like you're running from something."

*More like **toward** something — him.*

"Well, I do have some exciting news." I unzipped my bag and pulled the orange flier from my notebook. I'd kept it there, so it would be wrinkle-free and ready to present to him.

"More exciting than you becoming captain of your school?" he asked, pointing at my badge. "Did I tell you how proud I am?"

"About a million times, Dad."

"Well, it's true," he said. "I'm really proud!"

I smiled and held the flier out for him to see. "I wanted to tell you all about this amazing camp that Mrs. Halliday mentioned today. She showed us video footage from the website. It's so beautiful. It reminds me of that place where we went camping all those years ago. But at this camp, there are so many activities. It has this incredible aqua park, as well as a river with canoes and rope swings. There's even a go-kart track, rock climbing, and archery… oh my gosh, there are so many activities, I can't even remember them all!"

Dad took a quick glance at the sheet before pulling away from the curb. "That sounds like a great camp!"

"And if you let me go," I continued, "I'll be busy while you're working over the summer. So, you won't have to worry about me."

"Honey, I never worry about you," Dad said, ruffling my hair. "If this is something you really want to do, then I don't think I can say no, can I?"

"Really?" I asked, grinning. "It's okay for me to go?"

"I'll need to have a look at the website and talk to the organizers just to make sure it's safe and really is as good as they claim. But if it all checks out and you're keen to go, then I don't see why not. You haven't been to a summer camp in a long time."

"Well…" I added, trailing off. "There is one problem."

"What's that?" he asked. "If you're worried about the money, don't be. Let me handle that."

"It's something else…" I hesitated. "I really want Casey to come too, but she doesn't think Jackie will be able to afford it. I know it's expensive. I mean…it goes for several weeks. But Casey's never been to a summer camp because of the cost. It would just be so great if we could go together. Real sister bonding. And…I'd feel awful if I went without

35

her."

"Okay...so what did you have in mind?"

I laughed. "What makes you think I have something in mind?"

It was his turn to laugh. "I know you very well, Ali. You always think several steps ahead. Although I already have a feeling I know what you're going to say."

I beamed at him. "Well? What do you think? Would you be able to pay for Casey, so she can go too?"

He sighed; something I hadn't anticipated. Was this an issue I hadn't prepared for? I'd been so wrapped up in having the best summer ever that I hadn't even considered he would refuse to cover the costs. But Casey was my sister. It wouldn't be fair for me to go without her. He had to know that.

"I'm more than happy to pay for Casey," he said after a long pause.

"Great!" I replied. "So, what's the problem?"

He glanced at me. "There's more to this than the money, Ali."

"What do you mean?"

"Well, I'm not Casey's father," he said.

Technically, he wasn't my birth father either, but that never mattered. He was my dad. And I hoped that someday he'd be Casey's as well.

"Yeah, so? She's my twin." I frowned at him.

He cleared his throat. He seemed nervous. "As I said, this is a little awkward. I don't know how Jackie would feel about me offering to pay for her daughter. It's not as though we're in a relationship or anything. We're just friends."

My stomach dropped and so did my smile. Friends? What did he mean by that? He couldn't have changed his mind about Jackie in just one day? Right? What had happened in that time?

"I didn't think this would be a problem—"

"Then there is the matter of Lucas," Dad said, cutting

me off. "He could hardly be left at home on his own. Jackie works a lot and relies on Casey to watch her brother. This isn't a decision that I can make."

I sighed. "I thought that maybe Lucas could just stay with Grandma Ann."

"Ali, your heart is in the right place. But let's wait and see what Jackie says when Casey asks her. Perhaps you have their money situation all wrong and she'll be able to cover the cost herself."

"Okay," I nodded.

There was nothing I could do. I wasn't going to argue with him about it. But I hoped that Casey would at least ask Jackie and not just assume she'd say no because of what had happened in previous years.

Though Casey did seem pretty sure that Jackie couldn't afford to pay. And what if Dad still didn't want to get in the way? What then?

I didn't want to miss out on the opportunity, but would Casey mind if I went without her?

CHAPTER SEVEN

Casey

Even though I tried to block Ali out, I felt her excitement washing over me throughout the afternoon. It wasn't until she bolted from the classroom — probably desperate to tell her dad all about the camp — that I finally had a break.

Brie and I went to our lockers.

"Are you going to ask your mom if you can go to the camp?" she asked me.

"There's no point!" I sighed, shoving my books into the small space a little too forcefully. "I already know what her answer will be."

"Well, maybe this year will be different. Tell her that Ali wants to go. She wants you two to bond, right?"

"I guess," I said.

I didn't mind asking Mom, but I didn't want to get my hopes up. If she said no, it would make it all so much worse.

"Make sure you mention Ali," Brie insisted. "Your mom already feels bad about keeping your twin sister a secret. She might feel guilty and let you go. Besides, what's the worst she could do...say no?"

"I'll give it a try," I nodded half-heartedly. "But don't be too hopeful."

"Be positive," Brie said, patting my arm encouragingly. It was something that Ali would say to me. They were already becoming best friends...

On the way to the carpark to meet Grandma Ann, I thought about what Brie had said. Could I use Mom's guilt as Brie suggested? Or would that just upset Mom and make her angry?

By the time I reached Grandma Ann's car, I wanted to drop the topic completely. Maybe if I just forgot about it then I could avoid all the drama.

Lucas was already sitting in the front seat so I slipped into the back, happy that I didn't have to face my grandmother's questioning. For the entire ride home, Lucas didn't stop talking which gave me a chance to stare out the window and keep my thoughts to myself.

At home, Grandma Ann went straight into the kitchen to fill the kettle. It was something she did whenever she came to our house. She loved her tea. Normally, I might have sat with her, but I wanted to be alone.

"Did you have a good day at school?" she prodded.

"Yes," I said, not wanting her to pry any further.

I pulled my purple lunchbox out of my bag so I could wash it later on. Something brushed against my leg, and I looked down as I placed the box into the sink. An orange piece of paper landed at Grandma Ann's feet. With a grunt, she leaned over and picked it up.

My stomach sank. I hadn't planned on even mentioning the camp to Grandma Ann, and now she held the flier in her hands.

"What's this?" she asked.

"Oh nothing," I said and quickly washed my hands before walking over to the refrigerator.

Maybe if I didn't mention it again, she'd leave it alone. But I knew her too well.

"This doesn't seem like nothing; it looks like something fun!"

Of course it looked like fun, it was a summer camp. Summer camp had been my dream for years. I wished she'd just let it go, but I knew for her, that would be impossible.

"It's just some camp this summer." I sighed. Maybe if it seemed as though I wasn't interested then she'd stop discussing it.

The kettle whistled, and she turned the burner off. She placed the flier on the counter and poured the hot water into her mug. "Casey, this camp looks really good."

"Yeah," I said. "It does." *Too bad I can't go though.* The words spun in my head.

"I bet a lot of kids from your class are going." She raised her eyebrows curiously as she blew steam from the top of her mug. "Are Ali or Brie interested?"

I wished she'd drop it. I pushed back the tears in my eyes and turned away from her, pouring some cereal into a bowl. "They're both planning on going."

Why was she so curious about the stupid camp? Why didn't she just forget about it? Didn't she know what she was doing to me? She knew well enough that Mom would never let it happen. So why go on about it?

"Come, sit," Grandma Ann said. "There's no reason to stand there when there are three other stools right here."

I wanted to go to my room and be alone, but she wasn't having it. I knew if I tried to leave, she'd bring up the camp again later. Again and again and again. I dropped my bowl on the counter and picked out a few cereal puffs before popping them into my mouth. The crunching sound filled my head.

She glanced at the orange flier in front of her and then folded her arms questioningly. "Would you like to go too?"

I frowned and glared at her. "Yeah, I'd love to go. But look at the price."

She looked back at the sheet, taking in the details.

"Mom already paid for my school camp earlier this year." I shook my head. "There's no way she can afford to pay for another camp. Especially this one. It's way more expensive. Besides, what about Lucas? I'm his babysitter for the summer, remember?"

Why did I have to remind her of these things? She always pushed too hard and made me feel even worse.

Grandma Ann frowned and placed the orange flier on the table, smoothing her fingers over it.

41

I rolled my eyes. I wished she'd realize what her prodding did to people. Now she was upset because I'd snapped at her. But I couldn't dwell on the camp anymore. I already wished summer was over, so I could see what my life looked like after it all changed...again.

"I have to do some homework," I muttered, shoving off the chair. I wasn't even hungry anymore, but I took the bowl with me.

Inside my room, I closed the door gently so Grandma Ann wouldn't see how upset I was and want to pry into my life even further. I dropped my bag onto my bed. It was so much heavier than earlier in the school year. I had so many assignments to complete and tests to study for. But all I wanted to do was crawl under my sheets and close my eyes until September.

The sun poured in through my window, heating my room to an uncomfortable temperature. Striding over to the window, I lifted it open. Mom had been promising to install air conditioning units. I hoped that would happen soon or the summer really would be unbearable.

Turning to my mirror, I unbuttoned my shirt, revealing the tank top I was wearing underneath. I waved my hands under my armpits, wishing I'd stop sweating. I knew it didn't have anything to do with the warm temperature. The questioning from Grandma Ann had caused my entire body to overheat.

When I pulled off my shirt and placed it on the dresser, the vice-captain badge stared up at me. Earlier that morning, I was so proud to wear it to school, but what good would it do over the summer when I was stuck at home with Lucas?

Sighing heavily, I grabbed my bag and sat down at my desk. I then pulled out my books and spread them out in front of me. Flicking through my math book, I saw all the math problems across the pages. The math test was looming ahead and I needed to concentrate on the revisions. I had really struggled in class with the latest work and knew I still had a lot of practice to do.

But all I could think about was the upcoming camp that I would not be going to.

CHAPTER EIGHT

Casey

Using Ali's example, I made a list of the assignments I needed to complete over the coming weekend. If I was going to be home all summer, I didn't want to be grounded for bad grades. There was a difference between being stuck at home and not being able to leave the house altogether.

There were a few subjects I thought Ali could help me with but she'd be sure to ask about camp the moment we spoke. I wasn't ready to be reminded by her just yet and I didn't want to bring her down. Ignoring her was the only solution. Even though she and Brie had texted me several times, I knew what their messages were about and I didn't bother to read them. Eventually, I turned off my ringer so I could concentrate on my school work

After a while, my stomach began to growl and I hoped that Grandma Ann stayed to make something nice for dinner. I hadn't moved from my room since our conversation, and she hadn't bothered to check in on me. At least she had taken my hint this time. When I heard my mom arrive home, I didn't go out to greet her. Instead, I continued on with my school work.

When I'd completed as much as I could and began packing away my books, someone knocked on my door. "Come in," I said, hoping it wasn't Grandma Ann.

Mom poked her head inside my room. "Hey, Casey. How was your day?"

"Fine," I shrugged.

She smiled as she stepped tentatively towards me. My eyes landed on the orange flier in her hands. My cheeks flamed. Grandma Ann had told her about the camp. Now she was ready to tell me that I couldn't go. I already knew that, and I didn't need for her to rub salt in that wound.

She sat on the bed and placed the flier down as if it were a piece of thin glass. "Grandma Ann mentioned the summer camp. She said you'd like to go. She also told me Ali and Brie are possibly going as well."

She didn't seem sad or disappointed at all. Her expression was full of curiosity. My stomach fluttered. Had Grandma Ann convinced her to let me go? Did they work out some way that I could? Maybe Mom had put away some extra money for something like this. And was it possible that Grandma Ann could postpone her trip until school went back in the fall?

"I'm sorry, Casey," Mom said, immediately halting the questions in my head.

A breath whooshed out of me as she spoke.

"I'd love for you to go on this camp. It looks like a great experience. But we don't have the money right now. As well, with Lucas not being old enough to stay at home alone, I don't think it will work." She shrugged her shoulders helplessly.

That only irritated me even more. "I know…I know!" I snapped, unable to help the tremble in my voice. "Just — don't worry about it."

Mom winced and I immediately felt guilty for snapping at her. But the thought of my twin, my best friend, and the boy I'd hoped would ask me to be his girlfriend, all hanging out together at a really fun camp for the summer was all too much.

I whipped around, crossing my arms and trying to hold back my tears. "I have a lot of work to do before dinner."

We both knew that was a lie as I'd already packed my books into my bag. But I wanted to be alone before I started to cry. The weight of the day pressed down on me, and now that I had a confirmed answer, it was all too much.

Mom sat there for a moment, and I wondered if she was going to push me to talk about my feelings. If she didn't know how I felt, then she couldn't read people very well.

I wished I had thrown that flier away at school. Why did I keep it in my bag or even consider the idea of asking for permission? And why had I allowed Ali and Brie to get my hopes up?

"Dinner will be ready in about half an hour," she said, standing up from the bed. "I'm sorry, Casey. I wish things were different."

Yeah, so did I.

She closed my door behind her. The soft *click* gave me the opportunity to let out the breath I'd been holding.

I stared at the door. As much as I felt bad, I knew Mom felt terrible too. She did everything she could for our family and I had no right to make her feel guilty. But I struggled with that. Especially since my twin sister — who Mom had abandoned — was wealthy and could have anything she asked for.

Sometimes I wondered about my life if Mom had given me up for adoption instead of Ali. Everything would be so different for me right now. Growing up in Ali's household, I would not only be going to camp, I would have everything I ever wanted.

Shuffling over to my bed, I laid down on top of the covers and stared at the ceiling. My brain was tired from schoolwork, and I felt like curling up in a ball and falling asleep. But instead, I pictured my life if I had been the one to grow up as part of Ali's family. Designer clothes would fill my closet, clothes that were my style instead of Ali's. I pictured the organized shelves I'd have instead of the messy pile that fell onto the floor each time I opened my closet door, desperately searching for something nice to wear.

Framed photographs would line my bookcase from family vacations all over the world. Not to mention the beautiful house I would live in, one so beautiful it would be the envy of all my friends.

In reality for Ali though, I knew all of that had come with a cost. Her family had been through so much during her adopted mother's illness. And as if that wasn't bad enough, Ali had to accept the fact that her birth mother had given her away when she was born. While her adopted parents loved and adored her, at birth she had been the unwanted one.

Although there were a lot of things I didn't have, at least I had my mom. I'd grown up with her. And I supposed it was the one thing I had that Ali didn't.

My stomach twisted with guilt. I really should learn to appreciate my mother more. She did all that she could for Lucas and I. It wasn't her fault that we didn't have a lot of money.

But why did life have to be so difficult?

CHAPTER NINE

Ali

Once I arrived home from school, I had a constant urge to call Casey. I paced around my bedroom several times, texting her to find out if she had asked our mom about camp. But I didn't hear back at all. Either she was ignoring me, or the answer was no. I knew our mother usually didn't arrive home until late, so perhaps Casey hadn't even had a chance to ask her yet.

In a perfect world, our mother would tell Casey, *yes,* and I wouldn't have to put Dad in what he considered an awkward situation. To me, it wasn't a big deal. After all, we were practically family. Neither our mom nor my dad should feel bad about giving money to show how much they cared.

But Dad did.

I had to find a solution. It was the only way I could go to the camp and be happy about it.

Forcing myself to push my worries aside, at least until I heard back from Casey, I buried myself in my studies. Even though I kept up my grades, I still had to work hard. Math problems stared up at me from the textbook but camp remained foremost in my mind.

Eventually, I pulled out my camp bucket list and my skin tingled as I hovered in each of the thoughts that were soon to become memories. If only Casey could try harder to be in those memories, everything would be perfect. Was it so wrong for me to want that?

When Dad called me for dinner, I couldn't help myself. Ignoring his voice, I began texting. I had to know if

Casey was coming to the camp or not.

Have you told our mom? What did she say???

I pressed send and cradled the phone in my hands. Crossing my fingers, I hoped for the answer I wanted to hear.

Three dots appeared after my text and I knew that Casey was finally replying. My heart skittered in my chest. Please, please, please. The word repeated in my mind.

Her message came through, and it took me several seconds to accept what was in front of my eyes.

It's too expensive.

My stomach plummeted. I leaned against my bed, my legs turning to mush. That was it. As much as I was disappointed, I knew Casey felt even worse.

I sent a quick reply. *Did she say that?*

Yes. It looks like I'll be spending the summer with Lucas…

There must be a way for you to go. I typed back. *I don't want to go without you!*

My finger hovered over the send button. I chewed on my lip. Even if Casey couldn't go, it would still be so much fun to be at the camp with Brie, Jake, and his friend, Sai. I didn't know Sai very well but I loved hanging out with Brie and Jake. The best summer of my life was waiting for me.

My stomach twisted thinking about that. I'd never try and get between Casey and Jake, but I couldn't help the sliver of a crush that remained deep inside me. While it was nothing for Casey to worry about, I did want to maintain my friendship with Jake at the very least.

I moved my finger away and then back to SEND where it hovered above the button. I was hesitant to push it. Would Casey want me to remain at home with her over the summer? Staying behind with Casey would be the right thing to do, but even so, I didn't want to miss out on the camp.

It was such a dilemma. I wasn't sure what choice to make. I bit down hard on my lip, so hard that it hurt. Would

Casey stay behind if the situation was reversed and I was the one who couldn't afford the cost? I honestly had no idea.

I thought about it for a moment. My gut told me that I had to put my sister first. Without stopping to consider the matter any further, I pressed send and let the message go out into the airwaves. My palms were sweaty. I placed the phone down and inhaled a deep breath.

When Dad called me for dinner again, my original idea floated to the surface and a very small but hopeful smile played at the corners of my mouth. Now that Jackie had said no to Casey, surely there was something Dad could do to help.

I had to convince him!

CHAPTER TEN

Casey

There must be a way for you to go. I don't want to go without you.

Ali's text made my heart melt. All my fears of her abandoning me for the summer washed away. Those were the reassuring words I'd hoped to hear. I wasn't sure why I doubted my sister. She really did care about me.

At the same time, I was relieved. If I couldn't go to the camp this summer, then I didn't want Ali to go either. It sounded selfish, even to me. I also found it hard to admit, and it was something I would never share with anyone, but I'd be so jealous if Ali went and I didn't.

I'd see all her fun Snapchats and Instagram posts about how much fun she was having. I imagined Ali, Brie, and Jake smiling through the photographs, having the time of their lives. The thought made me sick to my stomach.

But I had to stop thinking like that. I tried to change my attitude. As the time passed by, I focused on Ali's message. She was smart, and she always had a plan. Maybe she'd find a way to help me get to camp after all.

CHAPTER ELEVEN

Ali

"I called you so many times for dinner," Dad said as he placed our plates on the countertop. We rarely ate at the table anymore, not since Mom died.

"Sorry, Dad. I was talking to Casey."

He handed over the basket of rolls, and I took one, breaking it open. It was still warm from the oven.

"I'm assuming Jackie said no?"

"She thinks it's too expensive." I might have turned up my whiny voice a little more than I had in the recent past, but it did the trick

"And you want me to call her to tell her that I'm willing to pay for it?"

I smiled. Dad knew me so well.

He ate a few bites before speaking again, "I looked up some camps for Lucas."

"You did?"

"Well, if Jackie agrees to let Casey go, then it's probably too much to expect Grandma Ann to mind Lucas every day, so he needs to be occupied with something."

"Oh my gosh, Dad. Thank you so much!"

I felt like throwing my arms around him right then and there. He'd already been thinking about the situation and was doing everything he could to make it all come together. At the very least, if Jackie allowed Casey to go, it would save me from telling my twin I was going without her.

Dad looked at me and smiled. "How was your day?"

"Really good thanks. We did a lot of revision for our

tests but all I could think about was the camp."

I told him all about the video presentation and while we spoke, I glanced at the table across the room. Sometimes, I imagined that my adopted mother was sitting there, listening to our conversations, smiling at us from a place with no more pain and suffering. I turned away as tears formed in my eyes. Thankfully, Dad didn't seem to notice.

When we finished eating, he reached for my plate but I stopped him from taking it. "How about I clean up tonight?"

He lifted his eyebrows. Normally we both cleaned up.

"I can stack the dishwasher while you call Jackie. Mrs. Halliday did say there were only a few spots left. The sooner we get this sorted out, the more chance we'll have of getting a place."

I couldn't imagine going through all of this, and then all the available spots were taken.

First of all, though, Dad had to call Jackie.

I could hardly wait to hear her response.

CHAPTER TWELVE

Casey

As I lay on my bed, waiting to be called for dinner, I heard the ringtone of my mother's cell phone. After the third ring, Mom's voice sounded in the hallway just outside my bedroom. "Chris? Hi, how are you?"

I chewed on my lip. Ali's dad? Was this the miracle I was looking for? I had a feeling that Ali was involved and I strained to listen. Sneaking quietly over to the door, I opened it slightly. Mom walked further down the hallway as she carried on with her conversation. Were they discussing their date this weekend? Or did it have something to do with the camp?

Whipping my door open, I headed toward the kitchen. I felt sneaky, probably because I was trying to eavesdrop and didn't want to be caught. I saw Mom in the living room with her back toward me. As if sensing me there, she glanced over her shoulder but then returned her attention to the phone call.

So it wasn't a secret conversation. She was probably relieved that I was out of my room. She might think I wasn't mad at her anymore. Although she should think twice about that. I was still upset. But as long as Ali was with me this summer, either at camp or at home, that was all that mattered.

"Dinner will be ready shortly," Grandma Ann said as she twirled a spoon around the pasta sauce bubbling in a pot on the stove.

"Okay," I replied, as I reached for a glass from the cabinet.

I opened the refrigerator, straining to hear more of the conversation. However, Grandma Ann flicked on the fan above the stove, creating a loud humming noise which made it difficult to hear Mom's voice. Grabbing the filtered water container, I poured some water into my glass. That had been my excuse for coming into the kitchen, but I was missing too much of the phone call.

Shoving the container back into the fridge, I moved toward the kitchen doorway where my mom's voice became clearer and the word "camp" stopped me in my tracks.

Mom and Chris *were* talking about camp.

I hovered there, leaning my back against the wall. If Grandma Ann noticed me eavesdropping, she said nothing. My heart pounded in my chest as I took a sip of water.

"No, I don't think so," Mom said. "It's much too expensive. I wish I could manage, but it's really bad timing."

I almost choked on my drink.

Grandma Ann turned around. "You alright, dear?"

"Yeah," I said, bolting over to the refrigerator. "I'm just thirsty." I needed an excuse to hang around and hear the rest of the conversation. There was no way I was missing out on it.

As I filled my glass again, Grandma Ann switched the fan above the stove to a higher setting and I could barely hear a word. With no other option, I walked into the living room. Mom acknowledged me and scurried to the window, peering out as if she weren't talking about the one thing that would make my summer a vacation I longed for.

"Oh no," Mom said, her tone changing. It sounded as if she was trying to be positive, but she chewed on her fingernail so hard, I thought it would snap. "I really couldn't accept that, Chris. It's very generous of you to offer, but no, that's out of the question."

I narrowed my eyes at her. As though she could feel me staring, she turned and looked at me.

"What?" I mouthed.

She frowned and shook her head.

My jaw dropped. This was unfair! She was talking about me, well camp, but that had to do with me. Why couldn't she include me in the conversation? I walked over to her, crossed my arms, and stared at her. Her eyebrows furrowed, and she waved me away.

I wasn't letting go that easily. I remained next to her, staring. This was about me. I needed to be included.

"What is it?" I whispered.

Her face scrunched up and she closed her eyes, pressing her finger against her free ear to listen; or maybe she was blocking me out.

I tapped her on the arm. She wasn't getting rid of me.

"Chris, I should be going. Thank you again. Have a lovely night and I'll see you soon." Mom hung up the phone and placed it on the coffee table beside her.

"What was that about?" I asked.

"Casey!" Mom said. "That was very rude. Please don't interrupt me like that again!"

"You were talking about camp, and that has to do with me." I frowned, ignoring the irritation in her voice. "What did he want? What can't you accept?"

She placed a hand on her forehead and swiped her hair away from her face. "He offered to pay for both you and Lucas."

"Lucas?"

"Yes. He checked online and found a day camp that he thinks Lucas might enjoy."

My heart leaped into my throat. Was I going to camp? The look on her face and her refusal of the money had to mean...no.

"If he's offering the money, why aren't you letting him pay?"

"Because I can't."

"Yes, you can."

"Casey, it's complicated."

57

"This is so unfair! It's like you want me to be stuck at home all summer with nothing to do."

"Casey, that's not what I want at all."

"Then why won't you accept his offer?"

"I don't want to discuss this anymore." She began to walk away.

However, I refused to back down. "He's trying to be nice. Ali is my twin sister. We're all family. Why not let him pay?"

"Casey!" Her warning tone rang in my ear.

Normally, I would have stopped, but she was being ridiculous. She couldn't afford the cost and Ali's dad could. He was more than happy to pay. His adopted daughter was my twin. We were family. What was the problem?

"I want to know why."

Her eyebrows furrowed into an angry frown. "I'm not discussing this with you. I've already said no, and that is final, young lady!"

"It's not—"

"Yes, it is!"

Her voice echoed in my head. Her cheeks flamed red, and I knew I'd crossed a line.

Heat coursed through me and tears welled at the corners of my eyes. When Grandma Ann appeared in the doorway, I fled to my room. I wasn't in the mood to discuss anything with her.

Lucas' blurry face abruptly appeared. "What's all the yelling about?"

I turned away from him and slammed my bedroom door shut. There was no reason for Mom to refuse the money. Ali's dad had plenty of it. Why couldn't Mom let me have this one thing?

I knew she worked hard to support us, but why couldn't she accept any help? Why was she so stubborn? She and Chris liked each other. Ali and I were more than happy to bring our families together. Did Mom's refusal have a deeper meaning? Was she not open to their relationship anymore? Surely, if she liked him, then she'd accept his money to send Lucas and me to camp.

I knew I had no right to stop Ali from going. I'd have to accept the fact that I'd be stuck at home all summer without her. It would be just me and my annoying brother for company.

It was all so unfair!

I fell onto my bed and sobbed.

CHAPTER THIRTEEN

Ali

When Dad agreed to make the phone call to Jackie, it had been hard not to focus on his smiling face. He had smiled more in the first few seconds of that conversation than he had in some time. That was until he told Jackie why he was calling.

"Ali has told me about the new camp this summer. It would be really great if the girls could go together. But Ali said Casey mentioned a financial issue?"

I watched Dad scratch his chin. It was a nervous tic of his and I could see he was feeling uncomfortable. I wished he and Jackie would come together on the fact that we were all family now. Casey and I didn't have a problem with that. There shouldn't be any issues.

"I found a day camp that Lucas might enjoy," Dad continued. "Its sports based and it's in the area so it would be easy to take him and pick him up each day."

He paused while Jackie replied.

"Yes, I'm happy to cover that cost as well as Casey's camp fees."

He then listened for what seemed like forever. The corners of his lips curved downward.

"I see," he said, scratching his chin again. "It's not a problem. I'm happy to do it for our children."

His words cut off. At that moment, I had no idea what was going on. I didn't know why Jackie wasn't accepting the money from him. There was no reason for her to refuse unless she didn't want Casey to go. If that were the case, no matter how much money Dad offered, it would never be enough.

"Alright, well if you change your mind, the offer still stands."

He paused again before looking at me.

"See you this weekend. Bye-bye."

The second he put the phone down, I confronted him. "What happened?"

"She won't take the money."

"But why?"

"As I said before, it's an awkward situation. Jackie is very independent. She wants to make her own way." He frowned again, clearly uncomfortable and perhaps a little embarrassed about offering the money, especially as Jackie had so flatly refused.

At Casey's expense? "That's not fair!" I said.

"She's in charge of Casey's life. I have to respect that."

Well, I was struggling to do the same. I wanted to pick up the phone and tell—no—beg her to take the money. Maybe that would work?

"I suggest you leave this alone," Dad said as if reading my thoughts. "She's made her choice."

"Not the right one," I muttered.

"Do you still want to go on camp without Casey?" he asked.

I nodded, not ready to say it out loud yet. I knew how Casey would react and I dreaded it. Maybe I could sign up and not tell her just yet. I felt horrible that she wouldn't be able to go, but I couldn't let that stop me from going. Could I?

As I trudged up the stairs to my room, my insides twisted uncomfortably. I wondered if Casey had heard the conversation between our parents or was Jackie sitting down with her right now and telling her the bad news?

Reaching for my phone, I checked my messages. There was nothing from Casey. I wanted to be there for her, but I knew her too well. When she was upset, there was no talking to her. I decided to let it go and see if she contacted me first.

I went into my bathroom to shower and get ready for bed. I'd already finished all my homework and felt prepared for classes the next day.

However, I wasn't prepared to face my twin. Not when I was going to camp without her.

CHAPTER FOURTEEN

Casey

Even though I was upset, I was hungry enough that I didn't want to skip dinner. Besides, Mom and Grandma Ann wouldn't have allowed it. Not going to camp wasn't a big deal for them. If I pushed too hard, I might end up grounded. I already had a boring summer to look forward to. I didn't need to make it worse.

So I sat at the table and ate as quickly as I could without saying a word to anyone. Luckily, Lucas talked everyone's ear off which helped to take the attention away from me.

I glanced at Mom across the table and her eyes turned down towards her plate. She seemed as miserable as me and only opened her mouth to eat. All I wanted was to go to the camp, and Mom didn't even have to open her wallet to make it happen. Why couldn't she have simply accepted Ali's dad's offer?

When we finished eating, Lucas announced that he needed someone to check his homework. Mom jumped on the opportunity to leave the room while Grandma Ann and I were left to clear the table. I gathered the dishes together and Grandma Ann scraped the leftovers into plastic containers and put them in the refrigerator.

The silence stretched on between us. I sensed she wanted to talk about Mom's conversation with Chris. No doubt Mom had told her all about it after we had our fight, but for once she didn't push the issue.

I wasn't sure why she wasn't discussing it since she rarely had a problem with meddling. I didn't question her though. The long summer stretched out before my eyes, and my mood deteriorated at the thought of it.

Grandma Ann hummed to herself while she washed the dishes. She placed them on the rack and I wiped them dry, thoughts of the following day with Ali and Brie going on and on about the fun they'd have this summer, flooding my mind.

When I finished wiping the last dish, I put it away and trudged off toward my room. My phone sat on my bed, facing downward. I knew Ali would have texted me by now after hearing her dad's news. He would have told her all about Mom's refusal. Ali would be upset for me, but even so, I knew she'd still want to go to the camp and I really couldn't be the one to stop her.

In an effort to distract myself, I grabbed my math book and the revision packet and started to make some notes. It helped a little. I even found myself focusing on the work and pushing thoughts of camp aside.

Almost half an hour later, someone knocked on my door. I groaned and sat up. "Come in."

I already knew it wasn't Lucas since he never knocked. Whether it was Mom or Grandma Ann, they were going to come in no matter what, so I had no choice but to get it over with.

Mom's head appeared around the door. She pushed it closed behind her and sat on the edge of my bed. "Casey, I want to talk to you about camp."

"What for? I know I can't go."

Her eyes were focused on mine as she continued. "I spoke with Grandma Ann and she's made a wonderful offer."

I shook my head. "I don't understand."

She paused as her mouth curved into a smile. "Grandma Ann has agreed to pay for you to go to the camp."

Her words took a moment to register and I stared

back in confusion. "She what? What do you mean? I don't understand. I thought…"

"She has some money put away. After all, you've been through since finding out about Ali, she feels you deserve a special summer with your twin. This camp looks amazing, and it would be the perfect opportunity for you girls to have some time away together."

"Really? I can really go?" I blinked as I tried to process what she was saying.

She nodded her head and it was then that I knew she meant every word. Overwhelmed with shock and excitement, I threw my arms around her shoulders. "I can't believe it! Mom…thank you so much! Thank you! Thank you! Thank you!"

Pulling back, I stared at her, struggling to believe I wasn't dreaming. Her news was so unexpected and I was still trying to come to terms with my new reality.

She smiled at me. "Well, Casey, it's your grandmother you need to thank. It's so good of her to do this. You're a very lucky girl. I told her it was too much. But she refuses to take no for an answer."

My grin widened. I knew Mom was stubborn and wouldn't accept help from Ali's dad, but once Grandma Ann decided on something, there was no arguing.

"What about Lucas? Who's going to watch him? Or is he going to camp too?"

"Grandma Ann has decided to postpone her trip so she can stay at home over the summer and be with Lucas."

I couldn't believe it. It seemed too good to be true. Grandma Ann had been looking forward to visiting her friend. Was she giving up that opportunity for me to have the summer of a lifetime with my sister?

I jumped off my bed and rushed out of the room. A lightness spread through me. I was actually getting what I wanted! From Grandma Ann of all people!

I found her sitting on the couch in the living room,

flipping through a magazine. I sat next to her, bumping my leg against hers in my excitement.

"Hello, Casey," she smiled.

I opened my mouth to speak and then closed it as a sudden thought popped into my head. This was the person I often complained about. I constantly grumbled about her meddling and the way she pushed into my life, but I never stopped to think about the sacrifices she made for our family. She was always there for us, buying groceries, cooking meals, washing clothes and driving Lucas and me home from school. As well, she gave up her time to stay with us when Mom was working or had to go out. Without Grandma Ann, our life would be so much more difficult. But how much gratitude had I ever shown her? And now she was making a huge sacrifice for me without any regard for herself. My cheeks burned with guilt and embarrassment.

"Grandma Ann," I said, knowing what I had to do. "I can't expect you to just give up your trip. I know how much you were looking forward to seeing your friend. And it's way too much money. I appreciate it so much, but I can't let you do this."

She gently pushed a chunk of hair behind my ears. "Darling, I think you deserve a special treat. I know how much you were hoping to go and you've been through a great deal this year. I want to do this for you. Make your grandmother happy and accept my gift to you."

"But what about your vacation?"

"Oh, that's okay," she said, waving her hand at me. "I've spoken with Margaret and she's going to come and stay with me instead. So Lucas will have the two of us fussing over him. Do you think he'll cope with that?" she chuckled playfully.

I laughed too. "Oh my gosh, thank you so much, Grandma Ann!" My smiled faded. I needed her to know how grateful I was. "I can't tell you how much this means to me." Tears welled in my eyes as I reached out and wrapped my arms gently around her neck. When I sat back, I saw there were tears in her eyes as well.

"All I ask is that you have a wonderful time. Take care but also take chances. Enjoy yourself. Enjoy being with your sister and your friends."

"I will Grandma Ann," I nodded. "I really will."

"And if you get the opportunity, I'd love for you to make me something," she added, smiling. "They usually do crafts at those camps. Maybe you could make me a bracelet, something I can treasure?"

"I'll make you ten bracelets," I said, hugging her again.

"Great," she laughed, squinting her eyes happily. "I'll look forward to that!"

For the first time, I realized how lucky I was to have

her around. As much as I thought she was annoying, she just wanted the best for me. She wanted to be a part of my life, and I had always been too busy to care. I promised myself that I would try harder and be much kinder to her in the future.

"Do you mind if I go and call Ali?"

"You do that," she beamed back.

I rushed off toward my room. Mom's door was open and she was at her desk. I wanted to tell her how happy I was. But I needed to tell Ali about my good news first.

CHAPTER FIFTEEN

Ali

As I was brushing my teeth, I heard my phone ring from my bedside table. I immediately recognized it as Casey's special ringtone, a Hailee Steinfeld song.

Throwing my toothbrush down, I ran to answer it. "Casey?" I breathed into the phone.

Her familiar voice sounded through the speaker. "You will never guess what!"

I couldn't lie about not knowing. "My dad told me—"

"No, not that."

"What?" I frowned. I didn't understand. What was she talking about?

"I have something to tell you!"

"What is it? Casey…just tell me!"

"Ali!" she squealed. "I can go to the camp! Grandma Ann said she'll pay for it. She just told me. She asked her friend to come here for the summer and stay with her instead. They'll both watch Lucas while I'm away. While *we're* at camp! Can you believe it? Ali, I can really go!" She was almost yelling the words and I could feel her excitement through the phone.

"What?" I squealed back. "That is amazing! Casey…I'm so happy!" I jumped up and down on the spot, totally overwhelmed. "When Dad told me what our mom said, I thought you definitely weren't going. There was no way I expected this to happen!"

"I know. One minute it was like the end of the world and then out of the blue, Grandma Ann saved me!"

"She really did!" I laughed. My whole body was

69

tingling. Everything had turned around in a heartbeat and I couldn't believe it.

There was a knock on my door and I looked to see Dad pushing it gently open. "Is everything alright?"

I covered the speaker with my hand. "Grandma Ann is paying for Casey to go to the camp."

A huge smile spread across Dad's face. "That is great news! So Jackie has agreed?"

"Yes," I said. "Grandma Ann can be very persuasive."

"I should get some tips from her," Dad said, chuckling. "I told you it would all work out." He waved at me before leaving the room.

"This is the best! Casey, we're going to have so much fun!"

"I know we are! I've never been to a summer camp before. I can't wait! Now, all we have to do is make sure we get a spot."

"I'll ask Dad to call first thing in the morning!" I grinned.

"I'll ask Mom to do the same thing," Casey replied. "I'll text Brie now and tell her."

"I don't think I'll be able to sleep tonight!"

"Me neither! A sleep-away summer camp. I've dreamed of this my whole life and now I'm actually going. And we won't even have to swap places!"

We laughed as we chatted about my bucket list and all the activities I'd listed. Casey was keen to do them all. We then group texted with Brie who was just as overjoyed as us. That morning, we'd had no plans for the summer and now we were going to have the best summer of our lives. Not just me and Brie, but Casey as well.

When we finally ended our call and I snuggled into bed, visions of the camp aqua park raced through my mind.

    I said a silent prayer of thanks as images of canoeing, rope swings, rock climbing, a high ropes course complete with a leap of faith, go-kart tracks and camping out under the stars filled my head.

    And the best part was that I'd have my twin sister to enjoy it with.

CHAPTER SIXTEEN

Casey

The next morning, the heavy weight that had been in my chest was gone. All the worry that had been pressing down on me had vanished. Grabbing my phone, I texted Grandma Ann with another thank you. I wanted her to know how grateful I really was.

It was still quite early, but instead of staying in bed and scrolling through my Instagram feed, the way I usually did, I decided to get up and make breakfast. When Lucas and Mom appeared in the kitchen, there was a stack of toast on the table. The bottom pieces were a little crunchy — they were from my first batch — but the thought was there. Fried eggs and toast was better than bowls of cereal, our usual breakfast through the week.

"Well, good morning, Casey," Mom said, shuffling toward the coffee maker. "This looks wonderful."

"Good morning, family. Today already feels like a good day," I said, as I placed a plate topped with two eggs down in front of Lucas.

As I turned back to the frying pan to cook more eggs for Mom, I spotted her amused expression. I was usually never cheery around my family in the mornings, but right then, I couldn't help it. Everything had worked out for me, and I wanted to show how happy I was on the outside.

Lucas grabbed two slices of toast and began scraping butter across the top. Too hungry to bother speaking, he munched on his first mouthful.

"I might have to send you to camp more often," Mom remarked with a grin. "Especially if it means having a delicious breakfast like this cooked for us."

Lucas dropped his fork. "You're going to camp?" A smear of yellow clung to his lips as he spoke.

I glanced at Mom. Hadn't she told him yet?

"Yes," Mom nodded. "There's a new sleepover camp being held this summer and Casey and Ali are going."

Lucas jutted out his lower lip. I winced, already knowing what his reaction would be. "You can't leave me at home by myself. Who's going to take care of me?"

"Grandma Ann and her friend Margaret," Mom said. "They have a lot of things planned for you."

"Like what?" Lucas asked, narrowing his eyes.

"Grandma Ann wants to show her friend around the area. I think they're planning on the zoo, some parks, museums, the cinema and maybe a few shows at the theater. There are heaps of great things for kids happening over the summer. If you behave yourself, they may even be open to some ideas from you as well."

"Wow, really?"

"Really!" Mom smiled.

Lucas dug into his food and Mom winked at me. As we ate our breakfast, we talked about the summer ahead. Lucas already had several ideas and I was surprised at how happy he was to be spending time with Grandma Ann. Although, if I had stayed at home, we wouldn't be going to half the places she had promised. So, it seemed that things really were working out for everyone.

The more we talked about the summer, the more excited I became. While only the night before, I had dreaded the months ahead, now I wanted the summer break to arrive as soon as possible.

On the bus ride to school, I group texted with Brie and Ali about camp. We chatted about all the clothes we'd need to pack. Ali invited us over to check out her clothing choices. She had so many and was willing to share with both of us. I'd borrowed clothes from Ali in the past, and it was so much fun. Everything surrounding camp was going to be incredibly exciting. And instead of our friendships breaking away from each other, after the summer we'd all be closer than ever.

When I met Ali and Brie at the entrance to the school, my mind was overflowing. I had no idea how I'd concentrate in class, but I was so happy, I didn't really care. However, my good mood disappeared when I heard Ronnie's voice screeching demands in the center of the hallway.

She wore a black tank top, which made her orange lanyard stand out even more. Her hair was tied back into a tight ponytail, making her eyes look narrowed and determined. She reminded me of a devious cat. She crossed her arms over her chest as she eyed everyone walking by. Most of the kids skittered out of her way, but when she spotted me, she charged in our direction.

"What is her deal?" Brie asked.

"No clue," I replied.

"She's taking this hall monitor job too seriously," Ali sighed.

Brie scoffed. "She's probably trying to make it seem really important, to make up for missing out on the captain position."

As we walked, Ronnie darted to the side, stopping right in front of me. "Littering is an offense. Pick that up now, or I'll report you." She pointed at the clipboard in her hands.

I frowned at her. "What are you talking about, Ronnie? I didn't litter."

An evil smile curved her lips and a cold feeling rolled down my spine as she cast her eyes downward. "Well, what's that then?"

We all looked at the floor to see a scrunched-up piece of paper near my feet. Right beside it was a trash can.

"I have no idea," I shook my head. "That's not mine." I pushed past her, not wanting to be in trouble for littering when I had done nothing wrong.

"I'm going to have to report this," Ronnie said, bringing her clipboard closer while she wrote on the sheet. "First offense, Casey Wrigley, littering in the hallway and refusing to collect her trash when asked."

"It's not hers!" Brie whipped around to confront her.

"We were with her the whole time!" Ali said, defending me.

Ronnie didn't seem at all bothered by their comments. She pursed her lips. "Casey, I should mark you down for two offenses, but since this is your first, I'll be nice."

Nice? "Ronnie, what are you doing? You know I didn't drop that piece of paper. It's not mine. I've only just arrived and that bit of paper was already there."

"No it wasn't," Ronnie said quickly. "I've been checking these hallways all morning. They were clean until now."

I glanced at Ali and she frowned at Ronnie. "Ronnie, don't do this. You know that paper isn't Casey's."

"It doesn't matter," Ronnie said, waving her hand at us. "Students are expected to keep the school clean and tidy, and you've blatantly refused to follow that rule."

My mouth dropped open once more. "You can't report me for something I didn't do!"

Ronnie raised her eyebrows. "Really? Watch me." She turned on her heel and continued down the hallway with the clipboard firmly in her hands.

I let out a little squeak of disbelief.

Ronnie disappeared into the crowd while I remained in my spot, struggling to believe what had just happened.

"What was that all about?" Brie asked.

"Someone woke up on the wrong side of the bed," Ali remarked, angrily.

"This is ridiculous. Is she going to report me for something I didn't do?"

Brie chewed on her lip. "Do you want a happy answer or the real one?"

Ali grabbed my arm. "Let's go."

It was easy enough for them to brush it off since they weren't the ones in trouble. I was aware of the badge attached to my shirt and that by the end of the day, Mrs. Jensen or the assistant principal, Mrs. Watkins, would be aware of Ronnie's list of offenders. Ronnie would hand the list of names to the main office and my name would be among them.

Everyone knew that after three offenses, students were required to do a session of detention. I certainly didn't want a detention. I didn't want my name on that list at all. In all my years at school, I'd never been reported for anything. How could this be happening to me? And how could Ronnie so easily get away with it?

The badge had only been on my shirt for one full day, and suddenly, I was about to be reported to the office. I couldn't believe it! When we reached the classroom, I walked over to my desk and slumped down in my seat.

When Ronnie and Holly entered the room, they both smirked at me with scheming smiles. Even though I already knew it, Ronnie couldn't be trusted. Since the election, she had a reason to get me into trouble as well as the power to do so.

Although I made a mental note to stay out of her way, I had no idea what to expect from her. She was obviously willing to lie to get what she wanted.

Knowing that caused my stomach to churn.

What did she have in store for me next?

CHAPTER SEVENTEEN

Ali

Throughout morning classes, I watched Casey from my seat at the back of the room. As Mrs. Halliday continued with revision exercises, my mind wandered. I already knew I would ace the tests, so I used the time to think about my twin. Her issues with Ronnie hadn't improved at all. Ronnie and Holly were ruthless, and I wished there was something I could do to make the bullying stop.

Sure, Mrs. Halliday was aware of one previous incident involving Ronnie, but now Ronnie had a position of power and teachers loved students who followed the rules.

In this case, though, Ronnie was also breaking the rules. We all knew Casey hadn't littered, yet Ronnie pushed forward with reporting her anyway. It wasn't fair. I didn't even know what to say in Casey's defense anymore. Ronnie and Holly listened to no one except each other.

Whatever plan they had in mind for my sister wasn't going to stop until Ronnie managed to get what she wanted. But that was the problem. What else could she want? Did she want to get Casey into trouble so that she could have her vice-captain job taken away from her? I'd never let that happen, but we couldn't wait and just hope for the best. Casey had to fight for herself.

As far as I knew, the bullying started after I arrived. I wasn't sure if those girls were jealous because Casey and I were twins and seemed to get a lot of attention. But there was plenty of attention to go around. Holly and Ronnie just needed to change their attitude. It would be so much better if we could all be friends. Though the damage was done. I doubted Casey and Ronnie would ever be friends again after this.

At recess, I huddled together with Casey and Brie, far away from our classmates. We didn't need any more trouble.

"I still can't believe Ronnie did that," Casey said, glaring in her direction.

Ronnie sat with Holly across the way and I hoped they would stay there. While they didn't look at us, I knew they were plotting something.

Casey turned to me with wide eyes. "Will Mrs. Jensen take away my badge and my title? What if Ronnie keeps doing this until I have three offenses? Mom won't be happy. And I can't imagine Grandma Ann would still be willing to pay my camp costs."

Brie shook her head. "We won't let that happen."

"Casey, try not to worry about it." I made my voice sound as reassuring as I could. "Maybe it was just a one-time thing. She's getting you back for being elected vice-captain instead of her."

I thought back to Ronnie's efforts leading up to the election. She had gone to so much trouble and expense giving out candy bars with the notes attached. She had tried so hard. If I did all that and ended up with a hall monitor position, I'd be upset too. Though that was no excuse to take it out on Casey.

"She's going to keep it up," Brie sighed. "She wants revenge!"

Casey's face fell. I bumped Brie on the arm and gave her a look. She wasn't helping Casey feel better at all.

Brie shrugged. "It's Ronnie. She's never going to stop."

I rolled my eyes and wished Brie would be a little more supportive and positive around Casey. But I supposed that was what best friends did.

"Should I say something to Mrs. Halliday?" Casey asked.

"I think we should just stay out of Ronnie's way," I replied. "She wants a reaction from you. If you ignore her, hopefully, she'll stop."

"But *you're* the school captain," Casey said to me. "Why isn't she doing this to you as well?" Casey waved her hands around helplessly. "Not that I'd want her to, but you know what I mean."

I nodded. It was true. Ronnie had begun targeting Casey long before the elections though. It was probably a combination of Casey being a twin, and becoming the leader of the cheer squad, as well as being elected vice-captain over Ronnie. I was sure it was jealousy, there couldn't be any other reason.

I locked eyes with Casey. "Maybe she feels threatened by you. Either that or she still thinks she can bully you. But you have to stand up to her, the way we talked about before."

"It's so hard," Casey moaned. "She probably has a list of ways to mess up my life. There's so much at stake and she knows I'm a pushover."

"Be confident," I reminded her, lifting my chin. Casey was sliding backward into her shyness, and that wasn't going to get her anywhere. We had a long year ahead of us in our captain positions, and we had to show everyone that neither of us was a pushover. "Ignore her as much as possible. If she sees that she's not bothering you, then she'll stop. I know it. Bullies thrive on attention."

Casey shrugged. "I'll try. But now that she's hall monitor, I feel like I can't even cough around her without being added to her list."

Brie groaned. "Okay, let's stop talking about Ronnie. Just pretend she doesn't exist. And besides, we have an awesome summer to look forward to. Casey, I still can't believe your grandmother is paying for it all. I never expected that to happen."

Thankfully, Brie's comment was enough to distract

Casey. "Me neither!" Casey nodded.

Brie encouraged her further. "What are you looking forward to the most?"

Casey listed all the activities that she couldn't wait to try, although she felt nervous about the Leap of Faith. According to Mrs. Halliday that activity was a great confidence booster which was exactly what Casey needed. I also hoped it would help with my fear of heights. As scary as it looked, I was determined that we'd all give it a go.

"I had another look at their website this morning," I added. "Since this is the first year, there weren't any reviews, but I found out that after your first visit, you're guaranteed a spot for the next year if you want it.

"That's so cool," Brie said. "We should book in for next year as well!"

Casey chewed on her lip and I took in her worried expression. She probably thought Grandma Ann wouldn't be able to afford another year, but there were ways around that. Either we could start saving in the fall, or if our mom and my dad became close, Dad could pay the costs without the awkwardness we'd dealt with this time around. From now on, I wanted to make it my mission to keep Casey by my side for all the fun activities in our lives.

"It's going to be amazing!" Brie let out a little squeal.

Casey's shoulders relaxed. With more talk of this coming summer, her mood perked up and mine did as well. I was happy when she was happy, and there was no one else I'd rather go on this adventure with. Having Brie there was an added bonus, and I knew we'd all have a great time together.

There was one concern though. Would Casey want to spend all her time with Jake? This was supposed to be a chance for Casey and me to become closer but with Jake around day in and day out, that might not happen.

Deciding not to be negative, I pushed that thought aside. I was sure my twin wouldn't let a boy come between us, even one as good looking and nice as Jake.

At least I hoped that was the case. But when I spotted him waving enthusiastically in Casey's direction, a shard of doubt hovered inside me.

Would having Jake there keep Casey and I apart?

CHAPTER EIGHTEEN

Casey

When we returned to the classroom, Ronnie and Holly snickered as I walked to my seat. Brie noticed and spoke up in a loud voice. "Casey, I can't wait for this summer at camp. It's so nice that we're not going to be stuck with our parents on some boring family trip!"

Holly rolled her eyes at Brie, but I could tell both she and Ronnie were jealous that we were going to the new summer camp and they weren't. Both girls settled in their seats and didn't say anything else.

"Thanks," I whispered to Brie.

She smiled. "What are friends for?"

I wished retorts like that came easier for me. Though Brie and Ali weren't the ones being bullied. I wondered if they'd think of good responses quite so quickly if they were being stared down by Ronnie. I was sure I'd be braver if I wasn't the one being picked on.

While I knew I should be concentrating on the lesson, Ronnie was all I could think about. If she continued with her bullying and I was given detention, Mom or Grandma Ann might stop me from going to camp.

Would Ali's plan work? Would ignoring Ronnie get me anywhere? I didn't have any other ideas. If I fought back, I was sure Ronnie would want to come after me even more. I had to be smart, and since Ali was the smartest girl I knew, listening to her would surely help my situation. So as hard as it would be to ignore Ronnie, I needed to try.

Maybe one of the teachers would catch her picking on other kids in the hallway and put her in her place or even report her to Mrs. Jensen. I imagined Ronnie losing that ridiculous lanyard and badge and then she wouldn't have any power over me. At least not in the hallways.

Hopefully, the summer away from her would help build my confidence. Making new friends at camp and going on new adventures might help. I still had to check that Jake was going too. Over the past two days, I had barely spoken to him. I couldn't wait to see his smiling face when I told him we were about to spend the majority of the summer together. I just hoped he'd managed to secure a spot.

As I turned in my seat to catch a glimpse of his handsome face, a thought occurred to me. He hadn't mentioned camp to me at all. What if he was planning on just going with Sai? Maybe he wouldn't want me hanging around for most of the summer? What would his reaction be when I told him I was going too?

My stomach was a bundle of knots when we went to lunch. Jake and his friends were already ahead of us. He hadn't looked at me once since leaving the classroom and I wondered if he was purposely avoiding me.

But as Ali, Brie, and I searched for a place to sit, he waved at us. "Girls! Over here," he called, indicating the spot at the table beside him and scooting over to make some room.

Beaming, I slid into the seat, my stomach fluttering as he smiled at me.

"Hey, Casey," he said. He touched my hand and tingles jolted up my spine. "Sorry I haven't been around much during breaks. I've been busy helping Mr. Pavoni with the sports equipment."

"That's okay," I smiled nervously.

Everyone was munching on their food, but my stomach was tied in so many knots that I wasn't even hungry.

"What's been going on with you?" he asked. "Any summer plans?"

It was the chance I needed and I decided to dive right in. "I'm actually going to that camp Mrs. Halliday talked about yesterday. What about you? Are you going too?" Visions of Jake and me holding hands by the fire caused goosebumps to run up and down my arms.

His smile disappeared. "That camp looks so good! Sai and I both really want to go. But my parents said it's too expensive. And Sai doesn't want to go without me. So he's going to miss out, too."

"Oh, no!" I was unable to hide my disappointment. I thought for sure that they were both going.

He cupped his chin in his hand and leaned on the table. "It's so unfair. It looks like the best camp in the whole country. The aqua park and the go-kart track will be awesome. I really wish I could go!"

I was surprised to hear that even his parents considered it too expensive. Once again, I thought about how lucky I was to have Grandma Ann. But I had been looking forward to having him at the camp. What was going to happen if we were separated for so long? I wouldn't see him for ages. My stomach lurched at the thought of us drifting apart.

"What are you going to do all summer?" I asked. Even though I knew Ronnie and Holly would be on vacation with their parents for most of the summer, I imagined them running into Jake at the movies or the mall and trying to steal him away from me.

A smile reappeared on Jake's face. "My cousin, Mike called last night and invited me to stay at his house. I'm so glad! Otherwise, I would have been stuck at home all summer. He lives on a big property with horses and motorbikes and a ton of land. When we were kids, we used to build forts and stay overnight in the woods. There's no aqua park or go-kart track but it'll still be fun." He touched me on the arm and his lips quirked in the corners. "I'll miss hanging out with you, though!"

The butterflies returned with full force. "I'll miss you too, Jake."

I realized instantly that if I'd stayed at home for the summer with Lucas, Jake wouldn't have been around at all. I silently thanked Grandma Ann once more.

"I read on the website that no phones are allowed, so I won't be able to text you, but I could send you a letter." I smiled shyly at him, not sure what he would think of that idea.

"That'd be great," he grinned. "And I'll write you back. I can give you Mike's address, so the letters get to me faster."

I smiled, broad enough that my cheeks hurt.

"Hopefully we'll have a few weeks at the end of summer so we can hang out. If you want to, that is?"

"Yes, definitely!" I replied, wanting nothing more.

Jake took a bite out of his sandwich and nodded a few times. "Maybe after you get back, Mike can stay with me for a little while, then we could go on a kind of double date? You, me, Mike, and Ali?" His hands twisted in his lap. For the first time ever, he looked nervous. "What do you think?"

I sucked in a breath. "That sounds amazing." I glanced at Ali who was talking to Brie. She hadn't heard the conversation, but I already knew how she felt about Mike. "I'm sure Ali would think so too."

"Awesome," Jake said, grinning.

I matched it.

Casey Wrigley
Vice Captain

On the way to class, I told Ali about the possibility of another double date. She squealed happily, even though the date was a while away. Camp excited us both, but now we had a reason to want to come back.

I noticed that Brie was quiet during that conversation, but I already had an idea for her. "I bet Jake can invite Wyatt and we can all go out together, just like before."

"Really?" Brie asked.

"Of course," I said, slinging an arm over her shoulder. "We wouldn't want to go without you."

"We haven't been out together since the day we went to Great Escape," Ali said, smiling.

I cringed. That day hadn't turned out very well for me. Ali's friend, Meg flirted with Jake the entire time. It was as if she wanted to mess things up between him and I as well as between Ali and me. I breathed a sigh of relief, knowing that so far, Ali hadn't made any plans with Meg over the summer and there had been no mention of her return.

Ali had said she'd had a great time though and would probably want to visit again at some stage. Apparently "a great time" meant torturing me, but maybe she wasn't even aware of what she was doing. I just hoped she didn't come during the last weeks of summer. That would ruin everything. It would turn our date into the Great Escape day all over again.

I shoved those thoughts from my mind. Maybe if I didn't mention Meg, Ali would forget all about her and just focus on our own amazing summer.

All I could do was hope that Meg didn't have ideas of her own.

CHAPTER NINETEEN

Ali

Since we still needed to get through our tests and end of year assignments, I tried to keep all thoughts of camp out of my mind during the school day. Casey had a harder time with that and Ronnie wasn't doing anything to help.

Ronnie seemed to be on a power trip, one she wasn't planning on ending anytime soon. She continuously wrote kids up in the hallways for the most minor and silliest of issues. Loitering was a big one. If someone stood at their locker too long, she wrote them up. With the long list of names that she was accumulating, I was certain detention would be packed during the last week of school.

She was so bad that most of us kept out of her way and walked the long path around the school to avoid her hallway.

Brie and I blocked Casey whenever we saw Ronnie coming. But that didn't stop her from saying rude things about Casey under her breath.

During our study sessions at night — either at my house or Casey's — our conversations veered toward Ronnie. While I tried to keep my twin feeling positive, it was becoming harder to do. That morning, Ronnie almost wrote her up for chewing gum. But Mrs. Halliday happened to be nearby and Ronnie backed down. She probably wouldn't blame Casey for littering again, but she had enough up her sleeve for us to be wary of her next moves.

Brie suggested reporting Ronnie, but Casey felt she didn't have enough proof. And most importantly, she didn't want either of us to cause problems only days after receiving our captain's badges.

I reminded Casey that we only had a week left of Ronnie and Holly and after that a summer of fun.

Casey worked harder than ever on her schoolwork, and by the time the weekend rolled around, I knew we were ready for anything.

Soon after I arrived home from school on Friday afternoon, I found my dad in his bedroom, searching through his closet.

"What are you doing?" I asked.

He peeked out from the walk-in robe, his hair messed up as if he'd rubbed a balloon across it. I opened my hands out questioningly in front of me. There were so many clothes laid across his bed that I could barely see the duvet. "What's all this?"

He raised his eyebrows sheepishly. "I'm looking for something to wear for my date tomorrow night."

I smirked and walked closer, rubbing my hands together. I'd never had a chance to dress my dad up before. "What have you chosen so far?"

He cleared his throat and pulled out two of his work suits.

I pulled a face. "Are you taking her for an interview?"

He shook his head and grinned. "Don't look at me like that. It's been a long time since I've been on a date. I don't have anything decent. My clothes are either too casual or too formal."

"It's also been a while since you bought anything new. How about we go shopping tonight?"

"Tonight?" he asked.

"Well, you have to work in the morning, don't you?"

"Yes, I do," he nodded.

"Then we should go shopping tonight. It'll be fun. And we could have dinner at the food court in the mall."

He scratched his chin thoughtfully. "I guess I'm not

really organized with food for dinner. So that's probably a good idea."

"Perfect!" I said, eagerly nodding my head.

Mom and I had always shopped together, but this was a whole new adventure. I was sure she would be proud.

As we drove to the mall, I questioned Dad about his plans for the date. He was going to buy some flowers for Jackie, and we talked about which type he should get. He had already booked a table at a local Italian restaurant, but it wasn't super fancy, so I had some ideas for the style of clothes he should wear.

When we reached the mall, I grabbed his hand and led him in the direction of the store I had in mind.

"I wonder who's more excited about this date?" he grinned as he quickened his pace to keep up with me.

I laughed as we entered the Brook's Brothers store. I really was excited and could hardly wait to search for something to impress Jackie.

As I browsed a nearby rack, a pretty saleswoman approached us. "Hello, my name is Gretchen. Are you looking for anything in particular? We have some great new stock just over here."

I turned towards her. "My dad needs a new outfit for a date!"

The woman raised an eyebrow at me and then looked at Dad.

He shrugged. "She's in charge."

She smiled at me. "Well, then—"

"Ali," I said.

"Ali, tell me what you were thinking."

I skimmed through the rack of clothing she had indicated and pulled out a long-sleeved shirt. "Something in this style would be nice! And maybe some pants like these." I said, pointing to a pair of beige chinos that were hanging on another rack.

Gretchen nodded and chose a few variations of color and style in Dad's size. She then carried them to the dressing room.

When Dad appeared, dressed in varying combinations, Gretchen went over to him each time and adjusted his shirt and complimented him on the choice. I beamed from ear to ear. He looked so happy. I knew he was anticipating the date with Jackie and I couldn't wait to see what she would be wearing as well.

Everything was falling into place for us. Something I'd never thought would happen when my adopted mother was so ill.

"I think this is the perfect combination," Gretchen said, tapping her finger against her chin. "What do you think, Ali?"

"I love it!" The pale blue shirt made his eyes pop, and the chino pants fit his style much better than the business suits in his closet. Those were too stuffy and formal. If he and Jackie were going to be a couple, they needed to be comfortable with each other.

"Are you sure?" Dad asked.

"Perfect," I said, agreeing with Gretchen. "Absolutely perfect!"

Dad smiled at his shoes, embarrassed at the compliment. I guess he hadn't been complimented in a while. We'd been too busy with Mom to worry about that sort of thing, and I doubted Dad was ever looking for one when Mom was so unwell.

Gretchen fawned over him and suggested that he buy a few of the other shirt options so he could mix and match for other occasions. I knew Dad appreciated her help but that was where his interest ended. He was already taken by my mother and he would end up marrying her. Well…eventually.

Tingles moved all over my body at the thought of that happening. It was way too soon to think about it, but I had a clear picture of their wedding day in my mind. I pictured Jackie all in white and me and Casey as bridesmaids. It would be a picture-perfect day that we would all remember. The image caused a shiver to run down my spine.

After leaving the store with two big bags of clothes between us, Dad and I walked down to the food court.

"What do you feel like eating?" I asked him.

"Didn't you say there was a good Chinese food place here?" he asked, looking around.

"Yes, it's just over there." I pointed across the way. Casey and I had eaten there a few times. The food was good.

As I glanced in that direction, a familiar face stood out amongst the crowd and I had to blink a few times, thinking that I was staring at a mirrored display.

"Casey!" I called out to the girl with my face.

"Ali!" She raced over to us. "What are you doing here?"

Jackie appeared behind Casey and smiled. "Hey, guys. What are the chances of bumping into you here!"

"We're shopping for the big date!" I said.

Dad cleared his throat.

"Us toooooo," Casey announced loudly.

"Okay, girls," Jackie mumbled quietly, an embarrassed expression filling her features.

I saw her eyes meet my dad's and amused smiles formed on each of their faces. Tugging Casey a few steps away so they could talk, I grinned at my twin.

"You didn't tell me you were coming here," Casey smiled.

"I didn't know until I saw what Dad was planning to wear." I rolled my eyes and laughed.

"That's so funny! Mom's bedroom looked like a bomb had exploded. She had clothes everywhere. So I convinced her to come shopping as well."

I nodded eagerly. "They both need to make a good impression!"

We glanced at our parents who were smiling and laughing. They could barely take their eyes off each other. Dad opened his bag for Jackie to look inside and she nodded in approval.

"Ali insisted," Dad said, leaning close to her.

"So did Casey," Jackie said. "They are twins though. They can probably read each other's minds."

Casey and I looked at each other before stifling laughter into our hands.

While both Casey and I were looking forward to starting our new lives together as a family, I had a feeling that Jackie and Dad were the most enthusiastic of all.

CHAPTER TWENTY

Casey

Mom took forever on Saturday afternoon to prepare for her date. She looked so beautiful in the little black dress that I'd insisted she-she should buy. Since it was on the clearance rack at the store, she didn't hesitate too long. And it was perfect for the occasion.

I braided one side of her hair and brought it all together at the back. She had the prettiest face, and I wanted to make sure Chris saw all of it. Ali and I were so hopeful of their relationship working out, that we'd decided to do all that we could to help.

As well, since Grandma Ann had offered to pay for my camp costs, my attitude towards my family had changed. I was lucky to have them, and I wanted them to know it.

When the doorbell rang, I raced to open it and beamed at my twin and her dad as I welcomed them inside. Chris looked so handsome in his new outfit. Like a gentleman, he had brought the most beautiful bunch of flowers, complete with a gorgeous white ribbon.

He smiled shyly as he handed them to Mom. They were so cute together, just like a couple of teenagers and I could almost feel their nervousness. As soon as I closed the door behind them, Ali and I squealed happily. Our plan was working so well and we were overjoyed.

After they left, we sat down with Grandma Ann and Lucas to watch a movie on TV. As we munched on popcorn, we imagined our parents at the restaurant together. A few times, Grandma Ann chimed in about how wonderful they were together. It was so good to know that we were all in agreement over the match.

At some point, I fell asleep on the couch beside Ali. I woke later when she went home for the night but was too tired to ask Mom about the date. So I questioned her on Sunday morning at breakfast.

"It was fun," she said, smiling into her coffee mug.

From her look, I could tell that she'd had a really great time.

"That's all you're going to give me?" I asked her.

"For now," she grinned.

I put a hold on that conversation since I knew Ali would probably get more information from her dad. When Mom drove me to Ali's house to do some test revision and Chris invited Mom in for coffee, it took so much willpower for Ali and me not to eavesdrop.

Instead, we went into Ali's room and closed the door so we could chat. Much to my disappointment though, Chris hadn't been any more forthcoming about the date than our Mom.

"He just said they had a nice meal and he really enjoyed himself." Ali was as frustrated as me.

I was impatient for more details. "Okay, so when are they going on another date?"

"I asked Dad that and he said nothing was arranged yet."

I gave a dissatisfied sigh. At the same time though, I felt sure we didn't have anything to worry about. Ali and I would just have to be patient and let the relationship take its course. I understood that Ali's dad would want to take things slowly after his wife's death. It had been a tragedy for him to lose her. Mom knew that as well. Ali and I wanted this new relationship to last, so starting it off on good footing was important.

Forcing myself to focus on school work, I turned to my books. By the afternoon, I finally felt confident about the upcoming tests. With Ali's studying methods and my desperate need to go to the camp over the summer, my brain clicked into place and absorbed everything I needed to know.

On Monday morning, I woke with excitement in my bones. It was the last week of school before the most amazing summer of my life. Exams were spread throughout the week so after each one, I could dump that information from my head and prepare for the next. Math was scheduled first. I'd spent the night before going over and over the formulas and hoped I would pass with a good grade. I was no longer happy with just squeaking by. With Ali's help, I now had the drive to be better. And I imagined Mom's face when my report card came back with A's and B's instead of all C's.

My confidence bloomed during the ride to school, but when the bus pulled into the curb and I spotted Ronnie and Holly heading into the building, my stomach flip-flopped. The summer was so close, yet I still had five days to deal with whatever they had up their sleeves. I already had one offense on my record, and I could not get any more. I wondered if Ronnie's aim was to see me on the detention list. I prayed that wasn't the case.

While I still had the option to ask for help from Mrs. Halliday or my mom, I wanted to do this on my own. I wanted to prove to myself and Ali that I wasn't a pushover and that I could deal with two mean girls.

Once I stepped off the bus, I grabbed my phone to text Brie and tell her I'd meet her at the entrance so we could walk in together. As I glanced at the screen, however, a notification from Instagram caught my eye. Clicking on it, I saw that someone had tagged me in a post. Someone with the username, *friendzone101*. I had no idea who that was. Could it be spam?

I clicked on the notification, and a photo of Ali and me sitting side by side in the courtyard stared back at me.

"What?" I muttered, scrolling down to the caption.

I didn't even know who had taken this picture or when. Ali and I were smiling but I couldn't recall the occasion.

My eyes tracked the wording of the caption and I had to read it three times before the message fully registered in my brain. That was when my pulse spiked.

Who is your favorite? Ali Jackson or Casey Wrigley? Comment below to vote!

I glanced up to see if someone was playing a prank on me. But everyone seemed occupied, chatting to friends or waving goodbye to parents as they drove away. My heart thumped wildly as I clicked on the picture and saw that a huge list of names had been tagged. Whoever had posted the photo and the caption wanted to make sure everyone saw it.

Already there were seven comments! Four kids had voted for Ali, two for me, and one had written…*I can't choose!*

My stomach dropped. I refreshed the photograph, and more comments appeared. Some of them were tagging other friends to make sure they saw the post as well. The newer votes were all in favor of Ali.

With my blood boiling, I stormed into the school, knowing exactly who was responsible. Ronnie had moved from bullying me in school to cyberbullying, and I wasn't going to stand for it. It was so cruel to pit me against Ali. Neither of us was better than the other; even though it seemed the kids in our grade thought otherwise.

As I entered the hallway, everyone was focused on their phones. I wondered if they were all in the process of voting for Ali or me.

Heat flushed my neck and cheeks, and I kept my eyes downcast as I walked to my locker. Once I opened it, I placed my phone inside and scrolled through the post. To anyone else, it would seem that I was looking for books, but I had to figure out a plan. Although I recognized a few of the voters' account names, most of the account names were random and I had no idea who they belonged to.

Names such as *crazygirl71* and *misspanda2* stared back at me. They were private accounts and I couldn't figure out who owned them.

It was the meanest and cruelest thing anyone could do. Staring in horror at my phone screen, I wondered what Ali would say when she saw it.

Ronnie had crossed a line with this prank. A voting poll to see who was more popular out of a pair of identical twins was not only cruel and mean, it was shameful. The word appeared out of nowhere and it was the only one I could think of to describe how I was feeling. To make things worse, Ali probably wouldn't even feel bad because almost everyone said she was their favorite. Whereas to me, it was the most hurtful thing ever.

Ronnie's laughter from the other side of the hallway drew my attention. Her smug grin was the last straw for me. Slamming my locker door shut, I stormed over to her.

Staring at her, I struggled to control my temper as the words burst from my lips. "Ronnie, how could you? You've gone too far this time. You have to take it down. Now!"

Ronnie glanced at Holly before looking back at me, the smug grin still attached to her face. "Casey, I have no idea what you're talking about."

***

Book 12

Staying Strong

CHAPTER ONE

Casey

The smug grin on Ronnie's face remained firmly in place. I could easily see that she was struggling to contain herself, to stifle the laughter that was bubbling inside her. To her, the Instagram post was a joke. And the firm shake of her head as she denied having anything to do with it, made me angrier than ever. I was certain she was lying. Who else could be responsible?

I moved away from her, speechless; there was nothing more I could say because she was obviously not going to own up. But I couldn't take my eyes off the post staring up at me from my phone.

Who is your favorite? Ali Jackson or Casey Wrigley? Comment below to vote!

I stared so long that the words started to blur and move together. It was the cruelest thing I'd seen Ronnie do. Even though she was adamant she hadn't done it, I didn't believe her. She and Holly had been torturing me for months. And since becoming hall monitor and finding herself in a position of power, Ronnie's bullying had escalated to a new level. I thought the littering offense was bad enough — especially as I had nothing to do with the piece of paper left lying on the ground — but targeting me over the internet was so much worse.

By the time I saw Ali coming down the hallway, my stomach was in knots. I waved to her frantically.

She tilted her head curiously and hurried over to me. "Casey, what's up?" She obviously hadn't looked at her phone since arriving at school. If she had, she wouldn't need to ask what the problem was.

"Everything," I said. "Here." I showed her the post.

She took in the image, read the caption and frowned. I chewed on my thumbnail as I watched her eyes dart all over the screen.

She shook her head. "Who would do something like this?"

"I'll give you one guess!"

She raised her eyebrows in recognition. "Ronnie?"

I nodded. "I just confronted her and she denied the whole thing! What a liar."

Ali glanced down the hallway. Ronnie and Holly had disappeared but everyone else seemed to be occupied by their phones. My skin heated up, and my cheeks reddened with embarrassment. Was everyone looking at Ronnie's post? Were they judging Ali and me and voting for the twin they preferred? It was so wrong.

"Where did she get this photo?" Ali asked.

"No idea," I sighed heavily.

Ali refreshed the page and more votes appeared. I moved closer to her and read through the comments. There were already twenty Likes and more than a dozen votes — most of them for Ali.

Two boys from our class, their eyes glued to their phone screens, laughed aloud.

One of them, a kid named James, pointed and laughed some more. I grabbed my phone from Ali to see if they'd voted. What else would they be laughing at?

Ali sighed. "Casey, I think you should just ignore this."

"Ignore it?" I frowned. "How can I ignore it?"

She reached across, turned off my phone screen and looked at me. "We should go to class."

As I walked alongside her, I refreshed the page again. I was right about the boys. James and his friend, Tomas had liked the photo. I could see their names added to the list; it was easy to identify their account names. Neither of the boys had voted, but seeing and Liking the post was just as bad.

Brie ran toward us from down the hallway. Her eyes were wide. "Casey, I was just looking at Instagram."

Ali frowned. "Brie, I told her not to worry about it."

Brie stared at her in surprise. "She should worry about it. And so should you. It's such a horrible thing to do. Setting you girls up like this is so mean!"

"We're not competing against each other," Ali said. "It's someone trying to create drama. All we have to do is ignore it."

"No more loitering!" Ronnie called out loudly. Two kids scurried along, moving away from her. "You're getting written up," she scowled. "Come here, give me your name." As if she knew I was looking, she glanced over at me and smirked.

I cringed. What was her problem?

"Alright everyone, it's exam day today," Mrs. Halliday said from the doorway. "All the kids from my class, please come in and take your seats."

It was hard to put away my phone but our first exam was math. And as much as I wanted to say something to Ronnie, I had to concentrate and get a good grade on the test. My summer at camp depended on it.

"Come on," Ali said, tugging me along.

I followed reluctantly behind her. When I reached my desk, I shoved my phone into my bag and pulled out my math notebook. I wanted to go over the material for a few minutes before the test started but I was unable to focus. Instead, I watched each person who entered the room, wondering if they had seen the Instagram post. Or worse, perhaps they had already voted. There were a few kids who glanced at me before sitting down. I couldn't be sure if it was coincidental or if they were judging me against Casey, just like all the others.

When Jake arrived at the door, he gave me a small wave. Ugh, Jake! Had he seen the post? Would he vote for Ali or me, or would he share the post with his friends? I wanted to believe he wouldn't, but I had no idea.

After the bell rang, Mrs. Halliday said, "Clear your

desks and put everything in your bags. This exam will take the entire period, so I want to give you plenty of time to start working."

While packing away my notebook, I discreetly checked my phone again. There were five more Likes and two more votes for Ali.

Mrs. Halliday stood at the top of my row, and I quickly zipped my bag up. I tried to remember the formulas I'd worked on but all I could think about were my classmates secretly judging me.

Mrs. Halliday placed the test papers face down on everyone's desks and then returned to the front of the room. "Okay, you may now turn over your sheets and begin."

I flipped the sheets over to the first page. There were five pages in total and each one was filled with problems. Blinking away the tears that were filling my eyes, I tried to concentrate.

Sometime later, I glanced at the clock and jolted. Our time was halfway through, and I hadn't even reached the third page. My mind swirled with thoughts about Instagram. I'd already wasted so much time thinking about it.

Glancing at Ronnie, I noticed she was already on the last page. How could she get through the test so quickly? More importantly, how could she be so mean and why did she hate me so much? Sure, I knew she was jealous, but no one deserved something so nasty.

As if she felt me looking at her, she looked at me and smiled. It wasn't a nice one.

My cheeks reddened and I wished Mrs. Halliday would open a window or turn on the fans. Though the rest of the class didn't seem affected by the temperature in the room.

Ronnie glanced at me once more then raised her hand. "Mrs. Halliday, Casey is copying my work."

I choked. "No, I'm not!"

Everyone in the classroom looked up from their tests. I felt their eyes on mine. Jonathon, the boy who was seated to my left, flipped his sheet over and glared at me.

I felt my face redden even more.

Mrs. Halliday pressed her lips together. "Ronnie, please keep your test covered. Everyone else, cover your work and keep your eyes on your own test paper." She gave me a pointed look and then sat back in her chair, crossing her arms.

Ronnie's desk was pulled too far away from mine and

there was no way I could have seen her answers even if I wanted to. But to avoid any more trouble, I focused on my paper and didn't look at Ronnie or anyone else again.

Sensing pairs of eyes still focused in my direction, Mrs. Halliday's as well, I became very aware of my vice-captain badge. It seemed to be Ronnie's mission to make me look bad in front of everyone both inside and outside the classroom. Would her bullying ever end?

I didn't want my teacher to think I was a cheater, so I avoided looking anywhere except at my own paper. However, even though it was in front of me, none of the questions made sense. Ronnie filled my thoughts, and my anger clouded my head. I tried to focus on one problem at a time, but each one seemed to take forever to complete.

The time raced by and before I knew it, Mrs. Halliday's voice rang in my ears. "Alright, everyone, put your pencils down and hand your tests to the front of the room."

I still hadn't attempted the last two problems, and those were worth the highest points. After quickly reading through each one, I did some fast calculations then scribbled down a couple of answers. I had no idea if I was even close to being correct but it was worth a try. At the very least, it was better than not attempting them at all.

I glared at Ronnie who was turned in her chair, collecting Holly's test. Her wide smile made me sick to my stomach. Would I even pass this test, let alone get a decent grade? I wasn't a high achiever like Ali. I would have been happy to settle for a B although I had actually considered the chance of an A. But who did I think I was kidding? An A was definitely no longer a possibility.

My vision blurred. However, I was determined not to show Ronnie my emotions. If I did, she'd probably feel good about herself and what she had done.

"How did you go?" Brie asked, handing me her test sheets.

"Okay, I think."

I turned back to the front of the room, not wanting to talk about the test. If I didn't get good grades on my report card, then Mom would probably ground me and say I couldn't go to camp, even though Grandma Ann was paying for it. My stomach churned. I wanted nothing more than to leave school and bury myself under my bedcovers where no one could find me. I'd worked so hard for this exam, and I'd messed up big time by allowing Ronnie to ruin it for me.

When the bell rang for morning break and we left the classroom, Brie smiled happily. "That test was easier than I thought it would be."

"I thought so too," Ali said. "How do you think you went, Casey?"

"Good," I lied. I couldn't help it. Ali had worked hard to help me study, and I couldn't tell her that I'd been distracted once again.

"So..." Brie's expression changed suddenly. "What are you going to do about Ronnie?"

"What can I do?" I asked.

"How about we all approach her and ask her outright if she was responsible for the post?" Ali suggested. "If she knows we're all against her, she might take it down."

Brie nodded. "It's worth a try."

I blew out a big breath. With Ali and Brie to support me, it might be easier. When we reached the hallway, Ronnie wasn't hard to spot. With the bright orange lanyard hanging around her neck, she stood out amongst the crowd.

My chest tightened as we approached her. She was already pestering a group of students which made me even more nervous. Many kids were now aware of her antics and doing their best to avoid her, not wanting to have their names added to her list. At least she was alone by the time we reached her.

"Ronnie," I said, my voice trembling. "I want you to take down that post."

"We both do," Ali said.

Ronnie sighed heavily. "Casey, I told you before, I have no idea what you're talking about."

I took in a deep breath. "Yes, you do!"

She rolled her eyes. "Stop accusing me of something I haven't done. It's pathetic."

"The post is pathetic and it's rude!" Ali scowled at her.

"Yeah!" Brie joined in. "You're the one who's pathetic!"

Even though Ali and Brie were also confronting her, Ronnie couldn't take her eyes off mine. It was as if she only saw me standing there.

"Please!" I said as my hands balled into fists at my side. "This has crossed a line. Take it down now!"

Ronnie shook her head and clicked her tongue. She then pulled out her clipboard and started writing something down.

"Casey, second offense," she muttered to herself.

"What are you doing?" I asked.

"Bullying and harassment," Ronnie said as she wrote.

She looked at me with raised eyebrows. "Wow! You're really setting a good example as a leader of our school, aren't you? Wait until Mrs. Jensen sees this one!"

My jaw dropped as Ronnie skipped away with my name written on her list. I couldn't even form words for what had just happened. How had she managed to win yet again?

CHAPTER TWO

Ali

"Can you believe she just did that?" Casey asked as Ronnie walked away from us.

I shook my head. I was as mystified as my sister. Once again, Ronnie had accused Casey of doing something she hadn't done. I was completely aware of the consequences of being written on the hallway monitor's list. Would Ronnie really cause Casey to have detention during the last week of school? When would she ever stop?

Casey's eyes filled with tears and my heart broke for my twin as the words stammered from her lips. "That's my second offense. If I get one more—"

"You won't," I said, trying to console her. Ronnie was such a horrible girl. I looped my arm with Casey's and felt her emotions through our closeness. She was so upset about all of this. I would be too if it were happening to me.

I tried to calm her down on the way to morning break, but her distress swelled through me.

When we arrived outside, I pulled Casey and Brie aside, away from Holly who was already across the courtyard. Being as far away as possible from both those toxic girls was the only way to keep Casey calm.

"Let's take a look at Instagram and see if we can figure this out," I suggested.

Immediately, I saw that there were more votes in my favor, putting me far ahead of my sister. As much as I felt sorry for Casey, a small thrill erupted inside me. I knew it was wrong but I couldn't help being pleased that I was the one winning the overall vote. To be in Casey's shoes would be so humiliating.

Something pinched at my chest and brought me back to reality. Casey's anger and hurt were strong through our connection and I turned to her with a sigh. Although at the same time, I was still relieved to be the one winning the vote.

"It has to come down," Brie said. "That's the only way this is all going to stop."

The despair was clear on Casey's face. "Ronnie won't admit to being responsible. And there's no way we can prove it was her."

From the corner of my eye, I caught a glimpse of someone jogging toward us. Looking up, I saw it was Jake and moved aside to make room for him next to Casey.

"Casey," he said, "I just saw the Instagram post. Who would do something like that?"

"Ronnie!" Brie exclaimed.

Jake quirked his lips. "Are you sure? She doesn't seem the type."

Casey rolled her eyes. Ronnie fooled everyone, except for us. "Yes, I'm sure."

"She's jealous of Casey!" Brie explained. "She's been targeting Casey for ages, and because Casey got vice-captain over her, she wants revenge. That's what we think, anyway!"

Jake's eyes widened in surprise.

"We want the post to come down," Brie continued. "But we don't know how to make that happen. Do you have any ideas?"

He shook his head. "Have you spoken to Ronnie?"

"Yes," Casey said. "She keeps denying it. But it's easy enough to make a fake email and create a new account with a random name. It's not like we can trace it back to her."

"Can you report it to Instagram?" I asked.

"Maybe." Casey nodded.

"But there isn't really anything inappropriate about the post," Brie said.

Casey's jaw dropped.

Brie waved her hands in front of her. "I mean, according to Instagram rules. It's not like it's showing anything gross or illegal."

"That's true," Jake said. "And it usually takes a while for them do anything about offensive stuff, anyway. I've heard that before."

Casey groaned. "So what am I going to do?"

I locked eyes with her. "What about reporting it to Mrs. Jensen? She's always going on about bullying and school rules."

Casey wrung her hands together. "I don't want to cause any problems during the last week of school. I already have two offenses written up by Ronnie."

"You do?" Jake's look of dismay showed exactly what

he thought.

"Yes. For no reason! She's so determined to make my life miserable this last week. If I get one more offense, I'll be put on detention. My mom will be so mad if that happens. Plus, Mrs. Jensen might even take away my badge!"

Jake frowned. "Maybe if we just ignore the post, everyone will forget about it. We have the awards assembly as well as all our exams coming up. Everyone will be preparing for those. They're not going to be thinking about some stupid post on Instagram."

"Maybe," Casey sighed.

I could see she wasn't convinced. Brie didn't look so sure either.

"Hang in there, Casey," Jake said, touching her arm. "It'll all work out."

"Thanks," she said, shooting him a grateful smile.

For a moment, I thought she was fine with everything. But as soon as Jake left, her smile disappeared.

I had to do something to cheer her up. "Casey, how about we just focus on other things, like Jake said? Let's all put Instagram out of our minds."

Unexpectedly, Casey whirled on me. "Easy for you to say!"

I gasped in surprise. Even Brie jumped in her spot. I shook my head. "What do you mean?"

"It's obvious you're the one everyone likes the most! The proof is right there on the post. Why would *you* be worried about it?"

"Casey," I pleaded. "Don't be like this. It's all just negative stuff that we shouldn't even be focusing on."

Casey scoffed and Brie stared at her shoes. She wasn't going to be any help.

"That's not fair, Casey," I said. "You're my sister. Of course, I'm worried about it."

I tried to keep my guilty thoughts from earlier locked away. I wondered if she could sense that I was glad to be the more popular twin. What Casey had just said was absolutely true, but I could never tell her that. If the situation was reversed, there was no doubt I'd feel exactly the same way.

"Whatever," Casey said, crossing her arms.

"Don't let Ronnie tear us apart. We're sisters. It's an unbreakable bond."

Casey's shoulder's dropped, but she said nothing else. I tried to distract her. "How about we go to my house after school so we can practice our speeches for the assembly tomorrow?"

It was the newly elected school captains' job to present speeches at the end of year awards ceremony the following day. Mrs. Jensen was writing the speeches for us, but it would be our first official assembly and she was expecting us to be prepared.

I looked at my sister hopefully. "Mrs. Jensen said we can collect the speeches from her this afternoon so we can practice going over them."

Casey started chewing on her nails. I knew she was nervous about the assembly but I thought it would take her mind off Instagram.

"I'll help you with your speech," I said. "We can practice together."

"Okay," Casey said. "And I'm sorry for snapping."

"Luckily we have the summer to look forward to," Brie sighed. "One more week and we can leave Ronnie behind."

"One more week," Casey murmured beside me.

I nodded, relieved that Casey was no longer angry with me. I just wished we could all forget about the Instagram drama but I knew it wouldn't be that easy. Whoever had added the post would be thriving on all the interaction and attention it was getting. I also knew that if Ronnie was responsible then until she was caught red-handed, she wouldn't be taking down the post any time soon.

CHAPTER THREE

Casey

For the rest of morning break, I couldn't think of anything else but the voting poll. Although I told Ali and Brie that I'd stop focusing on it, it was impossible. All I wanted to do was keep a constant check on any Likes and comments that were being added. So far, it was obvious which twin everyone liked most, but I was hoping that I'd at least get some more votes. If nothing else, I just wanted the votes to even out a bit, so that Ali wasn't so far ahead of me. But if Brie or Ali saw me looking at my phone, they'd know what I was doing.

That didn't stop Ali though. She swore she wasn't going to check the post, but as she discreetly scrolled through her phone, she smiled a few times. Why was she so happy? Was she going against her own rules and secretly looking on Instagram? Was she happy with the results? Of course, she would be, they were leaning toward her as the most liked twin.

A thread of doubt wove through me as a thought popped into my head. Surely Ali didn't have something to do with the post, did she? Could that even be possible? Ali was competitive, but there was no reason for her to be jealous of me and do something as cruel as an online voting poll.

Immediately, I brushed the thought away, but I couldn't stop it from lingering at the back of my mind. Even though it was most likely Ronnie who was to blame, I couldn't be absolutely sure.

Ronnie had all the reasons to mess with me, and she enjoyed seeing me squirm. Ali would never do that to me.

We were sisters, and we stuck together no matter what. Besides, there was no way Ali could be jealous of *me*. She had everything she wanted. If anything, everyone might think that I put up the post, even though if I had, the plan had clearly backfired.

Somehow, I managed to get through the rest of the day without running into Ronnie and ending up with a third offense. And I coped much better with our geography exam than I had for math. Ali and I had spent a lot of time memorizing the facts from class, and my confidence grew with each question I knew the answer to. It was also lucky that the test was multiple choice. It gave me options to choose from and one of them obviously had to be right. Even so, I was sure not to look up once for fear of Ronnie accusing me of cheating again.

After classes, Ali and I went to our lockers to exchange our books and then headed to the main office to collect our speeches. When we entered the foyer, we placed our backpacks by the door and walked over to Mrs. Jensen who was speaking to one of the secretaries. She looked at us and smiled.

In that instant, a breath whooshed out of me. Maybe Ronnie had been joking about reporting me for offenses in the hallway. Maybe she just wanted to get under my skin. I doubted Mrs. Jensen would smile at me if she thought I was a troublemaker. I wanted to explain myself, but I didn't dare mention the offenses in case she didn't even know about them.

"Good afternoon, Ali and Casey," Mrs. Jensen said, looking at the wrong person as she said each name.

Ali bumped my shoulder, and I tried not to laugh.

"Here you are," Mrs. Jensen said as she plucked several sheets of paper from the printer. "Hot off the press." She sifted through them and handed one sheet to Ali and one to me.

My hands shook as I took the page from her. There was no going back now.

She locked eyes with each of us. "The assembly tomorrow will be an important one. Make sure you take the time tonight to become familiar with your speeches. They're short enough, but the hall will be packed with teachers and parents, plus the entire student body. I've also invited some very influential people within our community too."

"No pressure," Ali said under her breath.

I swallowed. The sound was loud in my ears and apparently to everyone else as well. Mrs. Jensen leaned closer. "I'm sure you will both do very well."

I nodded a few times, but it wasn't until we walked through the doorway leading to the carpark that I was finally able to take a breath.

"This is easy enough," Ali said, reading over her speech. "It's not very long at all."

I hadn't even read past the part after I say my name. I needed a little more time to overcome my jitters first. I had known what I was getting into when I signed up for the position, but the thought of giving a speech at my first assembly as a new leader was daunting. I wished Mrs. Jensen hadn't said anything about the number of people coming — and the fact that there'd be important community members there made me even more nervous!

When I reached Ali's dad's car, my hands were so damp they slipped across the handle twice before I opened the door.

Chris smiled as we climbed in and sat down. "Hi, girls!"

"Hey, Dad," Ali replied "Sorry, we took so long. We had to get our speeches from Mrs. Jensen for the assembly tomorrow."

"That's great," he said. "I bet you already have them memorized."

Ali laughed. "Not quite."

When he turned to look over his shoulder at me, I smiled uneasily. I wondered if he realized how scared I was.

"I'll be there tomorrow to watch you both," he grinned.

Great. Another person to be nervous in front of.

It was a good thing he and Ali had a lot to talk about because it gave me a chance to be alone with my thoughts during the ride to their house. When the car pulled into the driveway, I was feeling a little less anxious. I'd already presented a speech in class and at a full school assembly. This new speech wasn't any different. The only thing that was different was me. I was now vice-captain and I needed to prove myself. I tried to pull from Ali's confidence and make the best of the situation. I was going to have to give a lot of speeches from now on, so I might as well get used to it!

We practiced for a large part of the afternoon. As usual, Ali was very confident and after the third time of reading through the words, she didn't even need to look down at the paper anymore. On the other hand, I stumbled quite a bit. When I had written my own speech previously, it was easier since the words were my own. In comparison, Mrs. Jensen's speech was quite formal and not at all my style. But if Ali could pull it off, so could I.

She continued to encourage me and by the time Mom came to pick me up, I was much more confident. I had Ali to thank for that. She'd also distracted me enough to give me a few hours break from worrying about Instagram.

As we headed along the hallway, we heard Mom and Chris talking downstairs. Ali and I shared a look and slowed our pace. Peeking around the corner we spotted the two of them standing by the front door.

"I had a great time the other night," Mom said, a beaming smile on her face.

Chris rubbed the back of his neck. Was he nervous? I waited quietly for his reply.

"Me too!" he nodded. "And actually, I was wondering if Ann might be able to watch the girls sometime this weekend so we can go out again. What do you think?"

Mom's smile widened further. "That sounds great, Chris."

I grinned at Ali and then spoke loudly so Mom and Chris would know we were there. "Thanks for helping me out, Ali!"

Ali covered her giggle with her hand. "I'll see you tomorrow, Casey."

I hugged her and then walked down the stairs where Mom and Chris were standing a foot apart from each other.

"How did you go with your speeches?" Mom asked.

"Good thanks!" I smiled. Turning to Chris, I added, "Thanks for having me over."

"Anytime," he replied, winking at Mom.

The thrill of seeing our parents together was enough to distract me for the entire trip home but as soon as I reached my bedroom, I closed the door and pulled out my phone. My hands shook with anticipation. So many new comments had been added since I'd checked last. My entire grade must have taken part in the stupid poll.

I quickly scrolled through and saw Ali's name mentioned in more comments than mine. How was that possible? I knew she was more outgoing, but we looked exactly alike, and I'd gone to school with most of these kids from the beginning. Whereas Ali had only arrived earlier that year. It didn't make sense. I recognized some of the names. Most of them didn't even know Ali and me very well since they were in different classrooms. Why did they bother to vote? Was everyone in the school against me?

Sighing heavily, I put my phone in my desk drawer and pulled my history book from my bag. As I stared at the review section, my anger grew. Ronnie had to be responsible. I wanted to follow Ali's advice and report her to Mrs. Jensen, but I knew I needed more proof that she really was the one to blame. Proving that she created the account was going to be impossible though. Regardless, there wasn't much time left in the school year, and I had to do something.

I took a deep breath. The following day, I would tell Mrs. Jensen everything. After the awards assembly, I'd approach her and tell her what was going on. I wanted to end this school year right, and as a leader, I had to stick up for myself. Something had to be done about Ronnie, and I was determined to take Ali's advice and be the one to do it.

CHAPTER FOUR

Ali

When I woke the next morning, I was excited for the day. I had the speech to look forward to, and as well as that, with each new day, the countdown to summer came closer and closer. I couldn't wait to go to camp with Casey and Brie, and we only had a few more days left of school until that happened.

I'd prepared as much as I could for my final exams. I had proved that by completing our history test in no time. After that, I also managed almost three pages for the writing task. When I did a quick edit of my narrative before handing it in, I was really proud of all the descriptive vocabulary I'd managed to include. Writing was my favorite subject and I hoped it showed.

During the exams, I occasionally looked towards Casey and tried to channel some positive energy her way. I also wanted her to avoid Ronnie, especially after Ronnie had blamed her for cheating which was obviously a lie. Ronnie was bad news, and it was best for everyone to stay away from her while she continued to be jealous and petty to Casey.

As well, I wanted Casey to get good grades in her tests so she wouldn't risk missing out on camp. I had no doubt that Jackie would follow through on her threat if Casey failed or did poorly, which was part of the reason I tried so hard to help her. I wanted us to have the perfect summer together. After the ups and downs of the school year, I was keen to have the best summer ever with my new sister and friend.

During lunch break, all the school leaders were asked to eat their food in the auditorium so Mrs. Jensen could prepare us for the assembly. While we sat in the front row, with our lunches in our laps, Mrs. Jensen went over the schedule and explained where each of us was to sit and stand on the stage.

Since Holly wasn't around, Ronnie spent her time actually focusing for once. She didn't even glance at Casey. As hall monitor, her job was to hand out awards during the ceremony and I could see that she didn't want to mess it up.

The auditorium was mostly empty. All the while though, I imagined it filling up with people in a short time and my stomach started to quiver. I took a deep breath and released it.

"Are you nervous?" Casey asked.

I nodded. "A little. But that's normal for me. I'm very excited too."

"I wish I was excited," Casey said. "When it comes to speeches, I don't think I'll ever get over being nervous."

"You'll be great, Casey!" I assured her. "These people are here to support us. You already have the position; you just have to show them you deserve it."

"I'll try," Casey said, gobbling up the rest of her sandwich.

I felt more prepared than ever when Mrs. Jensen ushered us backstage. As soon as the bell rang, the seats started to fill with people. Even though we were behind the curtain, the voices amongst us were loud and eager, feeding my energy. I sneaked a glance through the side of the curtain to see if I could spot our parents.

Dad sat at the side of the room, and he had his jacket slung over the two seats next to him, saving them for Grandma Ann and Jackie.

I turned to find Casey in a rear corner, quietly reading her speech.

I walked over to her. "Do you want to read it through

again together?"

"No, it's okay, thanks. If I'm not ready now, I never will be." She folded the paper and shoved it in her pocket.

Because Mrs. Jensen had our speeches in a binder on the podium ready for each speaker to present, we had those to use if we needed them. All we had to do was step up and read through the words.

"You'll be fine," I said, touching Casey's arm. I tried to push my excitement through our connection. I hoped it worked.

Casey gave me a shaky smile as the lights flickered backstage and went dark.

"Ladies and gentlemen, teachers and students," Mrs. Jensen's voice boomed loudly.

"It's showtime," I said to Casey and looped my arm in hers. We walked over to the side of the curtain, huddling with the other leaders who were also hidden from view, and watched our principal give her speech.

Casey squeezed my arm, but I didn't move away. I wanted her to be comfortable, no matter what.

When Mrs. Jensen's speech ended, she turned toward us and waved Mark and me over to her side. "I'd like to announce our girl and boy captains for next year."

"Good luck!" Casey smiled.

I gave her a thumbs up before walking across the stage with Mark by my side. The lights were so bright that I couldn't see anyone in the audience. Everyone in attendance applauded, and I heard Dad's familiar whistle from his side of the room. I smiled in his direction.

My speech was first. I delivered it clearly and managed not to stumble on any words. I could almost feel my adopted mom watching me from above. Warmth filled me, and when I stepped away from the podium, the entire room exploded with applause once more.

Mark was next. I made my way to the first seat on the stage and relaxed my shoulders. My job was done and I could enjoy the rest. I tried to pick out my family in the crowd, but I couldn't see much. Instead, I focused on Mark. I wasn't sure what to expect. During his speech for captain, he had been his usual funny self, making everyone laugh. But this time, Mrs. Jensen had warned him to avoid the humor and focus on giving a sensible speech. He fidgeted around and stumbled over the words a bit. I could tell he hadn't practiced at all. But at least he stuck to the words on the page instead of his usual silly antics.

Between the captain and vice-captain speeches, Mrs. Jensen invited our town councilor to the stage to present some awards. He had been newly elected to the local council and it was a huge honor to have him present at our assembly.

We listened to him give a short speech of his own and then Ronnie stepped up beside him to hand awards to the kids who he called onto the stage. She wasn't wearing her lanyard, but I could tell she was proud to stand on the stage as part of the school leadership team.

Awards were given for academic excellence to a girl and a boy in each grade for each of our main subjects. Even though I already had my dream leadership position, I was also hoping for an award. My parents had always taught me to reach for the stars and I wanted to make them proud.

When my name was announced for the writing award for our grade, I jumped up from my chair to receive it.

"Congratulations, Ali!" Ronnie said, handing over my certificate and shaking my hand.

I pulled away as soon as I could. She was so fake, and I couldn't wait until the summer where we could forget about her completely.

Casey didn't win any awards, but when the presentations were over, I knew she'd do really well with her speech, and I cheered the loudest when she approached the podium. From where I was sitting, I caught sight of her nervous expression and tried to send her some reassuring thoughts.

Ronnie moved away from her spot next to the podium to make way for Casey. I noticed a wide smirk on her face as she headed to her seat at the back of the stage. I didn't know why she was grinning that way, but I had a feeling she was up to something.

Casey stepped up to the podium, took a deep breath and began speaking.

CHAPTER FIVE

Casey

From the second Ali left my side to present her speech, my insides were a bundle of nerves. My speech was easy enough that I could have given it without the paper in front of me. But I was happy that it would be sitting on the podium, just in case. At least if I got nervous, I could look down and read from the sheet. I wasn't expecting to be as good as Ali, but I hoped I wasn't as bad as Mark. Without walking around and gesturing wildly, it was as if he didn't know what to do with his hands. Though there was no reason for me to judge him. My own hands were shaking more than ever before.

I didn't realize how long the awards presentations would take. It felt like hours until I was called onto the stage with Everett. At least he seemed nervous too and I was glad that I wasn't the only one.

When Mrs. Jensen announced our names, the sound of applause filled my ears. While it was a positive feeling that warmed my insides, I didn't dare look out into the crowd. I knew I'd become more nervous if I saw the faces of the parents, teachers, students, and the important people Mrs. Jensen had invited. Thinking of the empty chairs from before everyone arrived, I hoped I'd be able to hold onto that thought.

I tried to ignore Ronnie and her dumb smirk as she placed the certificates for kids who weren't in attendance, onto the small shelf of the podium. She wasn't going to ruin this for me. I had the vice-captain position, not her.

Taking a deep breath, I looked out into the auditorium.

So much for not seeing all the faces in the audience. Unrecognizable people in suits sat in the front row. Were they the important people I was expected to impress? Why did Mrs. Jensen tell us about them? Didn't she realize how much pressure she was putting on this single speech?

Even though their faces were in shadows due to the lights on the stage, I could still see them looking up at me, waiting for me to speak.

I tried to swallow, but my mouth was dry. My tongue felt stuck to the roof of my mouth and I longed for a drink. I felt my hands start to shake again and my mouth opened and closed, but no words came out.

I thought about Ali sitting behind me. I wanted to be like her. Confident. But the words from the speech completely disappeared from my mind and I was forced to glance down at the sheet in front of me.

"Hi, my name is Ali Jackson. I'm the school captain—
"

As soon as I heard myself speak, I realized the words were all wrong. Murmurs from the crowd caught my attention, and a few kids were snickering. Then the laughter became louder until that was all I could hear over the pounding of my heart in my ears.

Clicking high-heels approached me, and Mrs. Jensen appeared at my side, clearing her throat. She flicked over a couple of pages in the binder in front of me and located my speech, smoothing the page with her hand. Leaning toward the microphone, she said, "Let's start again. *Casey*, please continue." She emphasized my name and that caused more laughter amongst the crowd.

My cheeks burned. All I wanted to do was sink into the floor. I looked at the speech and began again, knowing that I wasn't able to get out of this that easily.

"Hi, my name is Casey W-Wrigley. I'm the school vice-captain—"

Even though I said the correct words, my body flushed with embarrassment. A sick feeling rose up from my stomach and sat in my throat, cutting off my words. I wasn't sure if I was going to throw up or not. I glanced into the crowd again. This was my first speech as vice-captain and I'd just humiliated myself in front of the school and some important people from the community.

I took several deep breaths and tried to keep the room from tilting.

Pushing quickly through the speech, I rambled over the words. I didn't even know what I was saying and all the practice that Ali and I had done the night before was wasted. I just wanted it to be over and done with.

The second I finished, I sprinted over to the chairs and sat down. There was scattered applause from the audience, and I had to fight the tears from spilling out of my eyes while Everett gave his speech. I didn't hear a word of it as I tried to figure out what had happened. How did I not notice that the speech on the podium in front of me was different? And why was the binder opened up at Ali's speech? It didn't make sense.

Ronnie sat alongside me, and her shoulders were shaking as she tried to hide her laughter. I blinked and remembered her smirking at me right before I began my speech. She'd been at the podium. Had she flicked over the pages, knowing that I was going to read whatever was in front of me? Or was it my own mistake? Was I looking for someone else to blame because I didn't check the speech that had been placed there? I didn't know what to think. My mind was a jumble of thoughts. My eyes welled with tears, but I tried not to show anyone that I was about to cry.

By the time Everett finished speaking, I'd managed to control my emotions so I didn't have to fear a stream of tears. When the assembly was finally over, I was more than happy to leave the stage. All I wanted was to leave the spotlight and escape. But just as I reached the area in front of the stage, Ronnie appeared.

"Good job, Ali, oops, I mean Casey," she mocked me. "Um…what's your name again?"

Holly and a couple of other girls from our class approached me and giggled.

"Are you Casey or Ali?" Holly said. "It sounds like that Insta post. Even you don't know who to choose!"

They laughed again, and I pushed past them all as tears threatened at the corners of my eyes. I knew I was never going to live it down. As well, I dreaded facing Mrs. Jensen. She probably thought I was trying to make a joke and would not be impressed.

Ali suddenly appeared at my side. "Casey, I was looking for you."

I shook my head. "I can't believe I did that! Ronnie and Holly are going to torture me forever about it."

"Don't be silly," Ali said. "It was just a little slip-up. You did great."

I turned away from her with annoyance, tired of her

always telling me everything was going to be okay. She had nothing to worry about. Her speech was flawless, as was everything about her.

I didn't dare say the words out loud. It wasn't her fault that I'd messed up. But unable to talk to her, I put on a fake smile and made my way through the crowds to find our families.

CHAPTER SIX

Ali

When I heard my name come from Casey's mouth, my jaw dropped. She stepped back from the podium, and from the angle where I was sitting, I could see that her face had turned pale. I felt her embarrassment. The laughter from the audience certainly didn't help. I knew the parents weren't laughing, but the kids were so cruel.

It was a good thing Mrs. Jensen was able to come to the rescue and switch to the correct page in the binder. But even though Casey made it through to the end of her speech, she really rushed it. Her head was down the entire time, reading every single word from the paper without looking at the audience once. She barely paused, and she mumbled so much it was hard to make out what she was saying.

Although I didn't believe it myself, I tried to tell her that everything was going to be fine. Deep down though, I knew she'd given Ronnie and Holly more fuel to make fun of her, and they wouldn't let it go easily.

But none of it was her fault. And I wished I could make it better.

On the way home, Dad talked about how proud he was of Casey and me. He didn't mention the name mess up, and I wanted to text her to say that he really had enjoyed both our speeches. He had already told her himself before leaving the auditorium, but I knew she wasn't convinced.

I thought about it and decided it would be better to just let the matter drop. The more I dwelled on it, the worse she would feel. So I checked Instagram instead, hoping the post might have been taken down.

But no such luck.

There were a lot more comments than there had been before and I clicked on the link, curious about what my classmates had said. While I was fully aware that it was a terrible and cruel joke, I couldn't help but feel pleased every time I saw another vote for me.

Dad glanced curiously at the phone in my hand and then looked up at me. "What are you smiling about?"

I almost jumped out of my seat. It was a good thing I had my seatbelt on.

"Oh, just looking at Instagram," I replied quickly.

He bobbed his head to the music on the radio, and I turned my phone away from him so he couldn't see the screen. I went to my main feed and saw that I had a ton of new Likes on my photos, a bunch of new followers, and several direct messages.

I opened my DMs and read through them. My smile

widened as I read each one.

So happy you're our new school captain!

You're the best school leader we've ever had!

You're so pretty Ali! I love the outfit you were wearing today!

Where do you buy your clothes? You always look so good!

Great job with ur speech. We think ur awesome!

What's it like being a twin? Weird how ur so much prettier!

I want to be a school leader just like you one day!

My heart warmed with each word I read. There were also similar comments added to the photos in my feed, more than I'd ever received before. I replied to all of them and hoped that more would come in return. A swell of pride rushed through me.

Flipping through my comments, I noticed one from Casey that she had added the week before. I clicked on her name, thinking she must have a bunch of new followers too. That would definitely make her feel better.

I didn't know the exact number she had before, but it looked as if there were only a few new ones. When I scrolled through her recent photos, I saw there were only comments from Brie and me.

I chewed on my lip. I'd hoped that there'd be more. Then I wondered if maybe she'd received a heap of DMs instead.

Returning to the *friendzone101* page, I looked to see if any more votes had been added. Immediately, I noticed five new comments had appeared in the last few minutes.

I vote for Ali...her speech at the assembly was awesome

Ali! Duh! If Casey wants to be a school leader she needs to remember her name. LOL!!

Ali, I mean Casey, no I mean Ali... What's my name again?? Hahaha!!

The good feeling I'd had before rolled into a tight ball and settled in my stomach. While I loved getting so many votes, I hated that it was at Casey's expense. There was no way I could feel happy about my success when this was happening to Casey. If the situation were reversed, I was sure she'd also feel bad for me.

The newer comments were from people I didn't know. I discovered that their accounts were on private and I didn't feel comfortable following them and asking them to delete their comments. I wasn't sure what else I could do except hope that Casey would stay away from the page. I doubted that would happen though. She was just as curious as me. She'd probably also visit my page and see all my new friends and followers. That would make the situation so much worse.

Would she think that I was enjoying this?

I debated on unfollowing the people I'd just followed, but I wasn't sure that would help. They might think Casey had logged in as me and deleted them.

I felt horrible that my twin was suffering while I was experiencing the exact opposite.

Placing my phone on my lap, I decided I would do something about this. It could not go on any longer.

CHAPTER SEVEN

Casey

After the assembly, Grandma Ann insisted that we go out for ice cream to celebrate my speech. I wondered at first if she'd been paying attention, because I didn't think there was much to celebrate. But when Lucas opened his mouth to say something, she quickly changed the subject, so she was clearly aware. I bet she told Lucas not to say anything negative about my speech, even though it was horrible. I wondered how long he'd last.

Mom and Grandma Ann both said I did a great job. I knew they were lying.

All I wanted to do was go home and hide under my covers until summer, but I knew I wouldn't be able to get out of eating ice cream with my family. It was a good thing Ali went home with her dad. Otherwise, everyone would have gushed over her and then felt bad that they couldn't say the same things to me.

It seemed as if Ali was everyone's favorite; from the kids at school to my family. They all loved her. As much as I tried to push away that thought, I'd always suspected it was the case.

Although at some point in the past, I'd actually managed to develop a little self-confidence and not feel intimidated by her, as time went on, I had started to realize how different we were. Ali was perfect, and I wasn't.

Now, along with a perfectly delivered speech from a perfect school captain, she was more on top than ever.

On the way to the ice creamery, my stomach sank so much that I doubted I'd be able to eat anything. I checked my phone again, desperate to see how many more people had voted for Ali instead of me.

Everything that I'd thought about Ali was true, and the evidence was on the screen. Ali didn't seem bothered by the poll, because she was winning. She probably enjoyed all the attention. Why wouldn't she? Out of the two of us, she was the most popular, everyone had admitted to it. By now, the whole school probably knew about the poll and were having a great time voting, not realizing how hurtful the entire thing was to me. I bet they were all laughing behind my back.

They wouldn't be if they were in my shoes.

I clicked over to Ali's page and saw how many new followers she had. Each of her photos even had a bunch of new comments, ones that she had already replied to. She must be so thrilled. I bet it wouldn't be long before the entire school followed her. She'd soon have way more friends at school than me and would probably prefer to hang out with them as well.

Would I be able to distract her from her new friends or would she rather be with them for the last week? I bet she'd make more friends at camp, then get even more followers on Instagram. She'd be the favorite at camp as well and leave me in the dust.

I went back to the *friendzone101* page and stared at it in disgust. I had promised myself I'd speak with Mrs. Jensen about it after the assembly, but when I messed up my speech, I wanted to avoid our principal.

Although I had been planning to tell her Ronnie was responsible, I was beginning to doubt that idea. What was Ronnie getting out of it? Sure, I was humiliated, but now Ali had tons more friends and followers. Could Ali be responsible for the post? She'd easily be able to hide that from me and blame Ronnie since Ronnie already disliked me so much.

If I told Mom or Grandma Ann about the Instagram post, then they'd most likely make me delete my page and ban me from Instagram altogether. Adults didn't realize how important social media was, and I didn't want to risk losing my account. At the very least, I wanted to keep track of Ali's list of followers and see how many of my classmates preferred her to me.

As I went through the comments on Ali's page once more, I saw that they'd become more personal. When I tried to check the account names, some didn't have a profile picture or were set on private, so I couldn't see who they belonged to.

Although Ali had benefited from the post, I went back on my idea that she was responsible. She'd already been voted in as school captain. She wouldn't do this just to get more Instagram followers, so it couldn't be her, could it?

Regardless, my problem still wasn't solved and I had no idea what to do.

I stared at the ice cream sundae that Grandma Ann had ordered for me. Strawberry Whip was my favorite and there was even a strawberry flavored love heart sitting on top.

But even the sight of that did little to lighten my mood.

CHAPTER EIGHT

Ali

Each time someone new started following me or made a comment, I felt worse, so I stayed away from Instagram for the rest of the night. Instead, I tried to focus on a solution and then finally, before going to bed, I came up with an idea.

The following morning, I asked Dad to drive me to school early. The comments had gone too far and may even continue to get worse. I had to move quickly.

As I brushed my teeth, I checked the post one last time. The *friendzone101* username had also added comments, making more fun of Casey's speech. I took screenshots and saved them on my phone. I hoped I wouldn't need them, but if the post happened to be taken down before I could speak with Mrs. Jensen, I needed proof that it had actually existed.

Cyberbullying had been bad at my old school, and my teachers were adamant that every incident should be reported.

My homeroom teacher's voice popped into my mind. "If the bullying is allowed to continue, then the bully gets away with it, and that is not acceptable. Even if you're not the victim, or you're not even a friend of the victim, it is important to stand up and support that person. If you prefer, you can report the incident privately, so no one knows it was you. But the bully must be reported so the behavior can be dealt with."

I didn't care about the increase in my number of followers, supporting Casey was the priority. If I didn't do that, then what sort of sister was I?

When Dad asked why I was going to school early, I

pretended I needed to speak with Mrs. Halliday in preparation for an exam. I felt bad about lying, but I didn't want to involve him or Jackie in the drama with the Instagram post. If they knew, they might make Casey and I delete our accounts and neither of us wanted that. As well, the person responsible needed to be punished. I just hoped that my plan would work. I also hoped Casey wouldn't be upset with me for bringing this to Mrs. Jensen's attention.

Once I reached the front office, my stomach was a bundle of nerves, and I had trouble preventing my hands from shaking.

The secretary took me to Mrs. Jensen's office and knocked on the door.

Mrs. Jensen called us inside. Her eyebrows shot up when she saw me. "What a surprise. Come in and sit down, Ali."

The secretary closed the door behind her. There was no going back now.

I took a deep breath as Mrs. Jensen spoke. "I want to congratulate you on your presentation at the assembly yesterday. Everyone commented on your proficient speaking skills. You did a wonderful job."

"Thank you, Mrs. Jensen," I replied, thinking of Casey. It was nice to hear a compliment from my principal, but I noticed she didn't mention my sister's speech at all.

"I doubt you came in here to listen to me go on about your oral presentation skills," Mrs. Jensen said with a smile. "So, tell me, what can I help you with?"

Grabbing my phone from my bag, I quickly opened the screen. "I have something that I want you to see. This Instagram post has been going around, and a lot of kids are Liking it and commenting. I don't think it's right."

Mrs. Jensen pursed her lips and put her hands out. I gave her the phone and twined my fingers together to stop them from shaking. She moved her finger over the page and tapped a few times. Her eyes darted rapidly back and forth on the screen as she read the comments. With a shake of her head, she looked up at me. "Do you know who this account belongs to?"

"That's the problem," I sighed. "I'm not sure, and I don't know how to find out."

Mrs. Jensen sat back in her chair and read through the comments some more. A deep crease moved across her forehead. After a few moments, her frown deepened. It felt good to be telling her and I was certain I had done the right thing.

"Thank you, Ali," Mrs. Jensen said, putting my phone on the desk in front of me. She gave me a reassuring nod.

"I'm very glad you've reported this. As you know, we have zero-tolerance for bullying at this school. Leave this to me; I will be dealing with it personally."

"Thank you, Mrs. Jensen," I said, picking up my phone and standing up from my chair.

"I won't reveal that you've brought this to my attention. Whatever is said in this office is between you and me."

The relief inside me grew as I thanked her once more.

On the way to class, I felt as if a weight had lifted from my shoulders. The hallways were empty, so I was able to compose myself before going into the classroom. Other than Mrs. Halliday, I was the first person to arrive.

My teacher smiled at me as I entered. "Good morning, Ali." She sipped from a coffee mug and appeared to be grading our exams from the day before.

"Good morning. Mrs. Halliday. Is it okay if I go over some notes for the exam today?"

"Absolutely! Great to see you here early." She nodded before going back to her work.

I moved to my desk at the back of the room, pulled my notebook from my backpack and opened it in front of me. I'd already studied enough, but I didn't want Casey to know that I'd spoken with Mrs. Jensen. I wasn't sure she wanted me to talk to our principal, so I decided not to tell her.

With our connection, I knew Casey well. With her messing up at the assembly and having two false incidents reported by Ronnie, Casey wouldn't want to draw even more attention from Mrs. Jensen.

I just hoped my sister wouldn't be upset if she ever found out I'd reported the incident. That was something I definitely wanted to avoid.

CHAPTER NINE

Casey

On the bus on my way to school, I read through all the new comments attached to the *friendzone101* post. Of course, they were in Ali's favor, and my classmates didn't have many nice things to say about my speech from the day before. Even if I wasn't sure that Ronnie had put up the post, I was certain she'd switched my speech. She probably then went home and made up a bunch of fake Instagram accounts to mess with me even more by commenting and voting under random account names.

By the time I arrived at school, it was hard to stand up and leave my seat. If it were any other day, I would have pretended to be sick, but I had to be there for final exams. Camp was at risk unless I at least managed to get passing grades.

I was the last person to step off the bus, and I kept my head down all the way up the front steps and down the hallways to Mrs. Halliday's classroom. I took the long way, so I didn't run into hall-monitor Ronnie, and I made it to Mrs. Halliday's class without an issue for once.

Ali was already in class and she waved to me as I sat down. I waved back but I didn't want to talk to her just yet. I already knew she had more followers because of the post and although I knew she wouldn't say anything to be mean to me, avoiding the topic was my plan. At least until the test was over.

During morning announcements, Mrs. Halliday didn't waste any time passing out the next test, which was fine with me. We were to keep the test turned over, so no one sneaked in a head start. I itched to begin, but I didn't want to get into any more trouble.

Meanwhile, Ronnie was talking quietly to Holly. I didn't miss the glares coming from her. Didn't she understand that she'd already won?

Without warning, Mrs. Jensen's voice suddenly sounded on the intercom. "Good morning everyone," My ears perked up. Normally, we didn't hear from her unless there was an important announcement. I listened intently as she spoke. "I want all classes in the seventh grade to gather in the auditorium for a short assembly immediately. You will receive extra time to complete exams."

Mrs. Halliday glanced around the room. She was as surprised as us by this change of routine. "Alright, class, let's head down there. Please form two lines at the door."

As we headed out of the room, Brie frowned at me. "What do you think this is about?"

Ronnie, in a rush to be at the front of the line, barged past me, shoving against my arm as she bolted through the doorway.

I rolled my eyes and allowed her to pass. If I said anything, she'd probably write me up on her list again, and I'd be doomed to spend the summer with Lucas. The thought made me shiver.

"I have no clue," I said to Brie.

"Ali?" Brie asked as my sister joined us in the line. "What do you think is going on?"

Ali shrugged, but she didn't look me in the eyes. I shook my head, shaking away the strange feeling coming from her. Even though I'd already convinced myself that she wasn't capable of the mean Instagram voting poll, there was still a sliver of doubt swirling through me.

As Brie continued to question what the assembly would be about, my head spun with possibilities. I wondered if Mrs. Jensen would take away my badge, saying that I wasn't worthy of the position if I couldn't deliver a speech properly, in addition to being reported for two hallway offenses. Surely, she wouldn't call an assembly over that and add to my embarrassment. Would she?

The auditorium looked empty compared to the day before as the classes settled in the first few rows of the hall. Everyone questioned why we were there, especially when we'd all been about to start an important end of year exam.

Mrs. Jensen walked to the center of the stage, and our teachers told us all to stop speaking and pay attention.

"Good morning, everyone," Mrs. Jensen said in a serious tone. "What I have to say to you today is not at all pleasant. I'm very disappointed to be interrupting classes while you all have tests to complete. But this matter is of the utmost importance and must be addressed immediately."

I frowned. Was this about the assembly the day before? Was she that disappointed in the leaders?

"Someone is in trouble," Brie whispered.

I caught her worried expression and the thread of fear inside me worsened. "But who?" I asked. And for what?

I glanced at Ali. Her eyes were locked on Mrs. Jensen, and she didn't acknowledge Brie or me at all.

Mrs. Jensen lifted her chin, scanning the faces in front

of her. "This morning, something was brought to my attention. Unfortunately, it appears that one of the students in this room is responsible for cyberbullying in its worst form."

A collective gasp sucked all the air from my lungs. Whispers filled the air as everyone questioned what she was talking about. But surely they all knew. They would have to.

I looked at Ali. She glanced towards me and then her eyes darted back to Mrs. Jensen. I shook my head. How did Mrs. Jensen find out? Who could have told her?

Ronnie and Holly sat in the row in front of us, but off to the side. Holly looked at her friend, but Ronnie was as still as a statue. Was Ronnie responsible after all?

"I'm also very disappointed because as well as the original post, there are some nasty comments on the page. We consider the comments just as serious. The people who added those are as bad as the person who created the post, to begin with."

That comment made several kids squirm in their seats. Murmurs filled the room and our teachers asked those speaking to be quiet.

Mrs. Jensen's voice rose. "I expect the post to be deleted by this evening. If not, I will involve the police to find out who is responsible. Have I made myself clear?"

Everyone agreed aloud or nodded their heads. My insides churned. Did my classmates think I'd ratted out the page since I didn't get a lot of votes? No one looked at me, so I wasn't sure what to expect. I hoped that I wouldn't be blamed for kids getting into trouble. But at the same time, I was filled with relief that the post would be taken down.

"I will be monitoring that page for any additional Likes and comments added from this minute onward." Mrs. Jensen spoke slowly and firmly as she waved her phone in the air. "Anyone involved will be dealt with by me. I can guarantee that your parents will also be notified at that point and it will lead to severe consequences."

I saw a few kids around me touching their bags, no doubt wanting to reach for their phones and delete their comments as quickly as possible. I wondered if Mrs. Jensen already had a list of account names.

"Cyberbullying is a monster that can impact innocent people in terrible ways. While the account and post might have been set up as a practical joke, there is nothing funny about it. I will not tolerate any form of bullying at this school." She stood in front of us, her arms crossed and her gaze scanning her audience. "I want you all to recall this moment next time you think something like this might be a good idea. While the person who informed me of this incident will remain anonymous, I want to thank that person for coming forward. I also want to encourage anyone else who witnesses bullying in any form to do the same thing and report it immediately. This is the sort of example that needs to be set, and I hope everyone has learned from it."

More murmurs moved through the group as Mrs. Jensen walked down the steps from the stage. "You may all return to class. Good luck with your exams and I hope that I don't have to see any of you in my office regarding this matter."

On the way back to class, all anyone could talk about was the assembly and Mrs. Jensen's warning Everyone, including myself, wanted to know who was responsible for adding the post in the first place, and who had reported it as well.

Several kids sneaked onto their phones, presumably to delete their Likes and comments. Was one of them the original culprit? I watched Ronnie. She and Holly were huddled together, deep in conversation. Apparently Ronnie's hall monitor duties had gone by the wayside. She ignored everyone as they made their way noisily along the corridor. She also appeared quite distressed, giving me a better idea that she really had been the one to post the poll.

Numerous pairs of eyes glanced my way and then

darted towards Ali, probably thinking one of us had said something. Ali didn't seem fazed at all. In fact, she was smiling.

Something light moved through me. "It was you, wasn't it? You told Mrs. Jensen?"

Ali pressed a finger to her lips and nodded. "Is that okay?"

"Yes!" I replied quietly. "Thank you so much, Ali. You saved me. I don't think I would have had the courage."

"What are sisters for?" she murmured back.

I felt a huge sense of relief. But at the same time, a heavy guilt pressed against my stomach. I couldn't believe that I'd suspected her. After all, she was my twin and my sister. Sure, she was perfect at everything, but she was especially perfect at being my sister. I was so lucky to have her.

When we entered our classroom, I headed for my desk and sat down. On the way to his seat, Jake stopped and touched my hand. Leaning towards me, he smiled. "Casey, I'm so glad this is all sorted out. But for the record, you've always had my vote. You know that don't you?"

My heart melted at his words. He was on my side and he had my back. He really did care about me. It made me believe that there were others around who felt the same way but didn't want to take part in the cruel bullying.

When Jake moved away, I noticed Ronnie glaring at me. She sat close enough that I knew she'd heard what Jake had said. I smiled at her as brightly as I could. This was sweet revenge, and I hoped she'd learned her lesson that bullies never won. Especially if they were dealt with. And thanks to my sister, Ronnie had finally been put in her place.

CHAPTER TEN

Ali

After the assembly about cyberbullying, I was relieved to see Casey finally smiling again. A lot of that had to do with Jake, who was loyal to my sister. I also noticed Ronnie eavesdropping and listening to Jake's conversation. Her scowl was obvious, and I had no doubt she was the one to set up the mean post, to begin with. I'd been praying I had done the right thing, and now I knew that I had.

As we began our final exam, I felt the connection between Casey and me lighten. The heavy darkness within her had vanished and I knew we'd both pass the exam with flying colors.

After lunch, Brie, Casey, and I walked through the hallways, laughing and talking about the summer to come. For once, Casey didn't seem worried when we approached Ronnie with her orange lanyard swinging around her neck.

The hairs on my arms stood on end, and I waited for Ronnie to say something to my sister. She had a little time left to report Casey for another offense, but I'd fight for Casey if she tried. No way would I allow her to cause a detention for my sister.

I shot a glare Ronnie's way, and for once, she looked away from us and actually skittered toward the lockers on the other side of the hallway. She stared at the floor as we walked by.

"Well, that's different," Brie said.

"Sure was!" Casey laughed.

I grinned. There was no need to protect Casey from Ronnie anymore. But there was one more test for Ronnie to pass.

"Let's see if the Instagram post is still there," I said, knowing that Mrs. Jensen planned on monitoring it. If Ronnie was smart, she would have taken it down by now.

The three of us huddled by our lockers. Since it was the end of the year and everyone was ready for summer, I didn't worry about Mrs. Halliday catching us. Most of the time between classes, she was on her phone too.

"I don't see it," Brie smiled. "I think she's already deleted it."

"I can't even find the friendzone account anymore," Casey snickered happily.

I put my hand up to high-five my sister. "It's over."

Casey high-fived me back. "Finally. Thanks to you!"

I beamed at her. "Like I said...that's what sisters are for!"

CHAPTER ELEVEN

Casey

Friday finally arrived. It was the very last day of the semester, a day for us to return books to our teachers and watch movies as we counted the seconds on the clock before the summer officially started. Brie, Ali, and I sat together as Mrs. Halliday gave everyone the chance to sit wherever we wanted for the final day.

Even though we didn't have much to do, I dreaded the end. Mrs. Halliday said she would return our exam papers in the last period. I wasn't sure why she wanted to torture us by making us wait so long, but I was so nervous that I'd picked my nails down to stubs. Though, when the time came, I wished the world would rewind and stop altogether.

As our teacher walked around the classroom and dropped our exam folders on our desks, I crossed my fingers and hoped my hard work had paid off. Without all the Instagram drama, I could have done so much better. But at least if I passed, I'd be going to camp with Ali and Brie over the summer.

I didn't share my nervousness with them. We'd had the perfect last day together. And I didn't want to spoil it.

I stared at the folder, happy my grades were hidden.

When I flipped it open, the first test paper I saw was math, and at the top was scrawled a large red B-. I let out a relieved sigh. For me, that test had been the hardest, and after racing through the final two problems, I was worried that I might not even pass. But except for the last two which were worth the most, I managed to get almost every other question correct.

For my other tests, I scored mostly B's, with a B+ for history and an A for geography.

"Report cards will be emailed to your parents by the end of the weekend," Mrs. Halliday announced.

I knew Mom would be really happy with my grades this year. For once, I didn't need to worry about her opening that email. Thanks to Ali, it would probably be the best-looking report card I'd ever received. I sat against my chair and sighed happily.

"How did you do?" Brie asked me.

I scanned through my tests to show her and she smiled, impressed. "Wow! That's so good, Casey!"

"Casey! Awesome job," Ali said, leaning over Brie's shoulder.

"How did you guys do?" I asked, even though I already knew their answers. Brie always did well and Ali would have passed with flying colors.

"Good," Ali smiled.

"Yeah, me too," Brie grinned, quickly flicking through and showing me some of her results. I spotted at least a couple of A's.

When Ali was talking to Brie, I sneaked a look in her folder and saw several red A+'s scrawled on her papers. I was happy for her. She worked hard at school and unlike me, rarely let distractions take hold of her. She deserved those grades. Brie had also done really well and I was happy for her too.

I beamed at both of them. "Hello, camp! Here we come!"

"Have you packed yet?" Ali asked.

Brie and I both shook our heads. "I haven't even started," Brie said.

Jake turned around in his chair and leaned over the back of it, resting his chin on his arms. "Hey, Casey. How did you do on your tests?"

Ali continued chatting with Brie about what clothes they were taking to camp while I focused my attention on Jake. "Pretty good. How about you?"

"Better than I hoped," he smiled. "I'm so busy with all the sport I do, I wasn't sure how I'd go."

"I knew you'd do well, Jake!"

"So...when are you leaving for camp?"

"Monday," I said. "When are you going to Mike's?"

"Tomorrow morning."

"So soon?" I kept my eyes on his while picking anxiously at my nails. I then shoved my hands in my lap in an effort to keep them still.

"I guess this is the last time we'll see each other for a

while."

I nodded. "I guess."

"I know phones aren't allowed on camp…so…maybe you could write to me?" he asked, raising his eyebrows.

"Of course…as long as you write back." I was so happy to hear that he wanted me to write.

"Absolutely!" he laughed.

My insides fluttered just as Sai caught Jake's attention.

Jake grinned at me, then turned to his friend.

The only downside to camp was that I wasn't going to see Jake until the last weeks of summer. But with the promise of keeping in touch, I had faith that I wouldn't miss him too much. And it gave me some hope that our close friendship would last through the summer and into the school year.

"You guys want to come over tomorrow and we can go through my closet?" Ali suggested just as the final bell rang. "You can borrow some things if you want."

"Yes!" Brie exclaimed as she stood up from her seat. "That'd be so good!"

"Definitely," I agreed eagerly.

Ali looked at me. "Dad wanted to barbecue this weekend. Maybe we can ask our mom to come for dinner?'

"As a family?" Brie cooed. "You two are serious matchmakers!"

Ali and I smiled at each other, knowing that with each day that passed, we were getting closer to becoming the family we'd always wanted.

When we headed out of the building, I waved goodbye to Ali and Brie as I walked to the curb to meet Grandma Ann. Over the last few days, she had made a habit of driving Lucas and I home. I had a feeling she was going to miss me this summer. Little did she know that I was going to miss her too. I hoped I'd be able to make her some nice things at camp to show her how much I appreciated her covering the cost.

As I glanced at each of the cars in the pickup line, I stood on my tip-toes to look for Grandma Ann's car, but it was nowhere in sight. It was then that I heard someone calling my name. Quickly whipping around, I found Jake standing in front of me. He hesitated for a split second and then wrapped me in a tight hug. My legs turned to jelly and my heart pounded as his arms held me in place.

"I'm going to miss you, Casey," he smiled shyly as he pulled away.

His hands still held onto my arms and I stared into his adorable eyes.

Before I could reply, he spoke again. "I should go. Be sure to write!"

"I will!" I called out as he sprinted toward his bus.

He climbed on board and I watched him walk to the back and sit down at a window seat. He waved to me and I waved back.

His heart-melting smile remained in place as the bus pulled away and the butterflies in my stomach erupted once more.

CHAPTER TWELVE

Casey

On Saturday, Ali, Brie and I cleared out Ali's closet and each of us put together several different outfits to pack into our suitcases. It was so nice that Ali was willing to share her clothes. A few times throughout the day, I felt bad for ever thinking that my sister was stuck up and spoilt. She was the smartest, most down-to-earth, and kindest girl I'd ever known.

A bonus from the day was spending the evening with Mom and Chris at dinner. It was our last opportunity for a while, and it was so great to see how happy they were together. Both Ali and I hoped their romance would continue over the summer and we'd come back to our parents officially dating and in a serious relationship. However, I knew that Chris would want to move slowly, and we shouldn't push them. They'd have a lot of alone time while we were gone and it would give them a chance to figure things out by themselves.

By Sunday afternoon, I finally had my bags packed. Thankfully, Mom was happy to lend me her good suitcase which I was so grateful for as I only owned a small shabby one. And when she came into my room and found me sitting on the bag so that I could close it, she insisted on snapping a photo.

The following morning, my house was a flurry of activity from the second my alarm went off at five. The bus for the camp was leaving much earlier than we were used to and by the time I reached the car, Lucas was already complaining.

"I'm hungry!" he moaned.

Grandma Ann turned in her seat to face him. "I told you that after we drop Casey off we're going to the diner."

"But I'm hungry now!" he whined.

For once, I wasn't bothered by his annoying ways. I wasn't going to see him for some time and I knew, deep down, that I'd miss him.

"Lucas," Mom warned from the driver's seat. Her glare cut through the rear-view mirror and Lucas crossed his arms and stared out the window.

She glanced at me and her eyes widened. Me going to camp was a big deal, bigger than I'd realized. I'd overheard her and Chris talking about it on the phone the day before. I had never been away from my mother for such a long period of time and she was saying how much she was going to miss me. I also knew she was the one who I'd miss the most.

Even so, my skin tingled with anticipation as we drove across town to the bus departure point. Outside the window, the sky looked bluer than ever before, giving me a good feeling about the summer ahead.

I rolled the window down — as the air conditioning in Mom's car didn't work half the time — and it was already sticky and warm outside. I couldn't wait for the water slides and the river with the rope swings, canoes, and all the other amazing activities. I bubbled over with excitement and wished Mom would drive faster.

"Are we there yet?" Lucas asked.

"Not yet," Grandma Ann said.

"Now?" Lucas asked a minute later.

Mom ignored Lucas. "Casey," she said, "the sun will be hot, so be sure to put sunscreen on. Getting burned is no joke."

"Even on the cloudy days the sun can still be harmful," Grandma Ann added. "You need to be prepared."

"Okay, I'll make sure I wear sunscreen." Normally, Grandma Ann's nagging would annoy me, but now I saw her in a completely different light. I knew how much I had to be grateful for. If it wasn't for Grandma Ann, I wouldn't be going to camp at all.

"Try and get plenty of sleep too," Mom said. "You might be tempted to stay up late at night, but you'll exhaust yourself and you'll be trudging around like a zombie. I know how grouchy you can get without sleep."

Grandma Ann turned in her seat. "And eat plenty of fruit and veggies. You always go for the sweets, but you'll get sick if that's all you eat."

"I also packed some spare batteries in your suitcase, if you need extra for your flashlight," Mom said.

"Take care in the woods," Grandma Ann warned. "I've heard all kinds of wild animals live in those nearby forests. Stay alert and look out for snakes. They may be deadly. When hiking, stay with your friends, always have a buddy—"

They didn't even give me a chance to chime in and agree with them as they prattled back and forth.

"What if Casey's attacked by a bear?" Lucas asked.

"I'm not going—"

He interrupted me before I could finish. "I saw this movie on TV yesterday, and these kids were camping in the woods, and a bear just jumped out—"

It was Mom's turn to interrupt. "I'm sure there won't be any bears, Lucas. Stop frightening your sister."

"Can I use your laptop while you're away?" he asked me.

"No way," I said. "You're not allowed to touch it. I've hidden it, anyway. You won't find it."

He snorted. "I know all your hiding spots. I'll probably find it the second I get home."

I glared at him. "You'd better not touch it!"

"You won't be there to stop me!" He stuck out his tongue to annoy me even more.

"Mom!" I pleaded. "Don't let him in my room or on my laptop!"

If Lucas happened to find the secret diary that I'd hidden away in a document on my desktop, he'd probably read it and show Mom and everyone he knew.

"Lucas, enough!" Thankfully, Mom's warning tone stopped him from saying another word.

I crossed my arms and fumed. How could I have ever thought I'd miss him? A whole summer without him annoying me was going to be bliss.

Then, as if Lucas had never interrupted them, Mom and Grandma Ann went on with their list of things for me not to do as well as what to look out for while I was away. It was as if they didn't trust me to walk from my cabin to the dining hall by myself. Eventually, I blocked them out and thought about all the fun that Ali, Brie, and I would experience together.

"Casey!" Mom said, breaking through my thoughts. "Don't forget to write when you can. You don't have to write every day but we'll be looking forward to hearing from you. And if you need anything, make sure you call me. I've checked and there's a phone available for emergencies or anything urgent."

"Yes, okay, Mom." Normally, this sort of thing would bother me no end, but today, nothing could spoil my mood. Not even Lucas.

"We're going to miss you so much!"

"I'm going to miss you too," I replied, really meaning it. My chest tightened a little thinking about it.

"Will you miss me?" Lucas asked.

I sighed and nodded. I couldn't tell him that he was the one person I probably wouldn't miss! There was no need to get into an argument about how much we needed to love our families right before going to camp.

"You're growing up so quickly," Mom said, choking up a little. "First your amazing report card —"

"Mom," I groaned, not wanting to hear her crying again.

Even Ali had seemed surprised when she saw my results. And to think that I was worried about doing so poorly that Mom would ground me for the summer. It ended up being the best report card I'd ever received. Ali was to thank for that. Without her and her study routines, I knew there was no way I could have done so well.

I was still in awe of Ali's report card though. She'd passed with nothing lower than an A-. But instead of feeling jealous, I was proud of her. She was a hard worker and deserved every single one of those A's.

When we finally pulled into the parking lot at the bus depot, my heart immediately began hammering in my chest. I strained to see who had already arrived and to catch a glimpse of the possible friends I'd make over the summer. There were already dozens of people around the bus, waiting to load their luggage and board. All thoughts of Lucas and report cards flew from my head as I searched for Ali and Brie amongst the group.

Mom parked a few spots over from the bus and when I hopped out of the car to help her with my things, my skin suddenly started to prickle. With my sleeping bag, pillow, tote bag, suitcase and backpack, I felt as if I'd brought way too much.

I took a closer look at the group by the bus and noticed that several kids had packed nearly double what I had. I thought my suitcase was big, but it seemed to be the smallest of all. What on earth could they be taking to camp?

I chewed on my lip, going over everything that I'd shoved into my bags over the weekend. Had I forgotten something important? Had I left some essentials behind?

Along with the clothes that Ali had loaned me, I thought I'd packed everything I needed.

I closed my eyes and took a deep breath, trying to calm down. This was all very new to me. Maybe these kids had gone to summer camp before, and they were bringing things for their friends? At the very least, I had my best friend and sister to borrow from if I needed to. I was going to be fine. Besides, we'd all agreed to share and swap with each other anyway. In addition to that, I was sure Ali had enough things for all three of us.

I took a step forward, knowing that the summer of a lifetime was waiting for me.

CHAPTER THIRTEEN

Ali

I was so excited for camp that I barely slept, but instead of feeling tired on Monday morning, my body was buzzing with pent-up energy. As soon as Dad drove our car into the parking lot, I spotted Casey waving and sprinting towards us.

As soon as I hopped out of the car, Casey grabbed my hands. "We're going to camp!" she shrieked.

Together, we bounced up and down, each of us just as excited as the other.

"Don't leave me out of this!" Brie laughed as she appeared at our side.

We were so overcome with the thrill of it all that our parents had to pick up our bags and usher us towards the line that had formed at the side of the bus.

When we reached the top of the line, the bus driver put our belongings in the storage compartment and we each turned to say goodbye to our parents.

Jackie immediately gripped hold of both Casey and me in a tight hug. When she pulled away, tears had formed in her eyes. "You two take care of each other, okay?"

Casey and I shared a look before nodding.

"And have fun," Jackie said before letting a tear slip.

Casey gave her another hug as I went to Dad and hugged him.

I couldn't believe his eyes were glossy as well. For a second, I wondered how this was all affecting him. Was this a mistake? Was it too soon after Mom's passing to leave him alone for almost an entire summer?

But when Dad and Jackie shared a look, I knew it was all going to be okay. He wasn't going to be completely alone. He had Jackie for company and hopefully over the summer they'd become closer. With Grandma Ann and her friend, Margaret keeping Lucas busy, Jackie and Dad should have plenty of time to themselves.

After we said our final goodbyes, we stood in line with the other campers. Casey and I glanced back at our parents and any fears I'd had subsided. Dad stood happily next to Jackie, and even Grandma Ann looked pleased as she chatted with them. That was until Lucas and his friend from school started chasing each other around the parking lot and she had to rush after him.

I smiled as I watched my family, the one that I dreamed of having united one day very soon. If everything went as Casey and I had planned, that was exactly what was going to happen.

Brie nudged my arm, bringing me back to the present. I smiled at her curiously and she nodded in the direction of the boy in front of us. I hadn't noticed him before. His dark hair was short in the back but longer up front and I watched him flick the wispy strands from his eyes. I couldn't see his entire face, but the parts that I did see as he chatted to the boy alongside him, made tingles roll up my arms.

"Do you know him?" I whispered to Brie, glancing at Casey to see if she had also noticed the good looking boy. But my sister was distracted by our mother who was still waving madly.

"No," Brie said with a smile. "But he's really cute."

I quickly shushed her and she clamped a hand over her mouth and giggled. I was so eager for camp, that a giggle burst from my lips as well. Then Brie's eyes widened as she glanced over my shoulder.

When I turned around, I found the boy looking right at me. He was much cuter than I'd thought. His brown eyes stared back and his smile widened. For once in my life, I was speechless. As the seconds ticked by without anyone speaking, my stomach flip-flopped. Brie hadn't been exaggerating at all. He was cute with a capital C!

Brie continued to grin, and I tried to ignore her as the boy glanced at Casey. He blinked a few times and then looked at me again, his eyes darting between us.

I geared up for the twin speech, letting him know that he was looking at two identical girls.

His mouth opened to say something, but before he could, the bus driver asked him to board. He shook his head and gave us one more look before walking up the steps of the bus.

Brie nudged me again and giggled. "Did you see the way he looked at you? You two would look great together!"

I rolled my eyes and shook my head. At the same time though, my mind wandered to that idea. Casey and Brie already had boys in their lives. Casey and Jake were a sure thing and by the way that Brie and Wyatt were always messaging each other, they seemed to be getting closer as well. There was no reason for me not to have the same thing.

The driver told us to board next. I squeezed my pillow and held onto the strap of my backpack as I stepped onto the bus. As I headed down the aisle, I glanced around for the boy. He sat closer to the middle of the bus, next to his friend. As I passed by him, he looked up and grinned, causing my heart to flutter wildly. There weren't three empty seats anywhere except for at the back of the bus so I headed towards them. I tried to turn my attention to the summer I was about to spend with my sister and friend but thoughts of the cute boy remained in my head.

"I saw him looking at you again," Brie said as she reached up to the overhead compartment. She shoved her backpack inside and waggled her eyebrows at me.

"No, he wasn't!" I shook my head, even though I knew what she'd said was true.

"Who are you talking about?" Casey asked, sliding into the seat next to me.

"That cute boy up there." Brie pointed along the aisle.

I reached over to grab her finger. "Brie! Don't point!"

Casey smiled as she stood up to get a better look. "I can't see who you mean."

I was surprised she hadn't seen the boy outside when he was staring at each of us. But she had Jake. I doubted she even noticed other cute boys. Jake was the only one she was interested in.

"Well, he'll be around all summer," Brie said to Casey. "You'll be able to see him and Ali holding hands at the fire and splashing in the pool."

Brie laughed. It was all in good fun and I couldn't help but smile too.

"Well, don't forget the double date we have planned with Jake and Mike for the end of the summer," Casey reminded me.

"Of course," I said. Maybe if Brie thought I wasn't

interested in the boy, she'd stop teasing me about him. "How could I forget?"

I glanced at Brie and she was already distracted by trying to untangle her headphones.

"Jake is going to organize the date," Casey said. "But if you don't want to go just let me know."

"Let's just have fun and not worry about the end of summer," I replied.

Casey blew out a breath and settled into her seat. "Okay. Sounds like a good idea."

About ten minutes later, the bus roared to life and we took off along the road. All three of us waved frantically at our families. Dad already had his arm around Jackie's shoulder as she mopped at her eyes with tissues. I hoped that the two of them together would be a familiar sight when we returned from camp.

As we drove onto the highway, my thoughts drifted to the cute boy sitting several seats in front of me. Apart from being really good looking, he had a kind smile. I wondered if we had the same interests. I would never tell Brie, but I did imagine holding hands with him at the campfire and splashing each other in the river.

Whatever happened, I knew this was going to be a very fun summer.

CHAPTER FOURTEEN

Casey

I was surprised to hear that Ali had a crush on a boy who was sitting just a few seats ahead of us. She hadn't even met him properly yet and I could sense she was already thinking about him. If Mike wasn't who she wanted, that was fine. Although selfishly, I was looking forward to our double date. If Ali and Mike liked each other, we'd all have so much fun together. But my sister deserved to be happy in all parts of her life and if she really wasn't interested in Mike, then I wasn't going to force the issue.

The ride to camp took several hours and when we pulled over at a rest stop to use the bathrooms, I searched for the boy amongst the group. There were so many people at the stop though, and I only caught a quick glimpse when Brie pointed him out in the crowd.

When we finally reached the campground, I forgot all about the boy as I looked out the window and took in the amazing sight in front of me. We were parked under a grouping of trees, and the river stretched out in the distance. I wanted nothing more than to get off the bus and experience all of it.

Brie leaned over the seat, to check out the view as well. "There's another bus coming." She stared in surprise down the driveway.

I followed her gaze and watched as the bus pulled up in a nearby parking bay. We hadn't realized how many kids would be at this camp. Once again I felt grateful that the three of us had managed to get a spot.

An older teenage girl stood at the front of the bus and spoke loudly, gaining everyone's attention. She waited for everyone to quieten down and then continued speaking.

"My name is Heather Watson. I'm one of the camp counselors. Before getting off the bus, you'll all need to check the overhead compartments and under your seats so you don't leave anything behind. You can form a line outside to collect your belongings. Once you have all your gear, you'll need to remain in that open area over there." She pointed out the window to a nearby clearing. "We don't have too many rules here, but we do expect you to obey the ones we give you. We'll tell you your assigned cabins and where to find them. Then you'll be able to make your way to your cabin and start unpacking. Welcome to camp, everyone."

A few kids cheered, and I looked at Ali who was still staring out the window with a wide grin. I had no doubt that she'd heard everything the counselor had said and planned on following the rules. But she was in awe of the sight in front of her.

Once we were outside, we lined up to get our bags and watched as the other bus also unloaded. There were so many kids, more than I could count. I imagined making life-long friends with some of them. I wanted to take all the confidence that Ali had given me and use it to be my own person. I wasn't going to be Shy-Casey anymore, I wanted to be more like Ali, but different at the same time.

After grabbing our bags, we moved to a shady spot and checked out our surroundings. In the distance were several buildings. All of them in the rustic log-cabin style.

Ali's expression was filled with excitement. "This is so much better than any other camp I've ever been to."

"Really?" I asked her. "We haven't seen much yet."

She inhaled a deep breath. "I can tell already. Come over here and take a look!"

"Aren't we supposed to stay in this area?" I asked, not wanting to get in trouble during my first minutes of camp.

"We will," Ali said, propping her pillow on her oversized suitcase.

Ali wasn't one for breaking the rules, so Brie and I followed her. We rounded the bus and saw a stunning view. The river flowed into the distance and from where we stood, we could see canoes on the riverbank and a timber jetty jutting out over the water.

My jaw dropped as I scanned the area and my eyes fell on the high ropes course. There were planks of wood and ropes running between the trees, high above the ground. I'd remembered seeing the same course on the video that Mrs. Halliday showed us, but it was even more impressive in real life. I knew that each person would be attached to a harness, so I didn't have to fear that I'd fall, but still, it was intimidating.

"That high ropes course looks so awesome!" Brie said.

"Kids from bus number one, over here please!" one of the counselors called out loudly.

Brie, Ali, and I scurried over to her. There were over a dozen more counselors standing behind her, all wearing similar green shirts. At least we'd be able to find them in a crowd.

The counselor held a clipboard in her hands and glanced at it before addressing us again. "Once I've assigned your cabin, you'll need to follow the signs to find it. Each person can also take a map. It will show you the full layout of the camp." She indicated the counselor beside her who was waving a pile of maps in the air. "You'll have the next hour to settle into your cabin. Lunch today is scheduled at noon. You'll need to arrive at the dining hall by eleven-thirty so we can go over the rules and give you a few instructions for how your summer will progress here. To reach the dining hall, just follow this pathway." She pointed behind her. "Everything is signposted and there are maps on display all over the camp as well. So you can't get lost. First off, Bobcat Hall..."

As she went down the list of kids, I noticed that the boys and girls were heading off into completely different directions toward their cabins, following the signs etched into posts across the way. It was like the school camp set up and I wasn't sure why I expected this one to be any different.

"That's us!" Ali said, nudging me. I hadn't been listening at all.

"Thank goodness we're in the same cabin!" Brie squealed.

I nodded my head, pretending that I'd heard which cabin we were headed to. After taking a map from the counselor, I followed Ali and Brie along the trail toward the place where we'd be staying for the entire summer. Together! If Ali was by my side, I could do anything.

The cabins were all similar with wooden exteriors, looking as if they shot up from the ground. We passed many of them with woodsy names…Buffalo Oasis, Rattlesnake Perch—I shivered, thinking of Grandma Ann's warning about wild animals, including snakes, and I hoped that the names weren't descriptions of what was found in the nearby woods— Bobcat Hall, Falcon Pass, Sundance Rapids, Aspen Chalet, Castaway Canyon.

"Here we are!" Brie said, running ahead as fast as she could, dragging her bags along.

I read the sign aloud. "Raindance Meadows." I smiled blissfully. The name of our cabin sounded wonderful. That had to be a good sign.

There were two steps to the door, and I braced myself for what was inside.

Once I entered, my jaw dropped. The rustic exterior hid the modern feel of the inside. The floor was a sparkling wood and the walls painted a pretty shade of blue. The windows allowed plenty of light but they also had curtains hanging at the sides for privacy. On either side of the room, were groups of closets with a storage area for our bags.

Brie stepped out from the bathroom. "Two showers! Two!"

At our other camp, we had to share one shower with all the girls in the cabin. It had been a nightmare every morning. Even so, I'd thought that camp was cool. But this one reminded me of staying in a hotel room. All the surfaces were clean and there was not a speck of dust or dirt to be seen; certainly not like the cabins at our school camp.

As our cabin mates hadn't yet arrived, we had the first choice of beds. "Let's pick bunks close to each other."

I looked around, trying to figure out which of the eight bunks was perfect for me.

"Over here," Ali suggested, choosing the beds furthest away from the bathroom and the front door. She placed her bag on a top bunk and just as I was about to put my bag on the next one across from her, the door burst open and three girls crammed into the room.

"I guess this is okay," one of the girls said as she rolled two suitcases alongside her. "Not sure about the name, though!"

She had wavy brown hair that hung in waves over one shoulder. On her lips was bubble gum colored pink lip gloss. However, they were tugged into an awkward grimace and she placed her hands on her hips as she looked critically at her surroundings.

Her eyes landed on Ali. "I'm Madison. This is Skye and Amy, my BFFs." Madison waved her hand at the girls behind her.

Skye played with the ends of her pigtail braids. She smiled warmly at us. Amy had a similar scowl to Madison as if copying her friend. How could anyone not be impressed with this place? Madison flicked her hair off her shoulder and looked around the room.

"Hi, I'm Ali," Ali said, introducing herself. "This is Casey and Brie."

Madison glanced at us then lifted her pillow and placed it on the bed by my side. She then turned to her friends. "Guys take the other top bunks. Lower bunks are for losers."

I swallowed as Madison claimed my bed.

"We were going to take these three," Ali said to Madison and pointed at the three beds, ending with the top bunk where Madison's pillow now laid.

Madison shrugged her shoulder. "Oh well, first come, first served." Then she climbed onto my bunk.

CHAPTER FIFTEEN

Casey

Ali chewed on her lip but said nothing else as Madison stole the bunk from me. There was no reason to fight over a bed, but I'd wanted to sleep next to Ali. I'd imagined us talking late into the night about all the fun we'd have together during the day.

Ali and Brie managed to keep their beds and Amy grabbed the fourth one. Sighing, I placed my things on the one below Ali's. At least we'd still be close. I shrugged off the confrontation and let it go. If only I hadn't hesitated, I'd still have the top bunk. I wouldn't make that mistake again.

Madison dug through her bag and pulled out a brush, stroking the bristles through her hair. The sunlight shone through the windows so brightly that her hair shimmered in soft waves.

"So," she said, without looking at anyone in particular, although it was clear she was speaking to us, "how many summer camps have you girls been to?"

"A few," Ali and Brie said.

I followed with my reply. "This is my first."

Madison dropped her brush and her jaw lowered as well. "This is your first summer away? Really? Wow!" She raised an eyebrow to her friends and Amy giggled into her hand.

What was the big deal?

"We go to camp every summer. Since we were kids...like, since kindergarten," Madison said in an insulting tone. "I just hope this place is as good as they've made it out to be."

"I'm sure it will be," Ali remarked.

"Well," Madison scoffed, "it wouldn't be the first time I've left an awful camp. After years of going to Camp Crystal, my mom wanted me to try somewhere new. So I went to Camp Green Lake, and it was disgusting. The lake was literally green, with algae! And they expected me to swim in that? No way! I called my dad, and he came to pick me up. I wasn't going to spend another hour there."

The other girls nodded, but I had a feeling that they'd remained at the camp.
Madison went on about how gross it was, although to me, it didn't sound so bad and I wondered if she was exaggerating about the green lake. She obviously thought pretty highly of herself, something that was becoming more and more obvious with each word that came out of her mouth.

From my bunk, I couldn't see Ali's reactions, but neither she nor Brie commented. As if Madison would give them the opportunity anyway, she didn't stop talking for one second.

I was worried about being late for the camp meeting, so I unzipped my suitcase, intending to unpack.

It was barely open when I heard Madison's voice again. "Is that all you brought?"

I looked at my suitcase, wondering if I had forgotten anything. But how would she know?

"Yes," I said.

"For the whole summer?" she asked.

I sighed. "Yes, why?"

"Wow, that's impressive." She pursed her lips. "I've never managed with so little. How do you get by with so few clothes? I mean, do you wear the same thing every day? That's a little gross—"

As she went on, I tried to ignore her while grabbing a few of my shirts. Just as I opened the closet, Madison jumped down from her bed and placed her hand on the knob before me. She pursed her lips once more as if daring me to say something. I thought of Ronnie and immediately

184

decided to stick up for myself. This girl wasn't going to ruin my summer the way Ronnie had ruined my semester.

"This is my closet," I said, indicating the number on the door, which matched the number etched into my headboard.

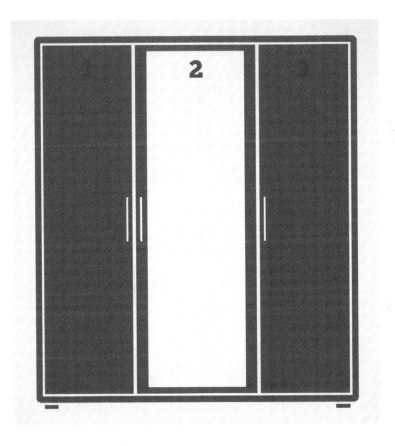

Madison flicked a glance at my bed. "Oh. I guess you're right." She glanced at Ali and then back at me. Realization flooded her expression. "Wow, you two look so much alike. Except for your hair. I swear you could be twins."

I smirked and turned to look at Ali. Brie and Ali started to laugh.

Madison crossed her arms. "What's so funny?"

"Ali and I are twins," I said. "We just wear our hair differently."

"Wow!" Amy commented, hopping off her bed and walking towards us. "I bet if you wore it the same, you'd be identical."

Skye also moved closer. It was obvious that both girls wanted to take a good look at Ali and me. "Have you ever swapped places?"

Ali cleared her throat. "A few times."

"That's so cool!" Madison moved in front of her friends, totally blocking their view. "Tell us more."

Skye looked over Madison's shoulder. "What was it like growing up together? Did your parents have trouble telling you apart?"

Madison placed her hand under her chin and nodded, interested in the answer.

Ali didn't mention our family history, and I followed her lead. That was too personal to be telling these girls, so we skimmed the topic and just gave them some general details about our lives as twins. The atmosphere became friendlier than when they first arrived and I felt better about having them as cabin mates.

"Guys," Skye said, checking the watch on her wrist. "We should go. We have five minutes to get to the dining hall."

"We haven't even unpacked!" Amy whined.

"We can unpack later!" Madison countered. "Stop stressing! Come on, let's just go."

The door opened, and two more girls stepped inside. "Sorry we're late!" one of them said, looking a little flustered. "My parents just dropped us off."

"There's a meeting at the dining hall, it starts in a few minutes," Ali said to the girls. "We'll see you down there.

Madison and her friends had already walked out the door and were on their way. But we didn't rush to keep up. Instead, we remained a short distance behind them.

CHAPTER SIXTEEN

Casey

"What do you think of Madison?" Brie asked. "She seems a little over the top. I hope she doesn't think she can boss us around all summer, the way she bosses her friends."

"We won't let her!" Ali turned to me. "Good job sticking up for yourself, Casey. She would have totally taken your closet if you hadn't spoken up."

"Yeah, I know," I said. "You've taught me well, Ali." I had to remember to stay strong, even when it felt uncomfortable.

"Does she remind you of someone we know?" Brie rolled her eyes. "I thought of Ronnie the whole time while she was talking. I can't believe we escaped Ronnie for the summer and then ended up with another girl just like her."

I nodded. "If we stand up to her, I think we'll be fine."

"I hope so," Brie sighed. "I don't want her thinking she can take charge of our cabin."

"Let's just be nice," Ali suggested. "But we can't let her dominate us, the way she does to her friends."

Brie and I nodded firmly in agreement. As we walked, however, I tried to build up my confidence. I knew that Ali and Brie would always be on my side, but if Madison ever cornered me, I'd have to be ready. She'd already stolen my bed and tried to take my closet. I wasn't going to ignore the fact that she hadn't picked on anyone except for me, which was exactly what Ronnie had done all semester. Madison had spotted someone who she thought was weak and I had to prove that I wasn't.

A while ago that might have been me, but after

meeting Ali I'd promised to change that part of me. It was the only way I could show everyone I wasn't a person who could be stepped on. Madison seemed to thrive on dominating others, but I was determined that I wouldn't allow her to do that to me.

When we reached the dining hall, the lovely new building that I'd seen when we arrived, there was a large group of counselors standing in front of it. Some of them were clapping and singing out camp rhymes and my mood began to perk up. Madison and the others were on the opposite side of the group and I made no move to go near them.

Ali and Brie seemed to have the same idea.

But, once Madison caught our eyes, she waved frantically and pushed past other kids to get to us.

I groaned but focused on the counselors in front of me. Most of them were very athletic-looking young adults and teenagers. The older supervisors were in good shape as well. I could see that we wouldn't be lounging around much this summer.

One at a time, the counselors said their names and something about themselves, but there were so many it was hard to keep track after the first five. Their shirts had their names embroidered on one side as well as the camp logo, a pair of American flags. I hoped they wore their uniform regularly, that way I could learn most of their names by heart.

"Wow, he's cute," Madison said loud enough for everyone surrounding us to hear.

She was talking about Greg, the counselor who did a back-flip when he was introduced. He was on the younger side, probably only several years older than us. He was lean and very muscular, and she was right, he was kind of cute.

"I'm signing up for all his activities," Madison said to her friends. Amy giggled the loudest, and the group got a few looks from some of the other kids.

Ali, Brie and I scooted away from Madison, but we wouldn't be rid of her for long. She was assigned to the same cabin as us. There was no escaping her there.

A woman stepped forward. She looked to be about Mom's age, but she had a pixie cut and wore her hair cut short. For a moment, I thought she'd start screaming at us like a military general, but instead, she smiled, and my insides warmed.

"Hello everyone. I'm Kristina Greene, I'm the co-supervisor of this camp. Now that everyone's been introduced, I'm going to explain the camp rules. There aren't many, as we do want you to have fun, but the ones that are in place need to be obeyed. That way everyone will stay safe and have fun at the same time."

Every one of the campers had stopped talking and was listening intently.

"First of all," Kristina said, everyone must assemble by eight-thirty each morning right where you are now for morning roll call. Then you'll go inside for breakfast. If your cabin mates are running late, then you won't be served until they arrive. So, think about that if you plan on sleeping in."

Madison made a snoring sound and Ali shot her an unimpressed look. But Madison didn't seem to notice.

"During the free time sessions each day," Kristina continued. "You are permitted to wander the grounds at your leisure. There will be free time activities written on the board in the dining hall ready for you to look through each morning. We don't mind if you spend some time in your cabins, but this summer is about making life-long friends and expanding your mind, so we suggest you take advantage of the activities listed. Lunch each day is at one o'clock and dinner is at six-thirty, followed by night time activities. After those, girls and boys must remain on their own sides of the camp."

Snickering and mumbling rolled over the group.

"Boring," Madison moaned.

"Morning snacks will be served at eleven each morning and there will be snacks available again each afternoon from three-thirty. There is always plenty of food. We don't want anyone going hungry."

Kristina paused, allowing us all to take in the

190

information so far. She scanned the group as she continued. "At this camp, no phones are allowed. If you've brought one with you, then you need to hand it into the office for safekeeping until you leave. The summer is about making friends and getting outdoors, not staying inside on electronic devices."

More groans rose up from the group. I waited for Madison to make a remark. She didn't let me down. She crossed her arms and said, "This sounds more like a prison than a camp."

"That's for sure!" a boy next to her said.

"What about emergencies?" Madison asked loudly, glancing at the people around her. She sure loved attention.

Kristina turned to Madison. "There are phones in the office in case of any emergencies. All the rules must be obeyed. They are clearly outlined on the website and on the brochures that were passed around your schools."

Madison snorted. "I don't remember reading that part. I wouldn't have come here if I'd known that. My other camps weren't this strict."

I cringed, but Kristina moved on, either not hearing or ignoring Madison. I wanted to ignore her too. She was so rude. But her friends and a few other kids rallied around her and continued to chatter about the no cell phone rule.

Kristina gave the group a sharp look and they quietened down as she continued. "No one is to leave the camp perimeter without permission. That side," she pointed at the water in the distance, "is bordered by the river and the rest is surrounded by trees. There are clear markers where the camp ends. I don't want anyone to be caught wandering past those markers. Also, the river is out of bounds except for supervised activity time. There are several sessions of activities daily, and each cabin group will be given the opportunity to sign up for the different activities that you'd like to take part in. While we promote cabin friends, you don't need to stick with your cabin group if you wish to explore other interests. To sign up, there is a whiteboard in the hallway of the dining hall. You can't miss it. It's your responsibility to add your names under each activity so that you can reserve a spot at that time. The rule is…once you sign up, you must attend because attendance will be taken for each session except free time. Everyone needs to be accounted for during activities. We encourage everyone to try each of the activities that are available so that you'll end your summer as a well-rounded camper."

"What if I don't want to sign up for jewelry making?" one of the boys closer to the front said.

"You can't force us to do things!" his friend called out, causing laughter from their group.

I rolled my eyes and so did Ali. Kristina didn't seem bothered by their remarks.

"Those boys sound like fun!" Madison said, standing on her tip-toes to see them.

Ali and I exchanged a look. She was going to cause trouble. Why did she have to be assigned to our cabin?

"One last reminder," Kristina said, her voice becoming firm. "There are consequences set in place for anyone breaking the rules. And we won't hesitate to call parents to collect any trouble-makers. Now, I will introduce your go-to counselor in case of any questions or problems. This is the person you will be checking in with at each meal," Kristina explained.

As the counselors were assigned their cabin groups, the groups entered the dining hall. I was so hungry and almost sprinted to our assigned counselor when she called our cabin name.

The pretty brown-haired girl named Heather, who had been on our bus, was our go-to person. I immediately noticed her kind smile. She also seemed very bubbly and I liked her right away.

"I'm starving," she said after checking that everyone was accounted for. "How about we get any questions answered so we can eat. Does that sound okay?"

Heather

Ali and I smiled and nodded at each other.

Madison sized Heather up and down, but Heather remained positive and happy. Maybe Madison had met her match. She was rude when vying for attention, but it seemed when confronted with our counselor, she clammed up. There was hope for us after all.

Madison and her friends walked alongside Heather as

they peppered her with questions. The two new girls who had arrived late to our cabin followed behind them. We could hear Madison's voice over everyone else's. She was very interested in Heather's hair care routine.

"I hope she's not sucking up to Heather," I whispered to Brie.

Brie rolled her eyes. "She probably is."

"We might have to do the same," I frowned. "We need Heather on our side."

I had a strong feeling that Madison wasn't going to be an easy cabin mate this summer and I wondered what was ahead for us.

CHAPTER SEVENTEEN

Ali

By the time we entered the main dining area, the line for food was huge. Instead of standing there waiting, I suggested to Casey and Brie that we head over to the activity board to sign up for some activities.

A few other kids had the same idea, but there were plenty of available spots on each of the lists, so we could choose whatever we wanted. Even though Kristina had asked us to branch out with other kids, I wanted to be with my sister and Brie. This was our summer together.

I bumped arms with someone and apologized, coming face to face with the good-looking boy from the bus. My face flushed. I'd been thinking about him but hadn't seen him since we first arrived.

"After you," he said, opening his hand out to me. He was holding a black marker and passed it to me.

"Thank you," I said, turning quickly to Casey and Brie. "Water slides?"

"Definitely," Casey agreed.

Brie winked at me a few times which made my cheeks redden even more.

I scribbled our names down and then handed the marker back to the boy. I wanted to ask his name, but my mouth was so dry that I knew nothing would come out if I tried. Besides, the group behind us was growing and we needed to move out of the way. For our first day, we were only required to do one activity and would then have free time. So I followed behind Casey and Brie toward the main food area.

As I walked, I took a quick glance back at the boy and

saw that he and his friend were adding their names under ours. When I turned back around, Brie was grinning at me. I shook my head as she nudged my shoulder. Casey looked at us and frowned.

Behind us, one of the counselors was calling out to the queue of kids. "The water slide activity is full."

Several kids groaned.

"I wanted to do that!"

"So not fair."

"You'll all get a chance," the counselor assured them. "There are plenty of other activities to choose from."

"It's a good thing you got us on the list," Casey said.

I smiled at her. She had no idea how good it was. As well as having fun, I would finally get to meet the boy from the bus. That idea excited me more than anything. Although I knew Casey was keen for us to go on a double date with Jake and Mike at the end of the summer, I hadn't heard from Mike since our day at the Great Escape and I wasn't even sure if he liked me. Casey already had someone, and she should be open to me finding someone too. She could easily go on a date with Jake, alone.

We joined the food line and after selecting from a choice of chicken nuggets and fries, or pizza and salad, we headed over to one of the only empty tables in the dining hall. It was by the windows so we could look out over the river. Even though the meal was straightforward, it was good, probably the tastiest chicken nuggets I'd ever eaten. They looked freshly made instead of from a frozen bag. Even the fries were from freshly cut potatoes. If this was any indication of the food for the summer, my stomach would be very happy.

Madison and her friends plopped down next to us and so did the latecomers to our cabin. During roll call, I'd learned their names were Hayley and Emma.

Casey, Brie, and I sat closer to Hayley and Emma. They both wore their hair in similar buns atop their heads.

We learned they were from the same town and took dance classes together. That explained the buns. They were much nicer than Madison's group, and I hoped to get to know them better over the summer.

"They call this Italian dressing?" Madison interrupted our conversation and threw her fork down on the table, startling me. "I can't eat this!"

"Get something else then," Emma suggested.

Madison shot her a look. Emma hadn't had the opportunity to discover how rude Madison could be.

Madison scraped her chair out from under the table. "I think I will."

She grabbed her tray and stormed toward the lunch line. I watched her cut in front of the kids who were waiting for food and slam her tray down then proceed to wave her arms in the air. Her mouth moved quickly, but there was too much noise in the room and I couldn't make out her words.

"Did I say something wrong?" Emma asked Hayley.

"She's like that," Brie muttered, keeping her voice low so that Skye and Amy didn't overhear.

They had both stopped eating and Skye had the same stunned look on her face as us. Amy didn't seem too surprised though. She had probably seen Madison behave like that before.

The woman behind the counter disappeared into the kitchen, and Madison stood there with her hands on her hips. A few minutes later the woman returned and handed Madison a bowl heaped with salad. Madison tore over to us and sat down again.

"Did you get a new salad?" Amy asked.

"Duh," Madison said, shoving her hair away from her face.

Amy hunched her shoulders.

Madison pointed at the bowl in front of her. "They remade the dressing and assured me it was the correct measurements of olive oil and vinegar this time."

She took a bite and nodded, seeming satisfied.

I let go of the breath I'd been holding. I didn't care if she got what she wanted, but I couldn't stand being near her.

I tried to avoid eye contact with her for the remainder of the meal, even though she constantly insisted on butting into every conversation.

Lunch couldn't be over fast enough. And when it was time to go to our activities, Brie, Casey, and I raced to clear our trays and head out the door. Hayley and Emma kept up with us as we walked back to the cabin to change into our swimsuits. They were going to a dance class inside the air-conditioned recreation hall. I liked them both and hoped that we'd be able to do an activity together soon.

We were all ready to go by the time Madison and her friends returned.

"I can't believe we got stuck with canoeing," Madison complained. "I don't think I have enough sunscreen to deal with this. I mean, do they want us to burn out there on the water?"

I breathed a sigh of relief. They hadn't signed up for the water slides. At the very least, our afternoon would be Madison-free.

Casey and I looked at each other, and I knew she was thinking the same thing.

CHAPTER EIGHTEEN

Casey

I was so grateful to escape Madison for the afternoon, and Ali felt the same way. As much as Ali always tried to be positive, Madison was even worse than Ronnie. We were glad to have a break from her. I put a t-shirt on over my swimsuit, grabbed my towel and flip-flops and headed out the door with Brie and Ali by my side.

As much as I was a little annoyed that Ali had a crush on the boy from the bus, I was pleased for her at the same time. Sure, Mike would be disappointed that she had met someone else, but it wasn't right for me to force a relationship between them. I already had Jake, and I wanted Ali to be happy too.

I expected a few water slides as I'd seen on the video for the camp, but when we arrived at the pool, my jaw dropped. There were three more than shown in the video, each one with varying sizes and twists. The pool was huge, and there was a bunch of white lounge chairs on the deck. As much as the camp had so many other activities, I wanted to be at the pool every day. The water was crystal clear, and I couldn't wait to jump in.

Brie picked out three chairs next to each other. "Let's put our towels down here."

We followed her lead and placed our towels and shirts down.

"Which slide do you want to try first?" Ali asked.

"That one," I pointed to the biggest.

I'd only been to one water park before, but I wasn't going to waste any time being timid about the slides. I was a new person, thanks to Ali, and this was my first opportunity to prove that.

"Risk taker!" Brie grinned. "What have you done with the old Casey?"

I laughed as we made our way up the steps to the openings for all the slides. Glancing over my shoulder, I noticed several other kids in a line behind us. We heard a loud squeal coming from a nearby slide and I watched a girl speed past, her arms outstretched as she slid into the pool.

Suddenly Brie grabbed my arm. "There he is." She proceeded to tap Ali on the shoulder.

"I see him," Ali hissed quietly, in an attempt to quieten Brie down.

Up ahead, the boy from our bus stood with his friend. There wasn't anyone between us, so we were about to stand right behind him. He was adorable. I could easily understand why Ali was interested in him.

Instantly, thoughts of Jake crossed my mind and I wished that he was there as well. I decided I would write to him that night. It would take several days for my letter to reach him, so it would be over a week before I received one in return. I smiled as I pictured him reading my letter and then writing back.

I could hardly wait until I had his letter in my hands. A wide grin stretched across my face and Brie had to nudge me forward.

CHAPTER NINETEEN

Ali

Brie made such a scene that I panicked and darted in another direction so I could go down a different slide. I wasn't about to stand in line behind the boy from the bus while she was making everything so obvious. I thought he was cute, that's all and I wished she'd stop going on about him.

I listened as the slide attendant told me to lay back and place my arms crisscrossed against my chest. I did as he asked and without warning, I found myself speeding down.

When I splashed into the pool several seconds later, I was breathless and grinning from ear to ear. Then someone came flying down the slide next to mine and abruptly appeared in the water alongside me.

It was the cute boy.

He whooped, and his eyes met mine. "Hey."

"Hey," I smiled.

He glanced at the slide I had just come down. "Was that fun?"

"It was really fast!"

He wiped water from his eyes, and a few droplets hung onto his eyelashes. "Mine was too!"

We were instructed by another attendant to clear the area so we swam to the side of the pool and climbed the ladder. As we stood by the pool waiting for our friends, we looked at each other awkwardly. It seemed that the two of us were lost for words.

Thankfully, Casey quickly appeared on the ladder with Brie right behind her. They were followed by the boy's friend. When each of them was standing alongside us, I broke the silence. "I'm Ali. This is Casey and Brie."

Casey and Brie smiled at the boys.

"My name's Liam," the cute boy said, "and this is Ethan." Liam's brown eyes were locked on mine. His gaze then darted to Casey. "You two look alike. Are you sisters?"

"We're twins actually."

Ethan clapped his hands together. "I told you, Liam!"

Liam and Ethan laughed. Liam glanced at me and then back at Casey once more.

Heat flushed my cheeks and I turned away. I'd only just met Liam, but I couldn't help liking him. Not only was he really cute, he seemed friendly too; just like Jake.

The two boys followed us up the steps leading to the slides and we had a few turns on every one of them, the boys whooping loudly. Casey, Brie and I squealed as well. The slides were so much fun and it was hard to choose a favorite. We then decided to try out the inflatables that were floating around in a sectioned off area of the pool. Several kids were floating around on a variety of rafts and tubes and when Casey, Brie, and Ethan grabbed an inflatable each, there was only one raft remaining.

"Do you want to share?" Liam asked me.

I hesitated, not sure what to say. I could feel the eyes of everyone else on mine and my skin flushed with embarrassment once more. But it would be more embarrassing to say no, so I nodded shyly. "Okay," I replied, ignoring the smirk on Brie's face.

Liam allowed me to get on the raft first before he maneuvered himself onto the other side. It took a moment to adjust our bodies so that we wouldn't fall off. Once we were settled, we were close together and his legs brushed against mine.

As we floated around, I couldn't help the tingles climbing up my arms. We had only been at camp for a few hours and it was already becoming the summer of my dreams.

CHAPTER TWENTY

Casey

I couldn't take my eyes off Ali and Liam. They were laughing and getting along so well. No matter where Ali went, she made friends. A pinch of jealousy rose within me, but I immediately squished it down. There was no reason for me to be jealous of her. I already had Jake.

Brie paddled over to me. "Ali's made a friend already. And we only just got here. Everyone seems to like her, don't they?"

"Yeah, they do," I nodded, realizing the reason for my jealousy.

This summer was supposed to be about us...getting to know each other better and being sisters. I didn't want her attention taken by Liam or anyone else. As Brie had said, it was only our first day but already Ali was occupied by a boy. We were supposed to grow closer instead of further apart. I also couldn't help feeling bad for Mike. I wanted Ali and him to be close so that we could all double date.

Visions of the weeks ahead flooded my mind, and my stomach churned. Would Ali and Liam spend all their time together and ruin our plans?

Ali completely ignoring me reminded me of when her friend, Meg came to visit. She managed to get between Ali and me, forcing a wedge into our relationship. I hoped that didn't happen with Liam. Since they'd officially introduced themselves, he had barely left her side. Now they were sharing the same raft?

Ugh!

I glanced over to Brie, who had floated away from me. She was chatting with Ethan, and they splashed each other a few times before breaking into loud laughter.

What was happening? Within an afternoon, those two boys had stolen my best friend and sister away from me. If the four of them paired up, I'd be the fifth wheel. I didn't want to be in that position all summer.

What could I do though? Would it be fair to prevent Ali and Brie from making friends just so I could have them to myself?

As the afternoon wore on, I wondered if I *could* do that. The four of them had been glued to each other's sides the entire time. They weren't even interested in going to the dining hall for an afternoon snack. When we were given the option to stay in the pool, they were having so much fun, they didn't want to leave. They didn't purposely leave me out, but unless I came forward, pushing into their conversations, they didn't make any effort to include me. The girls were too busy getting to know their new friends and laughing the afternoon away to be bothered with me. All I could do was try not to sulk.

When the counselors blew on their whistles, signaling the end of the activity, I was filled with relief. This was my opportunity to show Ali and Brie that they should hang out with me.

"Everyone head back to your cabins to change; you'll have some free time before dinner. Roll call will be taken at six-thirty at the dining hall, so make sure you're on time!" one of the counselors shouted over the group.

As soon as we climbed out of the pool and grabbed our towels, I looped my arms with Brie and Ali and tugged them away. "You heard her. We have some free time and we should make the most of it."

Ali glanced over her shoulder, and her mouth opened a few times, but Liam and Ethan were on the other side of the pool drying off.

"I had so much fun this afternoon," Brie said. "Ethan is so friendly and so smart!"

"Yeah, he is," I said, even though I hadn't talked to him much.

If Brie caught on that I was jealous, she said nothing.

"We should sit with them at dinner," Ali suggested.

"Why not just the three of us?" I smiled at her. "I'm sure we'll see those boys again soon. You don't want to look desperate, do you?"

Ali's eyebrows furrowed. "Did I seem desperate?"

I debated on telling her the truth or lying. If I lied, then maybe she'd back away from him, and we could spend our summer together. Could I do that to my twin?

I made a non-committal sound as we walked into our cabin. Madison, Amy, and Skye had already returned. They glanced our way but didn't bother acknowledging us, which was fine with me. The less complaining I heard from Madison, the better.

However, true to form, Madison managed to find something to complain about. "Casey, you're dripping water all over the floor."

I'd dried off at the pool and put a t-shirt on but water was still dripping from the ends of my hair which hung wet at my sides. Looking down, I saw there were a few droplets of water on the floor at my feet. Madison was clearly exaggerating.

Instead of arguing, I decided to take a quick shower and change. I opened my suitcase to search for some clothes. I wanted to wear something nice for dinner so I could make a good impression. But then I remembered I'd already hung a few things in my closet and stood up to pull open the door. I stared agape at the sight of someone else's clothes, taking up half the space.

Madison's closet was next to mine and clothes bulged out the door, preventing it from closing. She obviously had a heap of belongings and nowhere to store them. But why did she think it was okay to take up space in my closet?

"Madison, are these your clothes?" I asked her,

crossing my arms.

Her eyes flicked to the closet and she shrugged. "You didn't bring much, Casey. Surely you don't mind sharing?"

The other girls looked at me too, and my skin lit on fire. My hands dropped to my sides and I swallowed, trying to think of something to say. Was I going to allow Madison to step all over me or was I going to make a scene while sticking up for myself?

My heart pounded in my chest as I opened my mouth to speak.

Book 13

Camp Problems

CHAPTER ONE

Casey

A tickling sensation prickled the hairs on the back of my neck. I stared at my closet, overflowing with Madison's clothes. Everyone in the room had their eyes on me, waiting to see how I'd respond to Madison pushing herself on me once again. Was I going to allow her to step all over me like Ronnie had done during the school year? Or was I going to make a scene while sticking up for myself?

I glanced at Ali, but I could tell by her expression and the squelchy feeling through our connection that she didn't know what to do either. While she'd probably want me to stand up to Madison, it was the first day of camp. I barely knew the other girls and starting off with a big argument was going to divide all of us. Ali and Brie knew I wasn't a troublemaker, but clearly, Madison was. She and I had already discussed her not using my closet, and she'd stuffed her things into it anyway. There was now barely enough room on the clothing rod to fit anything of my own. And she'd also filled some of the small shelving units at the bottom with her things. It was her fault for bringing too many clothes to camp, but that wasn't my problem.

Her glossy lips pursed, and she shifted on her feet.

We both knew what she was doing. She was trying to take over. She was a girl who pushed, just like Ronnie, wanting to see if I would push back. The biggest thing about coming to camp this summer was escaping Ronnie, but here she was, in a prettier and pushier version. I had the worst luck!

My insides twisted and my entire body heated up as

if I were standing on the sun.

Before I could say anything, Madison scoffed and went over to her closet. "See?" Opening the door, she showed me all the other clothes shoved into her cubby. "My things will get so wrinkled if they're all stored in here or in my suitcase. I need more space."

My heart pounded in my chest as everyone waited for my reaction. I wondered what Ali would do in this situation. She'd probably have the perfect response, and then we'd all go on our merry way. But with Madison staring at me, I couldn't ask Ali for advice. I was on my own.

Licking my lips, I looked at my suitcase. Compared to Madison, I had brought very little.

"You have barely anything," Madison added as if reading my mind. Though her tone was a little insulting.

Looking at her assortment of clothes, I felt the same way I had when I first saw how many designer clothes Ali owned. Madison had gone overboard with her packing but that didn't mean she could take over my space.

Her gaze flicked to her friends, and the start of a smile crossed her lips. That annoyed me more than anything.

As much as I knew she would try to push all summer, I didn't want to argue with her on the first day. Maybe if I pretended it wasn't such a big deal, she'd back off. Hopefully for good.

"It's fine," I said to her and turned away. I didn't want to see her smug smile anymore. "We can share."

I focused on my suitcase as Madison flitted across the room to her friends. "Well, that was awkward."

My shoulders reached up to my ears. Even so, I managed to keep my cool. Madison could say whatever she wanted, and I was determined not to let it bother me.

Ali and Brie unpacked but neither of them said anything, which was fine with me. I didn't want to dwell on this for too long, or Madison might think she really had won out over me.

Ali and I locked eyes, and she shot a look in Madison's direction. I shrugged and shook my head. Ali unbraided her hair while keeping one eye on the troublemaker.

This was my fight. And just like with Ronnie, I had to be careful. Madison had more than one friend by her side, and we had to share a cabin with them all. This time, I'd let the situation go, and hope that she would back off from now on.

I placed my suitcase on the bed and went through all my clothes, putting aside the ones I wanted to keep in the small space remaining in my closet and choosing others that could stay in my bag.

I selected ones that would easily wrinkle and hung them up. Madison had brought velvet hangers for her things, so I used the camp ones that were remaining. Thankfully, she hadn't taken those as well. It wasn't as if I could tell her I'd changed my mind about sharing the space.

"Be careful with my clothes," she snapped, folding her arms and glaring at me. "I don't want them crushed. That would defeat the idea of hanging them up."

When she and her friends snickered, I frowned. It was bad enough that she had taken over my closet, but then she had the nerve to tell me how to put my things inside it!

As I moved toward the bathroom for a quick shower, I took a deep breath. Stepping into the shower cubicle, I tried to calm down as I let the warm water wash over me. But my pulse still spiked. If this was what the summer was going to look like, I was in big trouble. Madison's overpowering personality was already taking over the room and my space. I gritted my teeth and reminded myself not to be a pushover and stay strong against her.

Ali's words about confidence and showing bullies that they didn't bother me, rolled around in my head. I focused on that while shutting Madison out. It didn't last long though. As soon as I left the bathroom, she flicked a smug look my way before continuing to dominate the conversation with her friends. Her voice became louder and more screechy with each passing second. I wondered how long it would be before I snapped at her. She seemed so much worse than Ronnie and Holly put together. Was she going to ruin my entire summer?

"Let's head over to the dining hall for a snack," Ali whispered to me.

"Snack?" Madison butted in.

It was a good thing I wasn't facing her because my eyes rolled skyward. She had talked so much during the counselor introductions; she was clueless about the program.

"Yeah," Brie said. "Morning and afternoon snacks are available for anyone who's hungry."

Madison scoffed. "Well, I have to fix my hair, so you all have to wait."

"Not for a snack," Ali said, coming to my side. "We only have to show up together for morning roll call. We're on our own outside of that. See you later."

Ali grabbed my hand, and the three of us walked by Madison's friends and out the door. They didn't look too pleased about having to wait for Madison but that was their concern. While I wasn't upset with them for being friends with her, I wasn't going to help them either. She was causing me enough drama of my own.

As we left, I heard Skye grumbling about how hungry she was. This was followed by Amy's sharp retort. "We have to wait for Madison!"

When the door closed behind us, I could finally breathe.

CHAPTER TWO

Casey

Turning to Ali, I grinned. "Thanks for getting us out of there!"

Ali sighed. "I couldn't stand another minute of Madison's whining voice. And I can't believe she went and put her things in your closet. Especially after you told her earlier that closet was yours!"

I took a big breath of the fresh woodsy air and let it out. If I could avoid Madison for most of each day, I'd just have to deal with her in the cabin. Apart from sleeping, we probably wouldn't spend too much time in there, so surely, I could manage. At least I could ignore her while sleeping Unless she bullied people in her dreams, that was.

"You can put some of your things inside my closet," Brie said.

"Mine too," Ali nodded.

"Thanks, guys!" I smiled at them.

I knew neither of them had space but it was nice of them to offer. And I was so glad they were in the same cabin with me. If I'd been placed on my own with Madison and her friends, I wasn't sure what I'd do.

"Oh no," Ali winced and stopped walking.

"What is it?" Brie frowned.

"I forgot to grab my hat. I meant to bring it in case we go exploring before dinner. It's still so hot and I don't want to burn."

"We can go back after we've had something to eat," I suggested, not wanting to confront Madison again.

Ali shook her head. "It's fine. I'll just run back and get

it. I'll meet you in the dining hall."

"Are you sure you really need it?" asked Brie.

"I burn easily," Ali said, glancing at the sky. "It'll be easier if I grab it now. Save me a seat, and I'll see you in a few minutes."

Ali jogged in the direction of the cabin while Brie and I continued on ahead.

"Good luck!" I called behind me, and Ali waved.

I doubted Madison would mess with her though. No one did. Regardless of us looking the same, we were often treated differently.

Brie huffed with annoyance. "Madison is so rude!"

"Tell me about it."

"I'm sorry she's picking on you!"

I shrugged. "I'll just have to try and put her in her place. Practice for Ronnie, I guess."

"You know Ali and I have your back, right? I could tell you didn't want to get into a fight with her though."

"No. It wasn't worth it, especially being the first day. We have a whole summer ahead of us and I don't want to make an enemy so soon."

"Well, you were nice to her so maybe she'll leave you alone from now on."

I nodded at my friend, although I had a feeling it wasn't going to be quite that easy.

Brie then looped her arm in mine and changed the subject. "I still can't believe we're here. It's amazing, isn't it? I mean, I've been to camps before, but it's so much better with you here too. And this place is so good. Those waterslides are the best!"

I grinned and nodded in agreement. It really was an amazing camp. All I had to do was avoid Madison. And as long as Ali, Liam, Brie, and Ethan didn't become too attached, the summer would be incredible, I was sure of it.

Inside the dining hall, we discovered a lot of kids had

arrived for a late afternoon snack but there was still plenty of food left.

I pointed across the room. "There are three seats over there."

"I guess everyone's hungry," Brie said as we headed toward the table and reserved the chairs by tilting them over.

"Look at the food," I said, feeling my stomach rumbling. Across the room on long tables, there were cookies, brownies, fruit, muffins and an assortment of other snacks on large platters as well as water bottles and juice.

"Whoa," Brie said on our way over. Her eyes were just as wide as my growing stomach. "This looks delicious."

After swimming all afternoon, I was really hungry and loaded a plate with different options to share with Ali when she arrived. I might have gone a little overboard, but I couldn't resist.

Both Brie and I stacked enough on our plates, so Ali wouldn't have to wait in line. At least that was what I told myself as I balanced the pile of goodies on the way back to the table.

After sitting down, I snatched a blueberry muffin from the pile and sipped from my orange juice.

"This tastes like it's freshly squeezed!" I told Brie.

She'd already drunk half of her glass. "It's delicious."

The muffin was good too, super moist and fluffy with large chunks of blueberry poking out.

"Mind if we sit here?" a familiar voice suddenly asked from behind me.

I looked up and wiped the crumbs from my face as I stared into the smiling face of Liam.

Brie sat up in her chair and her chair legs scraped against the floor. "Sure!"

Liam sat down alongside me, and Ethan sat directly opposite, next to Brie. Brie shoved her food away as if she had already finished. Although I knew she hadn't.

"Did you have fun on the water slides?" Liam asked me as he bit into a giant brownie.

I glanced at Brie, but she was focused on Ethan. I then looked towards the door, expecting Ali to appear.

"Yeah, it was great," I said, turning back to Liam. I didn't want to be rude. Surely Ali wouldn't mind me speaking to him.

"I went to a water park last summer that had some massive water slides," he said. "One of them was, like, straight down and you had to hold your hands across your chest or else you'd fly off."

I shivered. "That sounds scary!"

"It was," Liam said, laughing. "But my big brother dared me, so I had to do it."

"Do you just have one older brother?" I asked.

He gave me a funny look and then said, "I have a younger brother as well. He's the annoying one. I told you about him before, remember?"

I raised my eyebrows and nodded, realizing why he'd looked at me strangely. He had obviously talked to Ali about his family earlier and he now thought he was sitting next to Ali.

"So, anyway," he continued on, "they had this other slide that twisted so quickly you almost did a three-sixty in the tube—"

As he spoke about the water park, a thought crossed my mind. If he thought I was Ali, maybe I could pretend not to be interested in him. If I said or did something to discourage him, he might back off, and Ali and I would be back on track to having the best sisterly-summer of our lives.

As the plan formed in my mind, my stomach flipped. I really couldn't do it. First, it was mean to both Liam and Ali. Second, she'd be back at any moment and Liam would find out that I was me and not her. Then, he'd dislike me for trying to trick him. That would be awkward.

Once I got the thought out of my head, I still didn't tell him I wasn't Ali, but I did keep talking to him. Time flew by as he continued chatting, and my cheeks hurt from smiling. He was so easy to talk to, and I understood why Ali liked him so much. Along with being good-looking, he was a really nice boy. He was also interested in what I had to say and gave me time to speak instead of talking over me. Madison should take some tips from him.

When I looked at the clock on the wall, I saw that fifteen minutes had already passed. I then checked over my shoulder in case Ali was in the dining hall looking for us. But she was nowhere to be seen.

"Who are you looking for?" Liam asked.

"My sister," I said, keeping Ali's name out of the conversation.

My earlier plan popped into my head again. If Ali didn't show up for some reason, I'd have a chance to discourage him. All I wanted was for my sister to go on the double date with Mike, Jake and I when we returned from camp. If I took advantage of Ali not being around and said something off-putting to Liam, neither he nor Ali would ever know.

I remembered Ali had taken out her braid earlier. Her hair was loose just like mine. When she arrived, there would be no obvious difference between us. It would be so easy to say something to him before she arrived. But what? Could I insult his family or say something about having more money than him?

Both of those things would be totally out of Ali's character and a sour taste flooded my mouth at the idea of it. It was so tempting though.

Brie was chatting intently to Ethan and was oblivious to Liam and I. Surely, my plan would work, and then Liam would get the hint that "Ali" wanted nothing to do with him. Then Liam and Ethan might find other girls to talk to and leave us alone.

Could I do that to both Brie and Ali? Would I get caught and then have to explain why I had done it?

I swallowed, almost choking on the lump in my throat. Should I discourage Liam or not? Things that I could say swirled in my head as I stared at the boy beside me.

CHAPTER THREE

Casey

Out of nowhere, Ali appeared at my side and smiled down at me. The broad-brimmed hat she had gone back for sat atop her head and her hair billowed around her shoulders. She slid into the seat next to mine, cutting off my words. After taking off her hat, she nudged my shoulder. I looked at her. Could she tell what I'd just been about to do?

She gave Liam a beaming smile before locking eyes with me. "Hey Casey, this food looks so good!"

My stomach dropped and my cheeks burned with embarrassment. I tried to force myself to remain calm so she wouldn't notice how uncomfortable I was feeling. My insides were all twisted, and it was hard enough to breathe, let alone smile and pretend everything was okay. I wanted to run from the room, but that would simply show my guilt. Then Ali would know I'd been up to something.

"Sorry I took so long, but I bumped into Heather," Ali said, unaware of my reaction.

I couldn't believe what I'd been contemplating. If she hadn't sat down, I would have said something I was sure I'd regret.

"She was telling me about the sports they offer here," Ali continued. "There are so many, but we did agree to check out water polo, didn't we, Brie?"

"Yes!" Brie said, pumping her fist in the air. "I've never been to a camp with water polo before."

"Heather said that during the last week of camp there's a big tournament with other camps. We have to do it!" Ali focused on Liam. "I made a bucket list for the summer, and that's one of the things we agreed to do. What about you guys? Are you interested in trying it out with us?"

"I'm in," Ethan said.

Liam cleared his throat and rubbed the back of his neck uncomfortably.

"If you don't want to, Liam, you don't have to," Ali said. "It's just something we all decided to try while we're here."

For a change, I saw Ali nervous. I could see that she really liked Liam, but he was clearly preoccupied.

"Water polo sounds great. I'm just confused, that's all. I thought *you* were Ali," he said, pointing at me.

I froze and with a gulp, I glanced at my sister.

Ali laughed and pushed her hair off her shoulders. "It's hard to tell us apart, especially when I have my hair loose."

I shifted in my seat and forced a laugh of my own. Liam never actually called me by Ali's name but he did mention talking with Ali about his brothers. Did he know I was trying to trick him? I crossed my fingers under the table, hoping he'd drop the whole thing.

He rubbed his cheek and then leaned closer, jumping into the conversation with Ali. The two of them fell into the same comfortable manner that was obvious at the pool. I had almost spoilt everything and my stomach knotted guiltily. I was also relieved that Ali arrived when she did. If I was caught out, it would have been a disaster.

Ali chatted in her usual friendly manner, the one that everyone was drawn to. From the minute I'd met her, she was always smiling and talkative. I wished I could be the same. Instead, I was the jealous twin, wishing I could be just like her.

There was no way Liam would be able to resist her, and it wasn't fair for me to try and prevent their friendship. This was Ali's summer too. She didn't have someone at home like I did. Ruining the chance of her becoming close to

Liam would make me a terrible sister and friend. She'd never have forgiven me if she found out.

"Casey, what do you think?" Liam asked me.

Both Ali and Liam were looking at me. I tried to recall what they were talking about. Something about sports. Were they still talking about water polo?

"Sounds good," I said, keeping my reply as vague as possible.

Liam smiled. "Great." He hooked a thumb at Ethan. "We're in too. Water polo looks fun. I hope it's not too hard."

"I'm sure you'll be good at it," I smiled.

Ali snapped a look at me.

"What?" I asked her, wondering what I'd said wrong. She shook her head. "Nothing."

"Didn't you say you played sports all year round?" I asked Liam.

He nodded his head. "Ethan and me both do. It's part of the reason we wanted to come here. They have so many cool sports to choose from. Heaps more than what we have at school."

Ali grinned at him, and I tried to forget about her odd look.

Liam and Ethan talked about all the other sports they had done at camps before, and Ali and Brie joined in. As they chatted, Liam asked me a few questions, bringing me into the conversation as well. He was easy to talk to and he showed interest in anything everyone else said.

"It'd be cool for us to be on the same team at the tournament." Liam turned to me. "All of us."

Ali nodded. "That'd be so fun! We'll have to sign up for water polo most days so we can practice."

"Let's keep our plan a secret," Ethan said with a wicked grin. "No other teams will see us coming."

"We could take turns signing us all up," I said, thinking of Madison and wanting to make sure we didn't get stuck with her for any activity if we could help it.

A strange sensation pooled in my stomach and caused me to turn to Ali. I could tell her head was swimming with thoughts as Liam asked me another question. Was Ali noticing the attention I was getting from him? I tried to shrug it off, but for the rest of our time at the dining hall, she was intently focused whenever I talked to Liam.

My skin prickled. I wondered what she was thinking. Did she know I'd just been planning to discourage him from liking her? Was it written all over my face? Had she caught me out?

Or was I simply filled with guilt over what I had been about to do?

I really wasn't sure.

CHAPTER FOUR

Ali

When I first walked into the dining room, I was so excited to see Liam and Ethan sitting at our table. I'd had so much fun in the pool and this was now an opportunity to have even more time with Liam.

Even though I'd just met him a few hours earlier, my crush was already growing stronger. I tried to keep it to myself. I didn't want to seem desperate, as Casey had suggested. But surely he also realized how well we clicked. Earlier, I wondered if he was just being friendly, but if he was keen to sit with our group, he had to be interested. Right?

When I sat down, I noticed that Casey was quiet, almost too quiet. I couldn't put my finger on it; something was different about her. I knew she was awkward around boys, but I was sure it was something else. She seemed to be acting guilty for some reason. What was that about? I stared at her, trying to figure it out.

Soon, that strange feeling vanished. Casey warmed up and began talking to both Liam and Ethan as if they'd been friends for life. If she didn't already have Jake, I'd have suspected she was interested in one of them.

After the confrontation with Madison, I was worried about her, but she seemed to have rebounded quickly and was now being confident and outgoing. It was also great to see her and Liam getting along well. Their conversation flowed easily, and I eventually sat back and watched them. I wanted my sister to like Liam. If she didn't like him, it would have been terrible. Especially when I thought he was the nicest boy I'd ever met, even nicer than Jake.

He tried to include everyone in every conversation. It was as if he drew energy from being friendly and nice. I watched him become more animated by the second. He was so funny and my cheeks hurt from laughing at some of his jokes.

As I watched him interact with my twin, my insides swirled. I wanted everyone to get along, and it was happening right before my very eyes.

"We should get on the list and start training for water polo ASAP," Ethan said with finger quotes around the word *training*. "If we sign up now, we can get in before everyone else has the same idea."

"Let's go," Liam said, clapping his hands together.

Casey and Brie grabbed their plates and headed off to the trash can. I followed behind with Liam and Ethan.

"Thanks for telling us about the tournament, Ali," Liam said.

I grinned. "No problem. I'm glad you guys want to do it too."

"Water polo will be so cool," Ethan chimed in as we made our way to the big activity board in the front room.

"I hope there are enough spots," Liam said. "It would be awesome if we could all do it together."

When Liam smiled at me, butterflies erupted in my stomach. I couldn't believe my luck with meeting him. All through the school year, I had to be careful of my secret crush on Jake. But after he chose Casey, there was no way I could keep my crush going without feeling guilty. Lately, I barely thought about Jake. And what I now felt for Liam was so much more. It scared me that I'd just met him, but sometimes people had an instant connection. And the best part was that I had the summer to get to know him.

Brie wrote our names on the board as the rest of us looked on. I just hoped I was good enough to play with the boys.

"Nice!" Ethan said after Brie had finished adding all our names.

She turned to him, a smile spreading across her face.

Casey pointed to the other lists. "I just spoke with one of the counselors. She said the activities in red are the most popular and we can only sign up for those a maximum of three times per week.

It was a good thing water polo was in black marker, which meant we could practice every day. I liked the idea of seeing Liam every day for at least one activity.

The aqua park was in red though.

"How about I sign us up for two more times at the water slides this week?" Casey asked with a smile.

"Can you add our names too?" Liam grinned at her. "We'll probably need some fun after kicking butt playing water polo."

Casey laughed, and I joined in too. I had a whole bucket list of things to do, so I didn't mind not going to the slides every day. There were so many activities on offer and I wondered if there would be enough time in the summer to try them all.

If I had my sister, as well as Brie and our new friends by my side, this summer was going to be great, no matter what!

CHAPTER FIVE

Casey

"What else should we do this week?" I asked Ali. I was still dwelling on what I'd almost done to sabotage the friendship between her and Liam. Thankfully though, she didn't seem to notice. She simply clung to Liam's side and his words.

"We should add our names to a heap of things for the week, so we don't miss out," Ethan said to Liam.

I glanced at the board. I couldn't believe that more campers hadn't taken advantage yet. But it was the first day. Probably by the following week, everyone would be aware that they could sign up in advance and then choose the most popular activities first. I wasn't much of a planner, but I didn't want to get stuck with having to do things that didn't interest me. While the counselors wanted us to try everything, there were some that I wanted to avoid if possible.

"Go-karts?" Liam and Ethan said at the exact same time. They high-fived each other and laughed.

"Oh!" Ali exclaimed. "Go-karts are on my bucket list." She jumped up and down.

Liam smirked at her and walked over to the board. "Go-karts it is."

We followed him. I tried to keep my eyes on the other activities, mapping out my week, but when I checked out the go-kart list, I saw my name.

Liam smiled at me as if to make sure it was okay he had already signed me up. I returned his smile, and he nodded his head before adding Brie, then Ali.
Ali beamed at him and relief spread through me as I watched her. If I had interfered and she found out, things would be very different between us.

Hopefully, we wouldn't spend too much time with Liam and Ethan though. While they were really friendly and Liam especially made sure to include me, I still wanted lots of time with just Ali and Brie.

Suddenly, my thoughts were interrupted by someone

228

barging past my shoulder. I jumped in surprise and turned to see Madison beside me. Instantly, I knew trouble was brewing. I nudged Ali with my elbow. She cringed.

"I can't believe it!" Madison shrieked. "The water park is filled up for tomorrow. Already? That's not fair! When did these people sign up? Who do I need to talk to around here to get on that list?"

Her friends huddled around her and commented, agreeing that the situation was unacceptable.

"Ugh," she grumbled and whipped around, probably wondering if her display had attracted some attention.

When she saw Liam, she did a double take, and her jaw dropped.

"Hey," Madison said, her expression rapidly changing. She smiled at him and offered her hand. "I'm Madison."

Geez, could she be any more obvious? I tried to feel Ali through our connection. She had to know that Liam wouldn't be interested in a loud-mouth like our cabin mate.

But I was going to be there for Ali, no matter what.

"Hi, I'm Liam," Liam said, shaking Madison's hand.

"These are my friends," Madison said, quickly rattling off their names as if she was obligated instead of being pleased to introduce her "friends" to someone new. "Which activities did *you* sign up for, Liam?"

Oh, no. If she signed up for the same activities because of Liam, we'd never get peace from her.

Liam pointed at water polo. "There's a tournament at the end of the summer. I've never tried water polo before. It sounds cool."

"Water polo?" Madison looked thoughtfully at the list.

I noticed the wrinkle in her nose, but it was gone before Liam saw it. She shoved another camper out of her way, grabbed a marker and signed her name under ours.

Brie, Ali, and I rolled our eyes, all three of us having the exact same thoughts. I crossed my fingers and hoped the rest of the activities we had signed up for filled up sooner rather than later.

"Great, thanks for the tip," Madison said, holding onto the marker and tapping it against her cheek. There were only a few markers, so other campers had to wait until she had finished.

"What else are you planning to do, Liam?" she asked, batting her eyelashes at him. "So many things are filled already, which is super annoying, right?"

"Well, the counselors did say —"

She cut him off. "Oh, you're doing canoeing tomorrow?"

He cleared his throat and glanced at me before talking to Madison again. "Um, yeah."

"Sign me up!" she said, giggling.

She scribbled her name under his and handed the marker to Amy.

"We just did canoeing today," Amy said with a

frown. "I thought you didn't like it?"

"What?" Madison said, shooting her friend a look. "I never said that."

Amy's eyes widened, and she clamped her mouth shut.

"Add your name, unless you want to do something else," Madison warned her. "You'd better hurry, or you'll miss out."

Amy nodded and rushed over to the board. When she finished writing her name, she passed the pen to Skye who was clearly not pleased about having to go canoeing again.

Madison continued to look for Liam's name on the lists and forced her friends to sign up for each activity where she saw his name. I was so glad that many of the spots were already taken.

While Madison was busy pushing her friends around, I caught a look from Liam. His eyebrows lifted as if saying, 'Who is this girl?' I covered a smile with my hand. Ethan continued to stare at the various options, oblivious to what was going on around him.

Madison, taking the pen from Skye, shoved other kids out of her way as she looked over the lists some more. Often, she didn't even bother encouraging her friends to join her. Although Amy was always there to grab the marker and add her name and Skye's.

I couldn't tear my eyes away from Madison. She was a whirlwind of whines and shrieks about not getting what she wanted. It was as if whatever she'd just eaten at snack time had gone straight to her brain.

"We should go," Brie said softly to Ali and me. "I don't want to deal with her any more than we have to."

As we said goodbye to the boys, Madison flicked her hair off her shoulder and smirked, pleased to see us leaving.

Liam leaned closer. "Save us spots at dinner?"

"Yes, sure," Ali said, grinning.

Brie, Ali, and I moved away with the sound of

Madison's voice ringing in our ears.

"So, Liam, where are you from?" Madison asked.

We all turned back to the pair who now stood side by side. A frown creased my sister's brow, but I tugged her along as Madison moved in on Liam. I felt certain that Ali wouldn't have to worry about Liam liking her. Surely, he wouldn't be interested in someone like that.

Outside, I was able to breathe again. Madison was so overwhelming, she stole the air around her and it was a relief to escape into the cooler temperature.

However, when I considered the consequences if I had deliberately turned Liam against Ali, I shuddered involuntarily.

CHAPTER SIX

Casey

We didn't walk too far before Madison was mentioned again.

"I can't believe how annoying she is!" Brie pouted in disbelief. "Did you see how she acted around Liam?"

I heaved a sigh. "She's ridiculous! She carried on this morning about that counselor named Greg, as well."

"Liam was so nice talking to her, but I think he'll regret it," Brie scoffed.

"Definitely," I agreed. "He actually looked scared of her."

Ali chewed on her lip. "He did?"

"Yes!" I exclaimed. "Didn't you see his face when we left? I bet he tried to get away from her as soon as he could."

Ali let out a big breath. "She's really pretty though. I wouldn't blame him for liking her."

"But she's so painful!" I frowned. "I doubt her friends even really like her."

"They're always doing what she says," Brie added. "It's like she has total control over them."

"They're probably too scared to do anything else," I replied.

Ali exhaled another deep breath. "Maybe."

I couldn't believe Ali thought Liam would prefer Madison over her. I squeezed her arm, letting her know I wasn't going to let Madison get in the way. Though, I wasn't going to have to do much. I knew Madison would get herself into trouble soon enough.

I thought of the small space I had in my closet

because of her. "I wonder if we could switch cabins?"

"I already asked Heather about that," Ali said.

"You did?" Brie and I asked at the same time.

Ali nodded. "When I spoke with her earlier, I told her about the way Madison's been acting around you. I hope that's okay, Casey?"

"What did she say?" I was so happy at the thought of escaping Madison.

"She said we can't swap."

My heart sank in my chest. "How come?"

"She said camp is about learning to get on with different people and different personalities. So we have to stay where we are. But she did say if there is ever a major issue to let her know."

"Well, she already stole Casey's closet," Brie groused.

Ali shook her head. "It won't be enough to switch cabins."

"What if Heather says something," I frowned. "Can you imagine if Madison finds out we've complained about her? She'll never let it go. Then she'll probably come after all of us instead of just me."

"I didn't think of that!" Brie's voice was filled with concern.

I pasted Ronnie's face on Madison, knowing how cunning bullies could be. I wasn't about to ruin everyone's summer because I didn't have enough closet space. It seemed silly. I just wanted to let it go.

"We could try avoiding her as much as possible," Ali suggested. "Find tables at the dining hall without enough space for her and her friends. That way, they won't be able to sit with us."

"We can make sure we sign up for activities sooner than her as well, so they get filled up quicker," Brie added.

Ali's tone became positive. "Maybe she'll do something that gets noticed by Heather or one of the other counselors and she'll get into trouble on her own without our help." She gave me a reassuring smile. "I'm sure it'll be fine!"

I nodded, trying to believe her words. But I was not prepared for what came next.

We headed to our cabin, so I could grab a zip-up hoodie and then leave again before Madison returned.
I opened my closet, and my jaw dropped. "What the — ?"

In the time since we'd seen her last, Madison had completely rearranged *my* closet to fit more of her things. Was this girl packing for six months instead of less than two? How many outfits did she need?

"What is it?" Ali asked.

"Look," I pointed at the closet.

She'd shoved the clothes I had already hung up, in one of the drawers at the bottom. I could see bits of fabric poking out. My entire body flushed with heat. I couldn't believe her! I barely had enough room before, and now I only had a drawer and a small shelf to myself.

"Move her stuff," Brie said. "She did it to you."

I grabbed onto her clothes and pulled them out. I wanted to throw them on her bed and show her she couldn't take advantage of me.

Hesitating, I thought better of it. I really didn't want to start a big fight on the first day. She would flip out if I touched her things. This was another game for her.

I looked at Brie in frustration. "That won't work." If there wasn't a way to switch cabins, I had to keep the peace, even though it was becoming incredibly difficult.

"Why not?" Brie asked. "She's so rude. Give her a taste of her own medicine."

I gritted my teeth and put the things back then grabbed all my clothes and placed them on my bed. Returning some to hangers, I pushed them into the closet so they'd fit. Then I remembered some packing tips from Grandma Ann and started rolling the rest of my clothes so I could place them neatly on the lower shelf. I knew it would annoy Madison to see that I'd rearranged things, but at least it wouldn't be me causing more trouble.

As I focused on restoring my closet, Ali began chatting from her bunk, ignorant of how Madison made my blood boil. "Liam is so nice, isn't he?"

I didn't respond but instead, tried to keep calm as I rolled my things.

"And super cute!" Brie added with a giggle.

She was on her bunk too. Her legs hung over the side. I wished we could all have top bunks. If only I'd stood up for myself about the bunk, maybe Madison would have left me and my closet alone.

"Ethan is really good looking too!" Ali grinned at Brie.

As I worked through my things, I kept quiet, listening to their conversation. It was obvious they both had huge crushes already. It was a good thing they were on the top bunks and couldn't see my face.

Though they didn't have someone forcing themselves into their closets, and they'd managed to get the beds they wanted. With their crushes, beds of their choice, and no one bossing them around, they were growing closer than ever. I imagined each day bringing them together while I was stuck being the fifth wheel. I then imagined there not being enough space for some activities, and I'd have to make a choice to do something else on my own...

I shook away those thoughts and focused on Jake instead. This immediately made me smile. But then I thought about the double date that wasn't going to happen anymore. Jake would be so disappointed. I pictured his adorable face and wished he could have come to camp as well. If that had happened, I wouldn't be the fifth wheel at all.

"Earth to Casey!" Brie called.

"What's up?" I asked, coming back to reality.

"What do you think of Liam and Ethan?"

"They both seem nice," I said, keeping my eyes down. "But we've only just met them. I don't know too much about them."

"Oh, come on, Casey," Brie laughed. "You and Liam were chatting it up in the dining hall. It's easy to see how nice they are."

"Easy to see how nice who are?" Madison's voice cut

through the room.

None of us had heard her enter. It was a good thing I'd already finished reorganizing the things in the closet. Her friends moved towards their bunks as Madison glanced at the closet without commenting.

Her gaze then landed on the three of us. "Who are you talking about?"

Brie frowned at me, and I struggled to keep my thoughts about Liam and Ethan to myself. If Madison tried to force herself on them, it would make Ali and Brie miserable. I couldn't allow her to do that.

"Oh, everyone is nice!" I said, hoping she believed me. *Everyone except for you, that is!*

"Well, I wouldn't say, everyone," Madison said, digging her hand into her hip. "Thank goodness there are some fun kids though. Otherwise, it would be so boring!"

I knew she meant Liam and Ethan. I wasn't going to push her into admitting it. Then, she'd know we were interested too. Well, at least Ali and Brie were.

She flicked her hair over her shoulder. "I'm going to shower and get ready for dinner."

She had already changed once already. I wondered what designer outfit she had planned. "Dinner isn't for a while yet."

"Yeah, well, I need time to get ready." She looked at her friends. "Amy, you should do the same thing."

Amy winced.

"There are two shower stalls," Madison reminded her. "At least that's a positive thing. Not like the last place we went to."

Doing as she was told, Amy gathered her things and followed Madison into the bathroom. With Madison gone, I settled onto my bed, relaxing until I had to deal with her once more.

"What did you think of canoeing?" Ali asked Skye.

Skye sat up as if she hadn't expected anyone to speak

to her when Madison wasn't around. "I thought it was fun. I'm excited to do it again."

I recalled her and Amy being upset when Madison forced them to sign up. Were they both pretending around her?

Brie and I joined in the conversation, and we asked Skye about her hometown. She was much friendlier without Madison in the room. I wondered if we weren't the only ones who were annoyed with that horrible girl. Amy would always fall into line, but perhaps we could drag Skye away enough to build a solid friendship with her. She seemed eager to do the same with us.

Hayley and Emma appeared at door and they joined in the conversation as well, telling us all about their afternoon at a dance class in the recreation hall. I almost forgot about Madison until she burst back into the main cabin area. Her eyes went straight to Skye who immediately closed her mouth as if Madison had caught her stealing or something equally as awful.

The mood soured as Madison moved to her bed. Her hair fell in bouncy waves over her shoulders and a fresh coat of lip gloss was smeared over her lips.

The atmosphere shifted in the room. Hayley and Emma escaped into the bathroom, and Skye opened her closet to pick through her clothes. I knew she was avoiding Madison and whatever mean thing she was about to say.

Amy, stepping out of the bathroom, stopped mid-step and glanced around her. She felt the awkward atmosphere too.

Madison sucked all the fun out of everything, and I was glad I wasn't the only one to notice.

CHAPTER SEVEN

Casey

Soon after Madison had finished in the bathroom, I knew it was time to leave. I didn't have the patience to deal with her drama. We'd had a fun time chatting without her, and I hoped Skye would see that too. I wouldn't mind hanging out with her as long as Madison didn't tag along.

Ali, as if reading my mind, hopped off her bunk and signaled to Brie and me to follow. "Anyone want to take a walk before dinner? I ate too much at snack time."

"Really? There was, like, nothing left when we got there," Madison said.

I huffed quietly. There was plenty of food there. She probably had some issue with every single item.

"Okay, well, we're going," Ali said. "The invite is open to anyone." I knew she meant Skye, but she stared at Madison, waiting for her response.

Madison flicked her hair away from her face. "I'm still getting ready. Besides, walking around the campground will only make me sweat. Duh!"

Skye's shoulders dropped, and she shook her head just as Hayley and Emma appeared again. I waved for them to come with us. "We're going for a walk."

They looked at each other and then Madison. They didn't hesitate to come along.

Once we were outside, I tilted my head back, breathing in the freedom of the outdoors and allowing the sun to warm my face. As I walked, I tied the arms of my hoodie around my waist, keeping my hands free.

"Thanks for inviting us," Emma said. "It's so

awkward when Madison's around!"

"Yeah," Hayley agreed. "What's with her? She's so pushy and rude."

I nodded. "I think she's used to having people do what she says."

"I can't believe we got stuck with her in our cabin!" Emma exclaimed, her tone full of annoyance. "I wonder if we can get her moved out."

Brie sighed. "Ali already asked Heather that. She said no."

Hayley and Emma groaned. At least I wasn't alone in how I felt about Madison.

"We shouldn't let her get to us," Ali said. "It's not like we have to spend every minute with her. We can just hang out with other people and do our best to avoid her."

I held back an eye roll. I knew the people Ali wanted to hang out with. Or the person.

"Good idea," Emma said. "I don't like drama. I have enough of that at home."

Changing the subject completely, we chatted about other things as we walked the perimeter of the camp. We even took a peek at the boys' cabins across the way. All the while though, I hoped we wouldn't cross paths with Liam and Ethan. If they showed up, I knew Ali and Brie would want to hang out with them.

While I tried to hold back my jealousy, it was hard. But once we left the boys' side of the camp, I was able to relax again.

The campsite was much bigger than I thought and the grounds were so well-maintained. We all agreed that our favorite spot was the river and we sat down on a wooden bench on the hill, overlooking the water below. The sun reflected off the ripples that were slowly pushing to the shore, making the water look so pretty in the late afternoon sunlight. With the mountains in the background, the scenery really was spectacular and we remained there, quietly admiring the view.

I forgot all about Madison and the boys that Ali and Brie were so obsessed with. I had never thought I would experience something as amazing as this camp. Having Ali and Brie by my side made it even better.

"I wish I had my phone to take a photo," Hayley commented.

I closed my eyes, taking a mental picture with my mind. I didn't ever want to forget this place.

After a while, Ali nudged me. "We should probably get going. We have to be there for roll call before dinner, and I guess we'd better not be late."

It was hard to tear my eyes away from the water, but there were many more days to come.

When we reached our designated spot, we found Madison, Amy, and Skye already there. According to what Madison had said in our cabin, they hadn't eaten much at snack time so I figured they must be really hungry. I knew if I had missed the snacks, I'd be ravenous.

"Wow," Heather said, after taking attendance. "First day and you're all on time. I love this. Let's keep this up every day, girls. That way, you get your choice of food and seats!"

We waited for Madison to push her way past so she could be first to reach the food line. She didn't disappoint. Even before reaching the counter, she was moaning about the choices of food.

Between Ali, Brie and me, we wanted to keep our distance. We were one of the first groups to enter the dining hall so there were more than enough options for food and seats to choose from.

"Let's wait for her to pick a table," Ali said.

"Yeah, so we can avoid her," Brie nodded. "Good idea."

Brie walked toward the hot food section. It looked like they were serving lasagna. And the breadsticks smelled amazing.

Ali went over to the salad bar, while I checked out the sandwich station. I'd already eaten a lot that afternoon and wasn't terribly hungry. After we chose our food, we looked around for somewhere to sit. Madison and her friends were already at a nearby table and her voice carried over the group. Did that girl ever stop talking?

"Let's go to the farthest table away from her," Brie suggested.

"We should hurry," Ali said, glancing around.

In the time it had taken us to get our meals, the rest of the campers had filed into the room. Some kids saved seats before jumping into line. I made a mental note to do that each time as well.

"Over there!" Brie said. "By the windows."

"Is there enough room for us, too?" Hayley asked, coming up behind us.

"Of course," Ali said.

Ali had promised she'd save a spot for Liam and Ethan but I wasn't sure there would be room. Before reaching the table, however, Ali stopped abruptly and I almost walked into her.

"What's wrong — ?"

I followed her gaze. Liam and Ethan sat with a group of boys at a nearby table. When she caught his eye, her face split into a wide grin. He waved at her and then waved at Brie and I as well.

I didn't have any hands to wave back, but I was sure he cared more for Ali's attention than mine so it didn't really matter.

He mouthed the word, *sorry*, noting the full seats around him. Ali waved him off as if it were nothing, even though I knew she'd been looking forward to sitting with him. I went over to the table that we had chosen and put down my tray.

"I told you he was friendly," Ali preened. She sat opposite me, so she'd have a view of Liam.

"Who's friendly?" Hayley asked.

Ali and Brie spent the rest of the time filling the girls in on Liam and Ethan. It almost sounded as if they were laying claim to them; which was crazy since they'd only met the boys a few hours earlier.

While I didn't mind doing an occasional activity with their new friends, it seemed like every second Ali focused on Liam, she and I were pushed further and further apart. This summer was about getting closer as sisters, not Ali getting close to a random boy.

I concentrated on eating while Ali prattled on about Liam. *Liam this and Liam that*. It was enough to make me lose my appetite, and I hated leaving my brownie untouched.

Maybe if we hung out with him too much, she'd soon get over him.

A girl could hope.

After dinner, the counselors led us to a huge bonfire that was situated in an open field. I had seen the stack of wood earlier, but it had now turned into a mountain of orange and red flames that flickered against the night sky. Rows of logs were set up around the bonfire for us to sit on, and we scanned the area looking for a suitable spot.

Ali motioned to Brie excitedly. "Liam and Ethan are over there."

Emma turned to us. "We're going to sit with some girls from the dance workshop. We'll see you later."

Ali nodded. "Okay, see you back at the cabin." She then grabbed Brie's arm, pulling her in the boys' direction and leaving me in their dust.

Brie's eyes tracked the boys. "Where are they going?"

They were with their friends from dinner and moving

to a different side of the fire. It looked like they wanted better seats.

Ali stopped and chewed on her lip. I felt her hesitation. Would Liam want her to follow? I could tell she was reluctant to make her way over.

"Let's sit here," Ali said, sitting down on the nearest log. "We'll see them tomorrow."

I couldn't help the smile that formed on my face as I sat beside her.

Glancing around, I took in the scene around me. One of the young counselors sang and played guitar and the sound of his music floated over the crowd.

He had chosen a popular song that most people knew

and the other counselors joined in, encouraging the campers to sing along as well. With a light breeze drifting up from the river and the warmth of the fire, I couldn't have been more comfortable. I fell into the rhythm of the music and sang along with the songs that I knew.

Ali bumped my arm, and I turned to her.

"Sorry," she said, her mouth spread in a wide grin. "Liam was looking at us. I just waved to him."

Across the way, Liam and Ethan were staring in our direction. It was so distracting. I wondered if Ali wanted to go and sit with them. There wasn't much room over there, but I was sure Liam and Ethan would make room. Would Ali and Brie agree to stay with me? Or would they prefer to be with the boys instead?

My stomach sank as Brie giggled to Ali and told her Liam was looking at her. With the light of the fire, it was easy to see he was staring our way. Brie and Ali were busy talking but still, he stared. A slow smile crossed his face and his eyes locked with mine. My stomach lurched when I realized he was actually smiling at me. I tried to shake it off and focus on the counselors instead.

As Ali and Brie chatted on about the boys, I thought of Jake. I recalled the bonfire at the school camp and the moment he sat alongside me. I could still remember everything right down to what he was wearing at the time.

He looked so good in his black skinny jeans and light blue t-shirt. Without even thinking about it, I caught his attention and waved him over. I surprised myself by doing that. It was something I would never have considered before, but it had been my chance to talk with him as myself, instead of Ali pretending to be me and doing all the work for me.

Smiling at the memory, I wondered what he was up to right then. If only he were at this camp with me.

If only.

CHAPTER EIGHT

Casey

My thoughts of Jake only lasted so long. Ali and Brie huddled together, giggling and talking on and on about Liam and Ethan. By the time the bonfire was over, I couldn't wait to leave. It was a relief when the counselors instructed us to head back to our cabins for lights out. We had about half an hour to get ready before the counselors would come by and make sure we were all in our beds.

As the entire camp split into groups, Liam and Ethan became lost in the crowd. Ali and Brie tried to connect with them, but there were too many kids between us.

Good riddance.

I thought I had some relief until we reached the cabin. I was barely at my bedside when Madison charged into the room and started blabbing to her friends about some boys she'd sat with during the campfire.

"They were so nice," Madison said. "And it's crazy…I think they both like me. How will I choose?"

Ali and Brie went into the bathroom, so I sat down on my bed with my back facing towards Madison. I didn't bother to look in my closet and see what else she had done. I was over it. Though, surprisingly enough, I didn't feel sleepy either.

With Jake on my mind, I decided to write him the first letter in our little pen-pal relationship. I had brought a notebook with me specifically for writing to him and I pulled it from my bag, along with a pen.

I thought for a moment and then began. When I started, the words flowed. There was so much to tell him.

Dear Jake

I hope you're having a fun time with Mike!

Today was the first day of camp and it was so much fun. We went on the waterslides. There are 7 different ones and we tried them all. After dinner tonight, there was a bonfire, the flames were huge. It was much bigger than the one at our school camp. One of the counselors even played guitar and we all sang. It was really cool.

This week, we've signed up for go-karting. I can't wait to try it. We're going to try water polo as well. It's such a great camp, there are so many things to do.

The only thing I'm missing is you...I wish you were here, too.

Tingles spread across my arms as I wrote the last sentence. Was it too much, too soon? He did hug me on the last afternoon of school and he made me promise to write. After the swapping mess earlier in the school year, I wanted to be honest with him. Didn't Ali want me to work on my confidence? I didn't have to mail the letter until the following day, so I decided to sleep on it.

I was about to write more when I felt someone looking over my shoulder.

"Who are you writing to?" Madison asked curiously.

I flipped over the notebook and sat up straighter, shifting my body so she couldn't see it. "No one."

"It doesn't look like no one," she said, smirking at her friends.

I shook my head. Ali and Brie were still in the bathroom, and Hayley and Emma were already tucked into their beds facing the wall, probably trying to sleep. I didn't have anyone on my side.

Madison sat next to me. The mattress wasn't very thick and her weight shifted the bed. "Do you have a secret crush?" She wrinkled her nose as if she couldn't imagine anyone liking me.

"It's none of your business," I stammered. My cheeks flamed as her eyes darkened.

Then her mood changed. "Come on, Casey. Aren't we friends? We're already sharing a closet. We can share our secrets too."

She made a point of looking at my notebook. Quickly reaching over, she snatched it right out of my hand!

I scrambled to grab it back, but she was already reading what I'd written.

"Ohh, *Dear Jake*? Who's Jake?"

Amy grinned from the other side of the room. It wasn't a nice grin; it was something that Holly or Ronnie would do.

"Who's Jake?" Madison repeated.

"Only the cutest and nicest boy at our school," Brie said from across the room. She and Ali had returned at the perfect moment.

I let go of a breath.

"Really?" Madison said, looking me up and down.

"Yeah," I said, grabbing the notebook back.

Madison waved her hand at me. "I'm not interested in your little love letter. But now I'm curious. What's he like? Do you have any photos?"

"They're on my phone." I hadn't brought it with me,

so at least Madison couldn't bug me if my phone wasn't available.

Madison crossed over to her bed and moved her pillow. "What about Instagram? You must have some photos of him on there."

"Yeah, there are a few," I said, unsure of where she was going with this. It wasn't as if we could check. Though, my jaw dropped when she revealed a smartphone.

Madison laughed. "I always have a backup."

I glanced at Ali and Brie. None of us knew what to say. Hayley and Emma didn't say a word; they clearly didn't want to get involved. If Madison were caught with a phone though, she'd be in big trouble. But I had a feeling she didn't care too much. She tended to get what she wanted.

Madison sat next to me again, opened her Instagram app then passed her phone to me. "Search for your username."

I hesitated.

She winked at me. "Come on. This is girl talk."

I didn't want to start another issue with her. It was too late in the day. There wasn't much she could do with it, so I guessed it was harmless enough. Sighing reluctantly, I took her phone and typed my name. She took it back and followed my account, then scrolled through my feed.

"There he is," I pointed at one picture, wanting this to be over.

Madison clicked on it and pinched the screen to zoom in. It was the group photo from the day we went to Great Escape. I couldn't help smiling when I saw Jake's face. I hadn't realized how much I missed him.

"Him?" Madison put her polished finger on Jake's image.

"Yeah."

"He's really cute," Madison gushed. "Who are the other boys?" She turned to Ali and Brie. "Are they your boyfriends?"

Brie smiled at Madison, but it didn't quite reach her eyes. "No, they're just friends."

Madison tilted her head to the side as she took in the image.

Ali and Brie climbed onto their bunks, completely brushing off the idea of Mike and Wyatt. How could they have forgotten about them already? Were Liam and Ethan that much better?

"There are plenty of cute boys at camp," Madison said, then laughed mischievously. "Liam is super cute; don't you think?"

I shrugged. I didn't want her to know that Ali had a crush on him. As much as the idea of Ali and Brie liking Liam and Ethan annoyed me, I wasn't about to tell Madison anything.

"You guys seem friendly with him. Did you know him before camp?" Madison asked.

Ali and Brie remained quiet, and I knew Madison wasn't going to stop pushing until she had an answer from us.

"No," I said. "We just met him today. He was on our bus this morning."

"Oh," Madison said, waggling her eyebrows. "I wonder if he has a girlfriend."

I chewed on my lip. It would upset Ali if Madison went after him. I had to say something to make her back off. "I'm pretty sure he likes Ali."

Madison's eyes widened. "Really?"

The bed above me shifted. Ali couldn't hide from the conversation any longer. While I didn't want her spending the entire camp with Liam, Madison irritated me so much that I was determined to keep her away from him. She didn't deserve to win over someone so nice.

Ali then spoke up. "Liam and I are just friends. We only met today."

I squeezed my eyes closed. What had happened to

"confident Ali"? Why did she always encourage me to stick up for myself when she wasn't willing to do the same? Liam clearly liked her, and she felt exactly the same way. What was the big deal in admitting it?

"You seem to think he's pretty nice," Madison said to me.

"I do," I said, meeting her eyes with as much self-assurance as I could muster. "We spent the whole afternoon with him. He and Ali are the perfect match."

Madison's face dropped, and a flutter of victory washed over me.

I felt Ali shift on her bed once more. What was the problem? Madison needed to know that she couldn't force herself into relationships with people who clearly weren't interested.

"We're doing heaps of activities with Liam and his friend, Ethan this week," I added.

Through our connection, I could tell Ali was uncomfortable. I wasn't sure why. Did she want Madison to go after Liam? It would have been the same thing if Ronnie went after Jake. Madison had to learn boundaries and if we were spending an entire summer with the girl, then why not start now?

My anger toward Madison grew, and I no longer wanted to be the person she overpowered.

Madison frowned at me. For once, she didn't have anything to say. Maybe Ali had been right. Sometimes bullies didn't appreciate others standing up for themselves. Though, I noticed she was thinking about something. Whether it was how to take Liam from Ali or something else, I wasn't sure. But I had the feeling this wasn't over for her.

Without another word, she went to her closet and picked out some pajamas. Ignoring her, I picked up my toiletry bag and went into the bathroom to brush my teeth. Once inside, I closed the door behind me and stared at myself in the mirror.

My cheeks were red, and I was a little out of breath. It was hard work standing up for myself, but at the same time, it felt really good!

CHAPTER NINE

Ali

The next morning, my alarm clock woke me up from a dead sleep. The beds were much more comfortable than I had originally thought, and we had done so much the day before that I fell asleep as soon as we'd turned out the lights.

"Whose alarm is that?" Madison whined from her bed.

I grabbed the small clock that sat on the small shelf at the head of my bed and hit the SNOOZE button. A minute later, someone else's alarm went off. I couldn't resist a smile when Madison groaned again and tucked her blanket around her with a huff.

Leaning over the side of my bed, I looked at Casey. Her eyes were barely open. I then recalled the events of the night before, unable to believe she had told Madison that Liam liked me. Of course, I wanted it to be true, but I didn't know if Madison would tell him what she'd heard. If she did, it would be so embarrassing. Although I was aware Casey was simply standing up for herself, I really wished she hadn't mentioned my name in connection with Liam.

All I could do though was hope that Madison kept that conversation to herself. Instead of focusing on it, I hopped out of bed and went to the bathroom. By the time I brushed my teeth and changed, the others were starting to get up. I had set my alarm clock earlier than I needed to, but I didn't want to be late for breakfast. And I wasn't sure what the morning routine was like for these girls. At least I was able to use the bathroom first. It was better to be over-prepared than not.

Surprisingly, we were all ready to go at around the same time. When Madison came out of the bathroom, Casey, Brie, Hayley, Emma, and I were heading out the door. We had ten minutes left to get to the dining hall, so I wasn't worried about rushing. Although, Liam had crept into my mind more than once that morning and I wondered if he was already there.

"Aren't you going to wait?" Madison objected in her whining voice.

I saw Casey stifle an eye roll as Madison pushed past her towards the door, flicking her hair over her shoulder as she went. "It's not like you can get into the dining hall without me."

The way Madison said that gave me the chills. Would she ever purposely be late for our meals just to be a brat? I shivered. She was such a control freak and to have a dramatic free summer, we'd have to stay on her good side. I knew not to give in to bullies, but in her case, it was the only way.

As we walked, Casey held her head a little higher. Her confidence seemed to be soaring, and I watched her with interest. Just in the space of one day, there was already a difference.

As we neared the hall, I looked for Liam in the crowd. Madison was unpredictable, and it would ruin everything if she ran right over to him and told him what Casey had said.

However, we were once again one of the first groups to arrive and after our names were checked off, we headed to the food counter. As I stood in line, I looked for Liam and Ethan but didn't see them anywhere.

Madison suggested we all sit together as a cabin group. Skye looked keen to do that, and I agreed, even though I would rather Madison sat with her friends elsewhere. But Skye was nice. It was just unfortunate that she was a friend of Madison's.

Brie, Casey, and I sat at the far end of the table while

we ate. Madison barely spoke to us, which was fine with me. When Liam and Ethan arrived with the other boys from their cabin, I pretended not to notice them. But I did steal glances while they were in line and looking for a place to sit.

As much as I wished they'd take the two empty seats at our table, I wanted to keep Liam as far from Madison as possible. She had wiggled her way into our activities for the day, and I was worried she'd say something about the conversation from the night before. Maybe if enough time passed, she'd forget about it altogether. When Liam and Ethan found a table several over from us, I felt relieved.

The rest of the meal went off without any problems, and when it was time to head to our activities, Casey, Brie, and I practically sprinted from the room.

"I can't believe she sat with us," Brie complained. "Why doesn't she go off with her friends and leave us alone?"

"As long as we stay on her good side, everything will be fine," I replied and then glanced at Casey. "But I don't think we can trust her. We should probably keep our secrets to ourselves from now on."

I didn't mean for it to sound like a warning, but I wanted Casey to keep my feelings for Liam out of any conversations with Madison. The less she knew, the better.

Casey gave me a look but then Brie lightened the mood by asking, "Does Madison have a good side?"

Casey laughed, and I did too.

As we neared the go-kart track, my stomach flip-flopped. I'd only go-karted once in my life, and that was a long time ago. Bumper cars were more my speed, but I didn't want Liam to think I was afraid of new things. Besides, maybe he'd spend a little extra time showing me how it all worked.

I smiled at the thought of spending more time with him.

However, I wasn't prepared for the size of the track. It was much bigger than I had imagined it would be and my insides started to twist as my eyes scanned the track and its many turns. We had over an hour doing this activity, and I hoped I would last that long.

"Wow," Brie said. "This is huge!"

"It sure is!" Casey agreed, her eyes wide.

Rather than sounding excited, she seemed scared. At least I wasn't the only one.

Liam and Ethan stood with some other boys lined up near the entrance. Apart from us though, there were no other girls. The boys all turned around and watched us as we came nearer. Liam smiled and waved at us.

Before I could wave back, he looked straight at Casey. She didn't even notice him. I'd worn my hair in a braid that morning so there'd be no chance of a mix-up. Maybe he still couldn't tell us apart. Hopefully, by the second week of camp, he'd recognize each of us.

"Hi, um, Casey, right?" he said to my twin.

"Yes," she smiled.

My heartbeat roared in my ears.

"You got it right this time," Casey said, glancing at me.

He scratched the back of his neck. "To be honest, the only way I can tell you two apart is because of Ali's braid. Since that's how you wore your hair when I first met you, Ali."

A wave of shyness washed over me and I smiled. He did know which of us was me.

He smiled back and butterflies danced around in my stomach.

But even though he had spoken about me and mentioned my braid, his attention immediately returned to Casey. He asked her how she enjoyed the bonfire, and if her bed was comfortable. I knew that Casey was only being friendly but he seemed to be giving her more attention than me and I couldn't help the sick feeling in my stomach.

Maybe he wanted to make a good impression with Casey, so we'd all be friends when we hung out together. The thought of him holding my hand as we sat in front of the bonfire warmed my insides.

"Gather around everyone," the instructor said. He was a balding man around my dad's age.

Liam turned to listen and Casey moved to Brie's side.

I watched her from the corner of my eye. She didn't look at Liam at all. Instead, she watched the instructor with interest.

I shook my head, releasing the jealous thoughts. I wasn't being fair to Casey. She liked Jake, and they were together. There was no way she could like Liam the way I did.

I focused on the instructor and listened to all the safety rules and the directions on how to use the go-karts.

"There is only one person per car," he said. "Three of you will be out on the track for ten minutes each. We'll rotate until the end of the activity time."

Some of the boys high-fived each other noisily, and the counselor, an older teenager named Jack, had to quieten them down. They joked around with him and I realized he must be their cabin counselor.

Pushing further to the front of the group so I wouldn't miss any of the instructions, I strained to listen. I wanted to be sure I had everything in my head before I stepped into one of the karts.

"For safety, there is a limit to the speed the karts can move. If you don't follow the rules, you'll have to sit out of the activity," the instructor explained.

A few of the boys groaned and nudged each other. Jack rolled his eyes but smiled too.

I wondered if it had been a good idea to do an activity with so many boys. They were already being loud and rough with each other and we hadn't even stepped foot on the track yet. Were they going to follow the rules or was one of us going to get hurt?

I wrung my hands together, worried we'd made a mistake. Though, I'd come to camp wanting new experiences. This activity was on my bucket list so I couldn't chicken out now.

After we were given all the instructions, we lined up together.

"How about we let the girls go first?" Liam said, then

smiled at me.

I smiled back.

Only one of the guys groaned, but Ethan bumped him with his elbow.

Jack handed Casey, Brie, and me a helmet each. It was a good thing I'd braided my hair that morning. The helmet fitted perfectly over my head, and I hoped I didn't look too much like a dork.

The boys watched us get ready. I wished there were enough karts for us all to have a turn so we wouldn't be the center of attention.

"I don't like how they're going to watch us," Casey whispered to Brie. "What if I crash? Everyone will make fun of me."

"Don't worry about it," Brie said. "I'm sure they're not perfect either. Just have some fun."

"At least there are safety barriers and we won't run each other off the track," I said, smiling.

Through our connection, I felt Casey's uneasiness grow. I tried to show her not to be nervous, but she overpowered my feelings. I just hoped she enjoyed herself and wasn't too frightened. I wanted her to have a good time with these activities or we might not finish the bucket list. My plan was to go home at the end of the summer with everything on the list checked off by each of us, and plenty of stories to tell our parents.

Casey was directed to the first kart, and Brie was given the one behind her. Being last, at least I had a little more time to become familiar with the kart itself. It seemed easy enough.

We did a few slow laps. I stayed behind, giving Brie enough room. I couldn't see Casey up ahead since I wanted to pay attention to the track just in front of me.

Brie and I bumped into the rubbery safety barrier a few times. She seemed frustrated, but I giggled each time. It was like bumper cars, which I loved. Glancing quickly at

Liam, I saw him cheer us on and so did the rest of the boys.

After the fourth lap, someone zoomed past me. Casey's long hair blew in the wind as she accelerated. The next time she came around, she nearly careened into my kart but kept going.

I gritted my teeth and tried to speed past Brie. But she continued to swerve enough that I had to putter along behind her. The instructor waved a red flag on our last lap, and I knew that meant our turn was almost over.

By the time I reached the start again, Casey was already in the center of the group of boys. One of them had taken her kart and sped away before Brie and I had even unbuckled our seatbelts.

I handed my helmet to another boy. Seb, I think was his name.

Brie and I walked over to Casey. She was grinning while some of the boys high-fived her.

"You were awesome!" one boy said.

"I thought you've never done this before?" Ethan asked her.

"I haven't." She shook her head.

"She's a natural," Brie said, scooting beside my twin.

Liam didn't say much, but he smiled at Casey while everyone congratulated her. This time, he didn't even bother acknowledging me.

Was I imagining his interest in Casey over me?

The question swirled around inside my head as I tried to figure out the answer.

CHAPTER TEN

Casey

We were each allowed one more turn on the go-karts before the end of the session. This time, I didn't bother to warm up. Once I hopped into the seat, I sped off, wondering how many laps I could complete in the allotted time. I loved the feeling of the wind on my cheeks as I nailed every corner and speedway. I couldn't believe I had never been interested in trying something like this before.

There was a track at home on the outskirts of town, and I hoped that before summer was over, I'd be able to try that one as well. I wondered if Jake would want to come with me. It was an idea for another one of our dates.

When the activity finally ended, we only had a half hour break before our next session which was water polo. Since our cabin was on the other side of the campground, Brie, Ali, and I decided not to worry about a morning snack and rushed straight back to our cabin to change.

Opening the door, we came face to face with Madison and her friends, dressed and ready to go. Hayley and Emma had signed up for water polo too and they were already in their swimwear as well.

Madison stood out even more than usual. She wore a bright red bikini with silver sequins stitched along the edges. It looked so good on her. From the way she strutted around the room, she knew it too.

"You aren't ready?" she asked. "You're going to be late. We're not waiting for you!"

"We were go-karting, and the track is all the way across the camp," Brie said.

Madison wrinkled her nose. "Is that why you smell like gasoline?"

I glanced at Ali, and she shook her head. I hoped we didn't smell.

For the waterslide activity the day before, I wore a bikini that I'd borrowed from Ali as she had a few pairs and was happy to share. Rather than borrowing from her again, I decided to wear the new set that Mom bought for me, especially for camp.

Rifling quickly through my bag, I pulled them out and followed Ali into the bathroom to change. She and I took a shower stall each while Brie took one of the bathroom ones. As I changed, I was still buzzing from the thrill of the go-kart track. Liam and Ethan, who were clearly impressed, had even made me promise to race them next time.

As soon as I walked back into the main cabin area, however, and saw Ali, Brie and the other girls, the excitement from go-karting faded. Although I didn't care about impressing anyone, I did want to fit in and I instantly became conscious of what I was wearing.

Brie wore the same floral print bikini that she had worn the day before and once again, the colors looked great against her skin tone. Ali's was covered in black polka dots with cute pink bows attached and I stared at it enviously. I loved the style and the design; it looked so pretty on her.

Glancing down, I frowned at my plain blue suit. The bottoms were higher, reaching my belly button, and they almost looked like shorts, while the rest of the girls had low cut ones. Why had I allowed Mom to talk me into buying this set? She convinced me that the style looked great and that the wider bottoms would be perfect for all the pool activities at camp. I should have checked with Ali first.

I thought about asking Ali if I could borrow from her again, but it was too late. There was no time for that now. No one said anything but I couldn't help the creeping feeling over my skin as the other girls pranced around the room in their nicer swimsuits.

Grabbing my towel, I wrapped it around my body

before slipping my flip-flops on.

"Come on!" Madison snapped and then flung herself out of the cabin. Amy chased after her while Skye struggled to keep up.

On the way over to the pool, Ali chatted with Hayley and Emma. Each of the girls held their towels in their hands instead of wrapped around them. At least once I got into the pool, no one would notice that I wasn't wearing the same style.

I stayed behind the group, not wanting to bring attention to myself. Brie stopped and waited for me to catch up.

"I like your suit," I said, wondering what she thought of the one I was wearing.

"Thank you," Brie said. "I like yours too."

"My mom talked me into this new style. I'm not sure I like it though."

"Are you kidding?" she asked. "You look amazing. The color is great against your complexion."

"You think?" I asked, opening my towel.

"Totally," she said.

I smiled, grateful that Brie was so positive. I instantly felt better and tucked my towel under my arm. Once we reached the pool, the counselors told us to leave our towels on the grass and sit on the pool's edge.

Glancing around at the other girls, I felt self-conscious again. But no one was looking at me. Instead, everyone seemed eager to get into the pool.

I took a spot at the end of the line of kids and sat down, leaving a space between me and the next person. Brie and Ali sat on the other side of me, and I hunched my shoulders, not wanting to be noticed. I couldn't wait to hop into the water so I could hide my body beneath the surface.

Down the line, some of the kids started kicking their feet and splashing. As I watched them being scolded by the instructor, someone sat next to me. I looked up to see Liam and Ethan squeezing in.

"Hey, Casey," Liam said with a smile. "What did I miss?"

I shuffled down towards Brie to make more room. "They haven't given us any instructions yet."

"Are you okay? You seem nervous," he commented.

I relaxed my shoulders and shrugged. I didn't want to be the girl who always talked about herself and her insecurities. Someone like Madison would do that for attention. Not that I'd say anything about my bathing suit to Liam but I wondered if Brie only said I looked good to be a kind friend.

Once everyone quietened down, the counselors and main instructor jumped into the pool to go over the instructions and rules. We were asked to move in closer together so we could hear everything. Liam leaned in, taking in everything the instructor was saying. He did a lot of sports and would probably pick this one up quickly. I was sure he'd be good at it so I hoped we'd be on the same team.

"We need to check everyone's swimming ability so we can sort out the teams fairly," the instructor said. "So everyone, please hop into the pool."

Liam and Ethan jumped in while I slid down the side, dipping my body carefully into the water. With the hot sun beating down, the water felt cold and my teeth instantly started to chatter.

"We'll get you to swim across the pool, six at a time," one of the counselors said, pointing to a group of us. "Spread out from each other. There you go. On the count of three, swim to the other side." He pulled out a stopwatch and waved his hand.

Liam and Ethan took off ahead and I followed. With them ahead of me, I pushed to catch up.

When I reached the other side, I turned to see Liam beside me. We had reached the edge first. Ethan came next, then another boy, followed by Ali and Brie. I was out of breath but pleased that I had beat the others.

"Great strokes, Casey," the instructor said before turning back to everyone else.

Liam grinned at me. I felt the same way I had after the go-kart track. I'd always been fairly good at sports, but except for swimming lessons when I was younger, I had never become involved in anything else outside of school. Now though, I was like a new person and excited to see where my confidence would take me.

"I can't believe you beat me," Ethan said.

"You should try and keep up next time," I teased him.

"Way to go, Casey!" Brie said, giving me a high-five.

The remaining groups had their turn and when Madison finally reached us, I noticed her glaring my way. The dark look in her eyes told me she was annoyed.

What was her problem?

The counselors asked us to hop out and sit on the pool edge while they teamed with the instructor and marked a list. I assumed they were checking the swimming times for each of us.

They then instructed us to get back into the pool as they called out names, splitting us into two separate groups with a counselor assigned to each one. Liam and Ethan, as well as Madison and her friends, were included in the group with Ali, Brie and me. I huffed inwardly. Why couldn't we just escape that girl?

"I need my group to divide yourselves into two teams, six people on each team," Gina, our assigned counselor said. She stared at the boy counselor across the pool and smiled.

It was the same way Ali looked at Liam.

"I'm on Liam's team!" Madison called out.

She leaped towards him, almost crashing into him and then proceeded to have a giggle fit.

I shared a look with Ali. We couldn't let Madison get in the way of our fun.

"Ethan," Liam said, waving him over.

Ethan nodded to Brie, and she moved closer to him.

"Casey, Ali," Liam said, and we swam over to his side.

Amy came over, and Madison put her hand up to stop her friend. "Can't you count? You have to be on the other team."

Amy's face fell, and she glanced at Skye then at the four leftover boys whose team she and Skye would obviously have to join.

"Okay, guys, Gina said. "Just go down to the other end and practice passing a ball around your teammates. I'll be back in a minute."

She headed towards the boy counselor while we swam to the shallow end of the pool.

"Let's get in a circle and toss the ball," Liam said, grabbing a ball from the bag at the side of the pool.

He threw it straight to me, and I tossed it across the way to Ethan.

"Nice throw," he said. "You have a good arm."

"Thanks," I smiled.

Even though there were plenty of people to pass to, Liam threw me the ball every single time.

I tossed it to Ali. She was frowning. Had she noticed too?

For the rest of the practice, I only passed the ball to Ali or Brie. I didn't want either of them to think I liked Liam as more than a friend. Surely, they had to know that.

"Is anyone going to pass it to me?" Madison whined.

Every time someone threw her the ball though, she either dropped it or tipped it so that so that it bounced across the pool. It was an effort to swim after it and no one wanted to pass it to her anymore. She was oblivious to this though and continued to complain. Meanwhile, everyone else seemed to block her out, the same way I did.

The instructor blew his whistle and asked all the

groups to gather around to hear the rules of the game. I was careful to stay away from Liam, but he always seemed to be nearby, no matter where I went. So I did my best to ignore him and stuck closer to Brie.

The game wasn't as complicated as I thought but I listened intently so that I wouldn't miss anything. It was hard since Madison blabbed with Amy the whole time.

I was happy when the counselors caught her and told her to be quiet. It served her right.

"The pool is split into two areas," the instructor said. "Each group is to stay in their area while we run through some practice games."

We split off into our groups. The water there was a little deeper, but I could still reach the bottom with my toes.

Liam had the ball first, and he asked each of us to spread out. Once the whistle blew, Ethan took off. Liam hesitated and then launched the ball toward his friend. Amy screamed and ducked as the ball almost smacked her in the head.

"You could have caught it!" one of the boys on her team said.

"No way," she scoffed. "He threw it too hard."

"It was a good throw," Ethan grinned.

Madison laughed at her friend which made Amy upset. Madison then continued to tease her. While Amy and Madison distracted everyone else, I swam ahead and moved closer to the goal.

No one tried to stop me and my heart pounded as I waved for the ball. "Over here!"

Ethan looked my way, and without hesitating, he tossed the ball over. I caught it, turned, and threw it as hard as I could into the net. It wasn't until the ball slammed against the back of the net that I realized what I had done.

Ethan and Liam let out a *whoop* and Brie whistled for me.

"Go, Casey!" she cried out.

I grinned.

The game continued. Ali and Brie were helpful in getting a few goals, but Liam, Ethan and I were clearly the strongest swimmers on the team.

Madison continued to call for the ball but every time it was thrown to her, she wasn't able to catch it and it ended up being lost to the other team. No one said it aloud, but we all tried to avoid passing to her.

It didn't take her long to catch on. "Why isn't anyone passing me the ball?"

None of us answered and when one of the boys on the opposite team said something not so nice, Madison went after him. Literally.

Then she cried out again. "Ouch! I stubbed my toe. This game is the worst. It's so tiring and dumb—"

She went on and on. I couldn't ignore her any longer. As it was a friendly game, I wondered if passing her the ball would stop all her fuss. But when I tried to pass it to her and the other team intercepted and scored on us, Liam and Ethan swam over to me.

"We can't let them win," Ethan said.

"What do you want to do?" I asked.

Liam bit down on his lip as Ali and Brie joined us. He went over a plan with us. A few seconds later, we broke from our huddle. Madison was still complaining and had no idea that we'd been discussing team tactics.

Liam and Ethan both thought it would be best to keep me near the goal since I had such a strong arm. Well, at least that's what Liam called it.

We scored two more times while the other team only scored once. When we ended up winning the first practice game, no one was more pleased than me.

"You guys did great!" the instructor said, from the edge of the pool. "Some of you are a natural at this sport," he added, looking directly at me. "You should take it up."

"Really?" I asked.

"Definitely," he said.

Madison, clearly frustrated at not being the center of attention, let out a loud protest. "This game is so stupid!"

Swimming towards the steps, she beckoned Amy over. Leaning close to Amy's ear, she whispered something to her then the pair walked up the steps and moved to their towels where they proceeded to lay down in the sun.

Gina blew her whistle and called out, telling them to get back in the water.

Madison sat up and moaned. "I don't feel well," she yelled.

Gina frowned but didn't comment. Because one girl from each team was out, there was no reason we couldn't continue playing. With Madison and Amy removed from the game, we had a much better time together. Even Skye joined in and tried harder.

At the end of the session, the counselors gave us some free swim time. The boys broke off from both groups and started passing the ball to each other.

"Want to get out?" Ali asked Brie and I. "Catch some sun?"

"Yes," Brie said. "My arm is killing me."

Mine was sore too but in the best way possible.

We went over to our towels. Madison sat up again and looked around. "Is it over?"

"No," Ali said. "They gave us some free swim time."

Madison whipped her head in the direction of the boys. Jumping to her feet, she raced back to the pool and hopped in.

"So much for not feeling well," I whispered to Brie.

"Over here!" Madison called.

Each time the ball was passed to her, she did the same as before. She either missed it, or it bounced off her hand and landed further down the pool. She then waited for someone else to chase after it.

At the sound of her voice, I laid back on my towel. It was nice to have some space from her and rest after the intense game.

"You should join the school swim team," Brie said to me. "Maybe even see if there is a local water polo team you could join."

"You think?" I asked.

"Absolutely," Brie said. "You did so well at it. Everyone said so."

I nodded eagerly, no longer self-conscious about my swimwear. My morning had been so much fun and those earlier thoughts were long forgotten. I'd tried two new things and it felt good to finally be better than Ali at something. I sighed and allowed my entire body to warm up to the idea.

Meanwhile, Ali's eyes were closed, but I knew she'd heard our conversation.

CHAPTER ELEVEN

Ali

After a long pause, I sat up. "You really should join the swim team, Casey." It felt weird for me not to say anything after Brie had just complimented her. "You're a really good swimmer."

"Thanks, Ali." The smile on my twin's face spread across her cheeks.

It hurt to smile back. I hated myself for feeling envious because she was a better swimmer than me. She'd been chosen as the head cheerleader during the school year and I hadn't minded. She was good for the position. But I didn't like how her performance at water polo attracted so much of Liam's attention; as well as that of the instructor and counselors.

It wasn't as though Casey was encouraging Liam during the game. He and Ethan had both taken the lead roles, and they used the strongest player on our team to score goals. It made sense. So why did I feel so annoyed about it?

Liam liked Casey, but I wasn't sure how much and if he preferred her over me. Had Casey told him about Jake? Maybe if he knew she had a boyfriend at home, he'd back off. Unless he just wanted to be friends with her. It was possible he just liked the fact that she was a good swimmer. She had also been much more confident on the go-kart track.

Overall, Casey *was* better at sports than me. It was one of the more distinct differences between us. I was quite good at sports, but Casey excelled, falling naturally into sporting events much more quickly than I did. It worked the opposite way when it came to academics. I was better at schoolwork than Casey.

I sighed to myself and laid back down. Perhaps I was overreacting. Then, a twisty feeling filled my stomach. Casey and Jake were together, and I knew how much they liked each other. There was no reason for me to worry about anything when it came to Liam. Right?

Why was I feeling so conflicted? Casey hadn't made any moves on Liam. He was super friendly, that was all. Maybe I just needed to try harder to get his attention.

On the way back to our cabins to change, I asked Liam if he'd like to sit with us at lunch. He agreed and we promised to save seats for each other.

After changing, our cabin group was the first to reach the dining hall again, so we immediately went over to a table by the window and saved enough seats for the three of us and Liam and Ethan. We kept the plan to ourselves and for once, Madison didn't barge her way onto our table. She sat with some of the boys from another cabin; one of them seemed really interested in her. As well, Hayley and Emma moved to the table with their friends from the dance class. So we had Liam and Ethan to ourselves.

I sat next to Liam and talked to him the whole time. While he still included Casey and Brie in the conversation, I held his attention for most of the time, and he didn't seem to mind.

Boys were so confusing.

When we walked back to the cabin to get ready for canoeing, I floated on air. I was sure that Liam did like me after all.

I felt so happy, at least, until we reached the cabin. When we opened the door, we found Skye sitting on the bottom bunk across the room, watching Amy and Madison argue.

"Just yesterday, you said you hated canoeing," Amy

said. "I don't want to sit on a boat again. It wasn't fun. I still have blisters from the oars. I can't believe you made us sign up for it again."

"You should have signed up for something else then," Madison countered. "I'm not your mother."

Amy glanced at Skye for help, but she said nothing. Amy, frowning at Madison, tried to stand up for herself. "Liam is the only reason you want to do it again."

"What?" Madison shrieked. It was too fake of a sound to be real. She gave Amy a pointed look.

Brie raised her eyebrows at Casey, and my twin shrugged. We'd left our bathing suits outside on the porch railing to dry, and I headed out to get them.
With a moment to myself, I leaned against the railing. Everyone seemed to have noticed Madison's interest in Liam. I wondered what he thought of her. She was incredibly pushy and obviously used to getting whatever she wanted. He couldn't be interested in her, could he?

Grabbing hold of the bathing suits, I headed back inside. I thought Liam wanted nothing to do with Madison but I wondered if I was wrong. She was really pretty. I gave her that. Plus, she was already dressed in a different bathing suit and this one was even nicer than the one she had worn earlier. While I knew that I had three bathing suits, two from last summer and one new one, she probably had about ten. All her outfits accentuated her looks. If she didn't constantly grimace and complain, she'd be stunning most of the time.

"We should get going," Madison said, ignoring her friend's objections about canoeing.

She rushed out the door, and her friends ran after her like lost puppy dogs. How could they stand her? I knew she wanted to meet up with Liam first. And as much as I wanted to beat her there, I was worried that if I played her game, he might think I was just like her.

As we made our way down to the river, my heart was

in my throat with every step. Casey and Brie didn't seem to notice. They were looking forward to canoeing.

I wished I didn't feel this way. It would be so much easier if I'd never met Liam. I could laugh and enjoy my time with my twin instead of worrying that she or another girl was going to get his attention more than me. That way I could avoid all the drama and just have fun.

I was unable to control my feelings and it didn't help that when we arrived, Liam and Ethan were surrounded by Madison and her friends.

"Let's go over there." I pointed to a spot that was away from their group.

Even if Liam wasn't interested in her, I didn't want to listen to her flirt with him. Casey gave me a strange look, and I shrugged it off. The river looked so pretty and I did not want Madison to spoil the experience.

Our instructor's name was Riley. He had a long brown beard and looked to be in his thirties. He seemed quite stern but was also very knowledgeable.

"I already heard about this stuff yesterday!" Madison called out.

Riley's expression darkened and a few kids moved away from her.

"Can't I skip this part?" Madison whined.

"No, you need to listen," Riley answered firmly.

I smiled. At least someone was showing Madison her place.

Madison groaned and rolled her eyes. Amy crossed her arms but Skye moved a few feet away.

Riley then asked us to break into pairs. I glanced at Liam, wondering if he would want to pair with me.

He barely had a chance to move before Madison grabbed his arm. "I'm with you, Liam. I'm an expert at this. I already did it yesterday."

"Oh, um…," Liam tried to edge away from her, but she moved everywhere that he did.

Noticing the irritation on his face, I exhaled a deep breath. My fear about him liking her more than he liked me subsided. He clearly wanted nothing to do with her.

"Brie!" Ethan called and waved her over.

Amy huffed as Brie skipped over to Ethan. I guessed Amy thought that if Madison was with Liam, then Ethan would automatically choose her.

"Want to pair up?" Casey asked me.

"Of course," I said, looping our arms together.

There were enough canoes for everyone, so we each took a life vest and hopped into our boats. We'd been given the instructions we needed to go off on our own. The main concern was to stay away from the marked trees in the distance where the river curved around a bend.

It took Casey and I a few tries to build up some momentum, but eventually, we were able to get a rhythm going and paddled toward Brie and Ethan. We bumped into the side of their boat, and all of us laughed.

"We'd better stay away from you," Ethan joked. "This isn't bumper boats." He paddled away, and Brie struggled to keep up.

"Let's get 'em," Casey said with a grin.

We took off and caught up quickly. Brie erupted into a fit of giggles and nearly dropped her oar into the water.

"You're sabotaging the race," Ethan teased, making Brie laugh harder.

I noticed Liam getting closer, his eyes were on mine, and my heart fluttered. "I want in on this race!" he called out.

Madison dropped her oar inside the boat and crossed her arms, forcing Liam to take control. But he didn't seem to notice her at all. She wasn't wearing her life jacket. Clearly, she hadn't followed instructions. Either that, or she'd taken it off before she started paddling.

"Let's go over here," Madison pointed in the opposite direction.

Liam ignored her.

"Ready, set, go!" Ethan said, even though he already had a head-start.

Casey and I pushed toward them while Liam remained slightly behind us.

"Ali," Casey said after a little bit.

"We've almost caught up to them," I said to her.

"The markers," Casey said, pointing as we floated past the trees. "We're not supposed to go this far."

I slowed down, giving Liam time to catch up. Ethan and Brie had already passed the markers and didn't appear to be stopping.

"I'm sure it's fine," I said, keen to keep going. I wanted to show Liam I was as competitive and good at sports as Casey. "We'll turn around soon. Once we've won!"

As we passed the bend, the water became a little

choppier and I started to think that Casey was right; we probably should turn around. Liam and Madison passed by us but I stopped rowing. Regardless though, the current pushed our canoe further downstream.

Just ahead, the boys had stopped and they were trying to keep their canoes stationary. As we approached them, we saw Brie and Ethan celebrating their victory while Liam jeered at his friend, saying he cheated and wanted a rematch.

"I want to swap places!" Madison demanded and stood up.

Liam's expression fell. "Whoa, Madison. Sit down."

Their boat rocked as she stepped forward.

"Don't do that!" Brie told her.

"It's going to flip," Liam warned.

Madison was determined to get what she wanted. "It's fine! Can you move out of the way?"

Ethan edged nearer and took hold of their canoe to keep it steady.

"Let go," Madison griped, "You're making it worse."

She took another step forward and overbalanced, causing one side of the canoe to dip into the water. Ethan desperately tried to steady the boat but it was no use. The boat rocked once more and right before our eyes, both Madison and Liam fell overboard, with the canoe flipping right over.

Casey clasped her hands over her mouth, unable to stifle a laugh. I burst out laughing too. The whole thing was hilarious.

Liam surfaced first and swam to the canoe as it began to float downstream. Ethan was close enough to grab onto the rope connected to the end but struggled to keep the boat in place. Taking hold of the side, Liam tried to push it upright but was clearly unable to do this on his own.

Casey and I stopped laughing.

"Should we go and help?" Casey asked.

"Where's Madison?" I searched the water for her. She should have already resurfaced.

I scanned the river but didn't see her at all. My heart thrummed in my chest.

"There she is!" Casey called, pointing downstream. Madison's head bobbed above the surface as she paddled her arms, but she was moving further away instead of closer. The undercurrent was pulling her in the opposite direction.

She wasn't a strong swimmer and appeared to be struggling. I gasped as the river carried her away from us.

CHAPTER TWELVE

Casey

As soon as we passed the tree markers, I knew our race was not a good idea. And the situation became serious very quickly.

With Madison floating downstream, it was obvious we needed help. Turning in my seat, I glanced back toward the calmer waters but there was no one in sight. We'd gone too far beyond the boundary and were on our own.

"We have to do something," I said to Ali.

She nodded. "Start paddling!"

"I can't believe she didn't wear her life jacket," I muttered under my breath.

She'd chosen fashion over safety, and we were all paying for that.

We heard a loud splash and saw Ethan popping up in the water next to Liam. Brie remained in her canoe, holding the rope to Liam's boat, while Ethan and Liam worked together to flip it upright. As we passed them, Brie looked frantically towards us.

"We're going to get Madison," I told her.

"Wait for us," Liam said.

Ali shook her head. "There isn't time."

I worked with Ali together, as we had done before, and pushed to get to Madison before she went under again. She was bobbing on the surface, but the current was taking her further away.

"Help! Help! Someone help me!" she screamed.

My pulse spiked. If she went under again, we might not find her.

"Come on," I said to Ali.

I bit down on my lip in concentration as we stroked in time, the way we'd been instructed. The current was so strong that with us paddling together as well as being dragged along by the water, we reached her very quickly.

"Madison," I called to her. "Grab onto the oar."

She immediately reached for it but pulled on it so hard, that our boat rocked dangerously.

"Whoa!" I said, and Ali reached out to help me hold the oar steady.

Madison didn't realize that she was about to capsize us too. And she didn't seem to care. "Get me inside!" she screamed.

I could see the oar slipping from her grip and she tugged hard on it once more. The canoe dipped wildly and my heart thumped as I yanked on the oar, trying desperately to pull her towards us. Once she was close enough, Ali and I grabbed her arms and dragged her into the boat, almost capsizing it as we did.

Finally, she was safely inside and the canoe was steady again.

Sagging against the side, she panted. "It took you long enough!"

I gritted my teeth.

"A 'thank you' would be nice," Ali snarled at her.

I'd never heard Ali use that tone before, but regardless, Madison pretended she didn't hear her.

Wordlessly, Ali and I worked together once more and paddled against the current to head upstream to the others. By the time we reached them, Liam and Ethan were both in the canoe with Brie. The capsized canoe was upright again, there was still a lot of water inside, and they towed it behind them with a rope.

"Are you guys okay?" Ali asked.

"Yes," Liam said, glancing at Madison who was busy twisting the water from her hair.

"You didn't ask me if I was okay," she muttered.

No one responded to that.

By the time we reached the calmer water, Ali and I were exhausted. But our relief at making it back with all of us intact was short-lived. Just up ahead of us, two of the counselors were already in a canoe, headed in our direction. They didn't look pleased with us at all.

"All of you, get back now!" one of them yelled.

I wanted nothing more than to reach solid ground, and Ali and I were the first to reach the bank.

Before we could tie up the boat, Madison leaped out and charged off. In the time since we'd left, everyone had returned to the shore. I guessed the instructor and the counselors had ordered them out of the water, while they searched for us.

"I almost drowned!" Madison shrieked loudly as campers surrounded her and she told them her story.

She overlooked the fact that it was her who capsized the boat. Instead, she blamed the current and Liam's canoeing skills. My cheeks flushed bright red as everyone stared at us.

"We're in so much trouble," I mumbled quietly.

"Maybe if we explain—" Ali said.

"Explain what? We went against the rules. I told you we should have stopped."

Ali was always a rule follower. It had taken one boy to change her, and I no longer recognized my twin. I could tell by her frown that she regretted her decision as well.

The counselors told us to go over and see Riley. He looked even more menacing than he had done earlier. But he stood in silence until we were all in front of him.

"The six of you ignored the most important rule," he said. "Do not paddle past the markers! That could have ended in disaster. And you...where is your life vest? He pointed angrily at Madison. "You had it on earlier. We have them for a reason."

"It's still in the canoe," she mumbled, crossing her arms. "It wasn't comfortable."

Riley's tone was filled with frustration. "There is no excuse for your behavior. It'll be reported and you'll all sit out for the remainder of the activity."

"What?" Madison screeched. "You can't do that. It wasn't my fault."

"I don't want to hear another word. All of you...put your life-jackets back in the trailer and don't bother me again." Riley walked away and gave everyone else a stern reminder about following the rules.

"This is so unfair!" Madison said, storming off.

She grabbed her towel and headed for the shade of a large tree. Spreading her towel on the ground, she stared at us as if she were expecting us to join her. I wanted nothing to do with her, and it appeared that everyone else felt the same way. We sat in the sun closer to the jetty, and as far from her as possible.

I didn't want to talk about what had happened, so I stared out at the water and watched the others. They had finally been given permission to return to their canoes and were all having a wonderful time.

Except for Amy and her partner, that was. She was in

a canoe with a boy whose name I didn't know. He struggled to paddle forward while Amy moved her oars in different directions, causing the canoe to go around in circles. Neither of them looked very happy, but it amused me. At least it kept my mind away from us getting into trouble.

CHAPTER THIRTEEN

Casey

After the canoeing episode, we followed the rules of every single activity while trying to stay as far away from Madison as possible. Each time I thought about what had happened, I recalled Riley's angry reaction and I cringed. Madison was bad news for everyone, and I wasn't sure what would happen if we went against the rules again.

I also remembered the panic I'd felt at the thought of Madison drowning. She could easily have been swept away by the current and pulled under. If that had happened, it would have been almost impossible to find her. While none of us liked being near her, we certainly did not want anyone to experience a tragic accident, not even Madison.

As the week went on, Ethan and Liam tagged along for several of the activities, including water polo, which we practiced daily. After the first attempt, Madison opted out of any follow-up sessions. This was a huge relief to all of us because we could focus on our skills instead of listening to her constant whining.

Ali continued to be excited whenever she saw Liam. Brie's reaction was much the same with Ethan. But as the days passed by, instead of feeling like a fifth wheel, I became more comfortable around the boys. Liam always made sure to include me and it really was a lot of fun having them with us.

Madison managed to jump in on some of our activities and made a show of trying to get Liam's attention. Though, to her dismay, he tended to ignore her most of the time. However, this only made her try harder.

At times, I could feel Ali's eyes on mine, especially when Liam and I talked or laughed together. I tried reassuring her by telling her that I missed Jake, which I did, and that I couldn't wait for his return letter to arrive. Though, when I thought of Jake, my stomach twisted a little because of all the attention I was getting from Liam. He often focused on me more than Ali. While it was disguised under a group setting, I still noticed. And I figured Ali would catch on eventually as well.

A thread of guilt became to wind through me as I considered the situation. If I were being honest, I'd admit that I was enjoying the attention from Liam. And try as I might, I could not make that feeling go away.

In the past, Ali had always been the more popular twin. Even Jake had preferred her at first. Ronnie's Instagram poll had proved that most kids at school liked Ali more than me. She had always been the favorite.

Until now.

It felt really good to have someone want to be near me as opposed to my sister. Though, it wasn't as if I'd give up Jake for a summer hanging out with Liam. That wasn't like me, and I would never want to jeopardize my relationship with Jake or Ali. She had the crush on Liam, not me.

To ease my guilt and try to improve the situation, I decided to help push them along a little, by giving them some alone time without me. Ali had done the same for me with Jake, and it was only fair to return the favor. It would be hard to go off on my own, but Hayley and Emma were nice, so I looked for an opportunity where I could sign up for an activity just with them and leave the others to themselves.

I kept an eye on the board for the following week's activities, hoping to find one from Ali's bucket list that had only four spots remaining. The opportunity finally presented itself on Friday afternoon.

As I stared at the list for the Leap of Faith, I knew it was the perfect scenario. There were only four spots left for Monday, with every other session for the week already full. It was an activity that everyone was talking about. The kids who had already attempted it said it was the most challenging thing they had ever tried. Those who completed it successfully were bonded and included in a special group that everyone else at the camp looked up to. At least that was how it seemed from the outside.

Once Liam saw Ali do the leap, I knew he'd give her more attention than me. He was a sports guy, and with Ali showing off her skills, it was the perfect opportunity to push him closer to her.

Everyone who spoke about the Leap of Faith talked as if it were the ultimate camp experience. I wanted to attempt it with my sister and best friend, but hopefully, we would try it together another time or I could just go with Hayley and Emma. I knew Ali would say something if I suggested they go without me, so I simply went ahead and signed the four of them up.

Ali caught me and tapped her hand against the board. "There aren't enough spots."

List with names

"Sure, there are," I said.

"What about you?"

I wrinkled my nose. "Nah."

"How come?" Brie asked, approaching us.

Liam and Ethan were behind her, and with their attention on me, my cheeks burned with embarrassment. I didn't want them to think I was scared, but I did want Ali and Liam to have time together. Why did they have to argue with me?

"I don't like heights," I said.

Brie narrowed her eyes. She knew I wasn't telling the truth.

"Besides," I said before she had a chance to push, "it's

on your bucket list, Ali, and every other session next week is full. Four spots have just opened up, so you guys should go for it."

Ali locked eyes with me. "I wanted us all to do it together."

"Well, I can go another time. It will be easier for me to fit in by myself than with five open spots. Or if you really enjoy it, maybe we can do it together later in the summer. Take this opportunity so you don't miss out."

Realizing Hayley and Emma had signed up for a craft activity at that same time, I quickly scribbled my name under theirs. "I'll be with the other girls anyway. We were talking about doing this craft activity earlier."

Ali looked at me as if she could see into my lying soul.

I tried to reassure her through our connection.

Finally, she shrugged and smiled. "Okay, then...Leap of Faith it is."

Liam and Ethan high-fived and started talking about the activity and what they'd heard from others. They discussed a strategy that they thought they could use.

At least it distracted them from wondering why I had opted out.

Later that afternoon, Madison appeared at our cabin door, a proud grin attached to her face. "We did the Leap of Faith today!"

Ali and I were sitting on my bed while Brie read a book on her bunk.

"Was it okay?" I asked.

"Oh, it was so fun," Madison said, glancing at her friends. "Right, girls?"

Amy opened her mouth to speak but Madison cut her off.

"Too bad Amy couldn't do it...she was too scared." Madison laughed.

Amy's face fell. "You didn't even hit the gong."

"But I jumped!"

"And you were crying when they lowered you to the ground," Skye added.

Ali and I shared a look. We weren't the only ones who were tired of Madison's over the top attitude.

"I wasn't crying!" Madison said. "I had something in my eye. It's a big jump, you know. You'd realize that if you didn't all chicken out." She walked over to my closet and whipped the door open, sifting through it. "Did you see that girl, Morgan? She clung to the tree so tightly I never thought they'd coax her down."

"Oh, yeah," Amy said laughing. "It took the counselors twenty minutes to pry her loose. Her hands were all scratched up from the bark."

Skye didn't laugh, but Madison made up for it.

"She looked terrified," Skye said.

That made Madison laugh even harder.

"Want to take a walk before dinner?" Ali asked me.

"Sure," I said. "Brie, you in?"

"I'll meet up with you. I want to finish this chapter." Brie said.

Ali picked up her jacket and wrapped it around her waist. I chose a hoodie and did the same before leaving the cabin. Madison continued to talk with her friends about the Leap of Faith and their voices carried outside.

"Wow," I said. "I doubt Madison is going to have any friends by the end of the summer."

"Do you think it's that bad?" Ali asked.

"Well, if she wants someone to go to camps with, she's going to need friends."

"No, not about Madison...the Leap of Faith. The other girls didn't do it. And what about the poor girl who clung to the tree. Is it that scary?"

I chewed on my lip. "We did the high-ropes course. You saw the jump from there."

Ali nodded. "Yeah, and it looked freaky! I was scared enough on the high-ropes, but the Leap of Faith is something else. What if I make it to the top and I can't do it, like Amy and Skye, or that girl, Morgan? What would Liam think of me?"

"First of all, Liam likes you. I don't think he's going to mind if you change your mind. And besides, I thought you really wanted to do it?"

"It's on my bucket list, but I'm not so sure now. All week I've heard rumors about how scary it is. If I didn't do it, would you mind?"

"Of course not," I said. "But you should at least try. Then you won't have any regrets."

She sighed and nodded. "Yeah, I guess you're right."

She dropped the subject but I could tell it was still bothering her. She had the entire weekend to get used to the idea though and I knew that the chance to impress Liam would be the encouragement she needed.

Still, I had never seen her so nervous before. Not since we'd met.

Would she manage the jump or not?

CHAPTER FOURTEEN

Ali

Throughout the entire weekend, I tried not to let anyone see how nervous I was about the Leap of Faith. But each day passed too quickly, and before I knew it, Monday had arrived.

Casey had signed us up for the afternoon slot. While it was hours away, I could barely eat my breakfast. If anyone noticed, they didn't say anything.

Liam and Ethan were across the way with their cabin mates and, for once, I was happy they kept their distance. If Liam knew how terrified I was at the idea of jumping from the ledge, he might stop liking me. He loved sports, and if I had any chance of him liking me more than the other girls at camp, I had to prove that I enjoyed the things that he did and that I was good at them as well.

I wasn't going to change myself for anyone, but Mom always told me to push through my fears as it would lead to amazing experiences. Though, I doubted my life would change if I jumped or didn't jump. It was just camp, not a defining moment in my life. Even so, I could not help wanting to impress Liam.

After breakfast, Brie, Casey, and I went to a performing arts session. We'd planned to learn a new cheerleading routine in preparation for the following year at school. The session was loosely structured, and we could split off and create a new dance, a play, or whatever we wanted.

When we originally signed up, I was excited by the idea of having a new routine to show Mrs. Caldwell at school. But the bundle of nerves in my stomach had tightened so much that I could barely concentrate on learning the steps Casey created. She noticed I was off and gave me a few odd looks but didn't say anything.

It wasn't until later on when we were heading to the dining hall for lunch that I made a split second decision.

"Casey, I forgot to give you that thing," I mumbled to m twin.

She shook her head. "What thing?"

I smiled at Brie. "Can you save us a table and we'll r eet you there?"

Brie shrugged. "Sure. Don't take too long. I'm tarving."

I tugged Casey along next to me. I'd had the plan since Friday night, but I wasn't sure if Casey would be up for it. Finally, I decided to ask her. She had to agree. I'd covered for her so many times before, surely she would do this for me.

"I need us to swap," I said, stopping next to a tree by the girls' bathrooms.

"What?" Casey asked. "Why?"

"I can't do the Leap of Faith."

Casey sighed. "Ali, you'll be fine."

"No, I won't," I said. "Please, do this for me, Casey."

I didn't want to point out all the times I had helped her in the past, but if she didn't agree, then I was prepared to remind her.

Casey was unsure. "You said we'd never swap again."

"I know. But please…I need your help. Just this once… I need everyone to think that I did it and I know you'll be fine. Please?"

Casey sucked in a breath and nodded. "Yes, of course, Ali. If you really want me to, I'll do it. You've covered for me before. It's the least I can do."

A breath of air whooshed out of me. "Oh, Casey, thank you, thank you, thank you!"

Casey grinned, and I wondered if she had hoped for this all along, or if she was simply happy to repay me.

"We don't have a lot of time," I said. "Let's change now. Then we can go straight to our activities after lunch. It'll be less obvious than disappearing later on to change."

"Okay," Casey said, "we can just go in here."

She led the way into the bathroom and we chose stalls, side by side. We then exchanged clothes by passing them under the wall, the way we had done in the past. As I put on Casey's t-shirt, I was reminded of our very first swap. My heart raced in the same way it always did, but this time, the swap also helped to ease my mind. I didn't care if I checked the Leap of Faith off my list. Everyone else would think I had done it and that was all that mattered.

I glanced at my shoulder and was relieved that Casey had worn a t-shirt with sleeves so I could hide my birthmark. I doubted anyone would notice, but Brie knew it was a way to separate Casey and me. Even though Brie was our good friend, I didn't want to risk her knowing.

"Ready for the braid?" Casey asked.

We went into the main area by the sinks and mirrors, and I braided Casey's hair before undoing mine. At that point we were expert swappers, and we made it to lunch right on time.

Brie turned to say hi to us, and immediately, her eyes widened. "You didn't!"

"Shh," Casey said.

"How did you know?" I asked her.

Brie dug a hand into her hip. "I know Casey too well."

"Fine," I said in a hushed whisper. "But don't tell anyone."

Brie smirked and pretended to zip her lips.

"And whatever you do, don't call her Casey."

"Well, duh," Brie said.

I'd underestimated Casey's best friend, but it did feel nice to include her in our secret.

Since I wasn't jumping anymore, I was able to relax and eat my lunch, chatting easily with Hayley and Emma. I watched Casey pretend to be me throughout the conversation. She was bubbly and friendly, even more so than normal. I wondered if that was how I appeared to the rest of them. I hoped so.

I was so lucky to have Casey in my life and grateful that she was doing this for me. When she first signed us up for the Leap of Faith without her, I was happy. I loved my sister, but I looked forward to having Liam to myself for once, so he could focus on only me. I also wanted to impress him not make a fool of myself in front of him. To be the girl clinging to the tree trunk would be so humiliating. If that happened to me, I'd want to run to our cabin and stay there for the rest of the summer.

Casey didn't know about my fear of heights. It was a weakness I didn't share with anyone. I'd added the activity to my bucket list thinking it was an opportunity to face my fear. After battling through the high-ropes course though, I was too frightened to try something as scary as the Leap of Faith. One challenge at a time. Maybe next year.

With Casey pretending to be me, I knew she'd complete the activity bravely. She had managed the high-ropes easily, so this one should be a piece of cake for her. Otherwise, what was the point of the swap? I hoped she'd get an extra boost of confidence as well. Although, since the beginning of camp, her confidence had grown a lot in the face of Madison, the bully.

I glanced across the room at Liam and wondered if he had anything to do with Casey's newfound confidence. He'd been paying her so much attention, lately. She'd never had a boy do that until we tricked Jake into thinking she was more confident than she was. But I wondered if Liam preferred her to me. It hurt to think about that.

Regardless of how he currently felt, it would all change after this activity. When he saw Casey do the Leap of Faith as me, I was sure he'd be so impressed, that I would stand out in his mind as his preferred twin.

I wished I could go and watch but that was impossible as "Casey" was committed elsewhere. When it was time to clean up and leave the dining hall, I wished

Casey and Brie luck before heading off with Hayley and Emma to take part in the craft activity.

I was looking forward to coming back to a really positive story about how Liam was so impressed with me.

I beamed with excitement.

Everything was about to change for the better between us.

I just knew it!

CHAPTER FIFTEEN

Casey

"Okay, tell me what happened," Brie said, pulling me aside.

Liam and Ethan were ahead of us, chatting about the leap we were all about to take part in.

"Ali didn't want to do it," I replied quietly.

"Why not? She seemed happy when you signed us up."

"She's afraid of heights, I think. Madison and Amy freaked her out with their stories the other day."

"Of course, they did. Madison has no idea when to shut her mouth."

I laughed.

Liam and Ethan turned around. Liam's smile made my heart race guiltily. "What's so funny?" he asked.

"Nothing," Brie winked at me.

I wished she wasn't so obvious. Though I was happy she knew it was me instead of Ali. I liked how we were such good friends that she noticed the swap straight away. I just hoped she could keep it a secret for the entire activity. Liam hadn't given me any strange looks, so I was sure he didn't have a clue and I prayed it would remain that way.

When we arrived at the meeting point, the instructor we'd had for the high ropes course was there. He went through all the safety requirements, explaining that we would wear a harness secured by a long rope which he and another instructor would control from the ground. If anyone slipped, the rope would stop us from falling.

To access the jump, we had to climb up a really tall

vertical post with small footholds secured at various points. At the very top was the platform from which we'd need to leap out and hit the metal gong with the wooden hammer provided. Then the rope attached to the harness would be used to lower us back down.

When I stared skyward and took in the sight, my hands started to sweat. I was nervous, but at the same time, excitement overpowered my anxiety. I had wanted to do this from the moment Ali added it to her bucket list. I loved high-adrenalin activities, and Ali's help with boosting my confidence gave me the extra push I needed. I certainly didn't want to miss anything because I was worried what others would think.

As we watched the first boy in line approach the tall post, my heart raced faster than ever before. This was the scariest thing I had ever attempted, but at the same time, the most thrilling. He took quite some time to climb to the top and I didn't think he would even make it to the platform. Once there though, it took even longer for him to leap. From where I was standing, I could see the fear in his expression, but the whole time, the instructors encouraged him patiently. When he finally leaped and managed to hit the gong, we all cheered loudly. It was such an achievement and the look of relief on his face was mixed with pure joy.

When I stepped up to the front of the line, the *click* of the harness around me made my pulse rate soar.

"Are you ready?" the instructor asked with a smile.

"Yes," I breathed.

"Go, Ali!" Brie squealed.

I wasn't making this leap as myself but it was still a huge accomplishment that Brie and I could share together. Liam and Ethan cheered me on as well.

I stepped up onto the first foothold then with one foot securely placed on the next one, and my hand gripped tightly to an even higher one, I heaved myself up. Pushing with my thighs, I managed to raise myself to a higher position. The main platform loomed above me and I still had a long way to go.

Daring a glance downward, I saw my friends watching me closely.

"You can do it, Ali," Brie called.

"You're doing great!" Liam shouted.

I gave them a small nod and then returned my attention to the task, taking one steady step after another. Listening to the instructor's advice, I pushed with my legs to help me reach the next foothold. He had already told us that boys tend to rely on their upper body strength to lift themselves up, whereas girls usually push with their legs, and this was the most effective method. Before I knew it, I had reached the platform at the very top and I heard my friends and the rest of the group cheering crazily from the ground below.

When I dared to look down, my pulse soared even more. I was so high in the air, and I looked anxiously out at the gong that was hanging from an upper tree branch several feet away.

I reached for the hammer that was attached to a loose rope. If I had any hope of hitting the gong, I had to leap out into mid-air.

"Take your time, Ali," one of the instructors called loudly. "You're doing great!"

The gong swung gently in the breeze and I stared at it, while at the same time, gulping down a nervous breath.

The instructor's voice rang in my ear once more. "You'll be fine. You're secured by the ropes and you're safe. You just have to reach for that gong and whack it as hard as you can!"

Holding securely to the hammer, I inhaled again. Without hesitating any longer, I leaped off the edge and lunged forward. The distinctive sound as the hammer in my hand connected with the metal surface echoed through the airwaves.

The sound roared in my ears and my heart pumped wildly as the bungee line caught. I floated in the air, high above the ground and looked down to see Brie, Liam, and Ethan clapping, yelling, cheering and pumping their fists skyward.

I let out a breath and a massive smile spread across my face.

I did it! I really did it!

When I was lowered carefully to the ground, Liam beamed at me. "That was so awesome, Ali!"

At first, the name didn't register and I looked around for my twin before realizing he was speaking to me.

"Thanks, Liam," I grinned back.

Ethan joined him in congratulating me along with several other kids in our group. I was pumped full of adrenaline and pride. It was the most exciting thing I had ever done.

Every pair of eyes then turned toward Brie who was already harnessed and had started her trek to the top. Her foot slipped on a ledge and the breath caught in my throat as she fell. But the rope secured to her harness immediately tightened and she floated in the air as she swung herself back towards the post.

I willed her on, watching as she reached for each foothold, one after the other. Eventually, she was standing on the upper platform. She then moved to the edge but instantly backed away. She repeated this a few times and I crossed my fingers, wondering if she would actually attempt the jump.

"You can do it, Brie!" I called up to her.

Her body suddenly sailed over the edge, and she reached out, slamming the hammer into the gong.

I screamed louder than I ever had before.

Brie waved at me as she was lowered to the ground. Once her harness came off, I hugged her tightly.

"Oh my gosh! That was the scariest thing I've ever done in my life!" she laughed.

I laughed with her. "I know! But how good was it!"

"It was the best!" she squealed.

We then watched the boys have their turns and cheered each of them on as well. Every single person in our group managed to leap and hit the gong. Not one person chickened out and our instructors said that we were the best group they had ever supervised.

"You not only listened to the instructions," one of the instructors smiled, "but every one of you faced your fears and tried your absolute hardest. As well, you encouraged everyone else. You supported your friends and helped them through what was probably the biggest challenge of their lives so far. You're an awesome group! You should all be very proud."

I was overwhelmed with a pride so deep, I'd find it hard to describe if someone asked me to. I thought about Ali and her reluctance to take part. If she had tried, she would probably have managed, but I was so happy to have done it in her place. To achieve something that Ali was so afraid of, felt better than I could ever have imagined.

"We've got free time now. Let's head to the rec room," Ethan suggested. "There are always fun things going on there."

We readily agreed and as we walked together, we chatted about the amazing feat every single one of us had just completed. It was so fun to be sharing our experience together. Although a couple of times, I forgot to respond to the name, 'Ali.'

"Sorry. My head's still spinning from that leap."

Brie smiled at me, knowing exactly what the issue was. But thankfully, she hadn't let on and our secret was still safe.

Inside the rec hall, I didn't see Ali and realized that she must still be in her craft session. While I felt a little guilty thinking it, I was happy to be a part of the foursome for just a little while longer.

Adrenaline still coursed through me, and when I realized that karaoke was in session, I turned to my friends eagerly. "We have to do this," I shouted over the blaring music.

A girl was singing a popular song. She screeched some of the high notes but no one cared. It all looked so much fun.

When she finished, a boy stepped up for his turn. He started with a song I'd never heard before, and I wasn't sure I wanted to again after his performance. He was so out of tune, and his voice cracked as he "sang".

We looked through the karaoke book, and I found the perfect song for Brie and I. Because of how bad the boy had sounded, several kids changed their minds and all of a sudden, Brie and I were up next.

I grabbed her hand and tried to drag her over to the microphone.

"No way," she said, tugging her hand away from mine.

"Come on, Brie. It'll be fun! I can't sing on my own," I told her.

Liam touched my hand and electricity sparked through me. I turned to face him.

"This is one of my favorite songs. I'll sing with you, Ali. Come on!" He pulled me toward the microphone. The music had already started, and the first set of lyrics were on the screen in front of us.

I looked down at our clasped hands, and my stomach swooped.

As soon as the lyrics started changing colors on the screen, indicating for us to sing, he nodded encouragingly.

The words came out of my mouth so easily, even though on the inside, I was really nervous. Though, I was playing Ali. Would she be afraid to sing? Probably not!

Liam smiled at me, and something fluttered in my chest. I convinced myself that everything was fine. Ali wouldn't have given up the opportunity to sing with Liam, so neither would I.

A pop of color flashed in the corner of my eye, and I spotted Madison with her friends. Madison wore a bright purple top that stood out amongst the crowd and she was staring directly at me. Every time I looked over, she was still staring. Something was definitely off.

At the end of the song, everyone applauded us. Well, everyone except for Madison.

Old Casey might have cared, but I didn't care one bit. That girl wasn't going to ruin my fun.

Liam and I sat down to watch the next performance and Brie nudged my shoulder. "Great job, *Ali!*" She winked.

Liam grinned at me. "That was so much fun, Ali!"

I smiled back. Our plan had worked, and Liam liked Ali more now that she had done the Leap of Faith and sang karaoke with him. From now on, I imagined Ali would be the girl he preferred. For once, that was fine with me. Ali deserved to feel as good as I did when I was around Jake.

We stayed for a few more songs, but I still didn't see Ali anywhere. Brie and I decided to go back to the cabin to find her and shower before dinner. Between the heat and the anticipation of the jump, I needed to cool off.

When we arrived at the cabin, Ali, Hayley, and Emma were inside. Ali's eyes widened when she saw me. It still felt strange to see her in my clothes, with her hair out, looking identical to the way I usually looked. We had to keep up the charade though, so everyone thought Ali had gone through with the Leap of Faith.

"Oh my gosh, you have to tell us all about it," Emma said. "I'm super freaked out to try it."

Ali walked toward me, excitement all over her face. "How did you go, Ali?"

"Was it scary?" Hayley asked.

"Yes! It was freaky but it was so much fun!"

Brie and I went over every detail of the jump and we were squealing with laughter when the door opened and slammed against the wall.

"Casey!" Madison said, locking her eyes accusingly on mine. "What do you think you're doing?"

I glanced at Ali, wondering what Madison was playing at. Surely she had no idea about our swap. She must have us mixed up.

"What's your problem?" I asked her.

"Singing a karaoke song with Liam and holding his hand? Are you serious?"

The other girls looked at me, and I felt my jaw drop as Ali stiffened at my side. I had done nothing wrong! It was all a charade so that Liam would like Ali more. I couldn't care less what Madison thought. I would just tell her that she had Ali and me confused. Liam wasn't interested in Madison, and she didn't deserve him anyway. It was good for her to see him with *Ali*.

But I hadn't had a chance to tell Ali about the karaoke yet. I wanted to explain, so she would know the hand holding meant nothing to me.

A twisted feeling of guilt surged inside me. Ali frowned and refused to meet my eyes. I could almost hear her mind ticking over with Madison's words while I still felt Liam holding my hand.

I knew it hadn't been a part of the deal with Ali, but Liam did think he was holding Ali's hand. That had to mean something, right?

Though, when I thought about it, a warmth swept through me. I'd had such a wonderful time with him, and I didn't want to let it go that easily.

What was wrong with me?

Ali finally looked at me, and I felt her sadness through our connection. Somehow, she knew it meant more to me than I was letting on.

I'd tried so hard not to admit that Liam had made an impression on my heart. And even though I adored Jake, I couldn't help but have feelings for Liam as well.

What could I say to my twin without sounding like the worst sister in the world?

***

Find out what happens next in the continuation of the
TWINS series.

Twins - Book 14: Envy

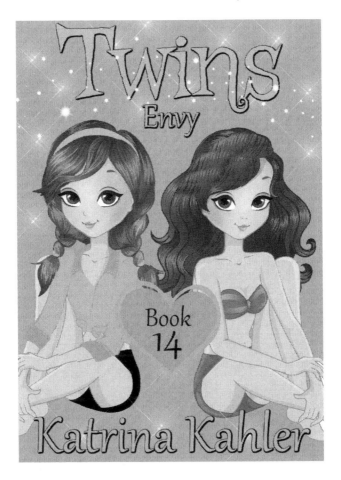

You can also buy the next 3 books as a combined set at a DISCOUNTED price.

Twins - Part Five: Books 14, 15 & 16

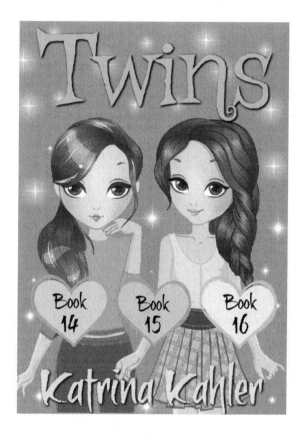

If you enjoyed this story, would you mind leaving a review?
Reviews encourage other readers and they also encourage me to
continue to write more books.
I really appreciate you taking the time to do this and I can't wait to
hear what you think!
Thank you so much!!!!!
Katrina xx

Here are some more of my books. I hope you enjoy these ones as well…

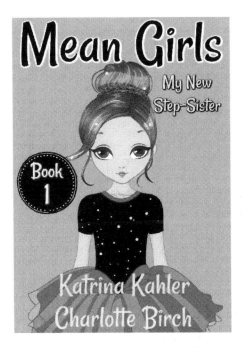

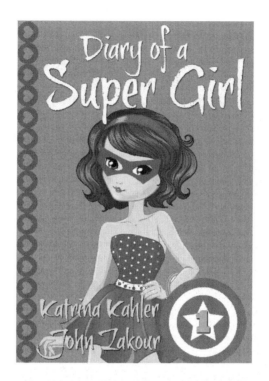

Made in the USA
San Bernardino, CA
22 May 2020